SILVER THREADS

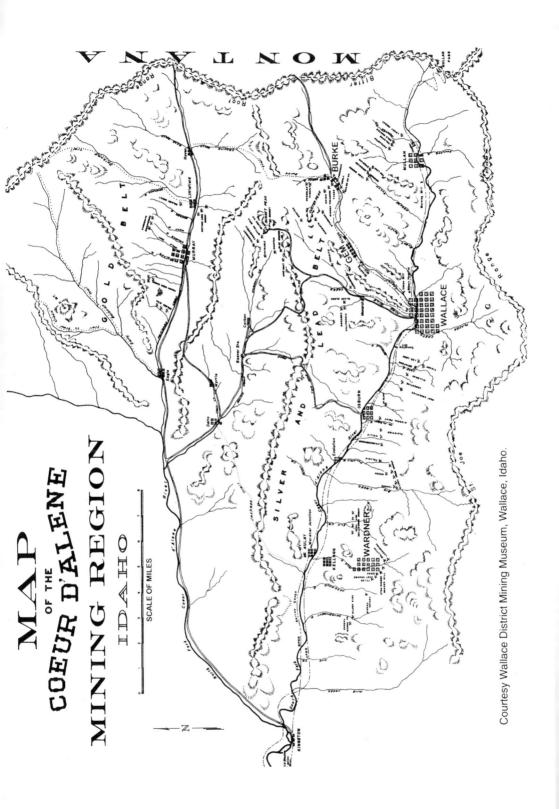

MAP
OF THE
COEUR D'ALENE
MINING REGION
IDAHO

SCALE OF MILES

Courtesy Wallace District Mining Museum, Wallace, Idaho.

SILVER THREADS

War in the Coeur d' Alenes
1891-1892

A NOVEL
BY PAT CARY PEEK

ISBN: 978-0-9753335-1-8

Library of Congress Control Number: 2007909553

Printed in the United States of America by
Maverick Publications • Bend, Oregon

To the mothers, wives, sisters and daughters
whose hearts are broken by war.

⤳ AUTHOR'S NOTE ⤳

M en flocked to the beautiful mountains of North Idaho for gold, but
discoveries in the 1880's found the region held vast amounts of precious silver. By 1891, millions of dollars worth of ore was being
shipped from the area, but the miners whose shoulders and backs carried
the tons of valuable ore barely made a living. Then the unions were
formed and the workers finally had a voice. That voice became a scream
of protest against the dangerous working conditions and low pay. Government troops were called in to control the miners.

This is a novel set in the North Idaho region known as the "Coeur d'
Alenes" when the "mining wars" were at their peak. The Coeur d'Alene
Mining District is a large area located in the panhandle of Idaho in the
heart of rugged mountain country on the western edge of the Bitterroot
Mountain Range that separates Idaho from Montana.

Later known as the Silver Valley, here a strip of rich mineral deposits
about eight by twenty-five miles long became one of the most productive
areas in the world. It was up the narrow rock-walled canyons that rich
lodes of gold and later silver were located and where vast riches were
made for the owners and shareholders of the mines.

The district is tied together by the north and south forks of the Coeur
d'Alene River, which flow into the huge glacially-formed Coeur d'Alene
Lake. The rivers follow canyon floors at about twenty-eight hundred feet
and the mountains rise almost straight up to heights of up to seven thousand feet.

Railroads also tied the region together and connected it to the markets
and population in the east. Built soon after the rich lodes of silver were
discovered, they threaded across the country through this remote wilderness and out to the more populated West Coast. Thousands of miles of

silver track and huge steam engines made the mines possible and profitable.

"The Coeur d' Alenes" in the 1890's included the mining camps and towns of Wallace, Wardner, Burke, Gem, Kellogg, Mullan and Osborn. In 1892, about five thousand people lived and worked in these towns with Wallace, population 2,500, and Wardner being the largest.

The city of Coeur d' Alene today, population 38,388, was called Coeur d' Alene City and is located about forty miles west of what was considered "The Coeur d' Alenes."

Wallace, population 960, and Kellogg, population 2,395, are the two main cities of the Coeur d' Alene Mining District that remain today. Wallace is located on the South Fork of the Coeur d' Alene River and is situated at the confluence of five major canyons on the historic Mullan Road and Canyon Creek. It was, and still is, a natural supply center and business district for all the mines in the area.

About eight miles downriver from Wallace was Wardner Junction. Also along the Mullan Road, it was at the mouth of one of the largest drainages in the region, Milo Creek.

The settlement of Kellogg, which came later, was above the Junction up Milo Creek, then farther up the narrow canyon, called Milo Gulch, was what was in the 1890's the larger town of Wardner. Its main street took up the narrow bottom of the canyon and the houses were perched along the sides of the mountain like sparrows on a clothesline. One thousand people lived in the three settlements in 1889.

At the top of the gulch, looking down on the villages below, like the king's castle, perched above Wardner, was one of the greatest and most productive silver mines in the world, the Bunker Hill and Sullivan. The mine, discovered in 1885, was an engineering masterpiece for its time. The most modern methods were used.

In 1891, a new tramway, the pride of the mine managers, was built. Snaking up the canyon, hanging high above the three settlements, the tramway cables carried raw ore more than 8,000 feet from the mine at the top of the mountain to the concentrator mill down below at the junction. The cables had huge supports along the route, the highest, more than 89 feet above the ground, was in the center of town at Wardner. One hundred thirty-three buckets whizzed above the town for twenty-four hours a day, each one carrying seven hundred pounds of ore.

The mine was a marvel, but the miners worked under conditions that were from the dark ages.

When gold was discovered in the wilderness of North Idaho Territory in the 1880's, miners arrived by the thousands. Each man was his own boss or worked with a small group of friends to flush the gold from the mountains. Nuggets the size of a man's hand were plucked from the crevices of the earth by miners who had little machinery or skills except for a strong back to wield a pick and shovel or to haul ore with a wheelbarrow. Some became rich, but most didn't.

Then silver was discovered, and in a flash, mining in the Coeur d' Alene district changed dramatically. It took vast amounts of capitol and hundreds of men to build a shaft into the bowels of the mountains and haul out tons of rocks to be pulverized and treated to give up precious silver. Big money was needed to finance the operations and the big money generally came from back east.

Workers from the east and recent immigrants from other countries who came west following a dream of freedom and autonomy found themselves trapped in conditions that were in many ways worse than the factories and big industry in the places they came from. Men worked ten to twelve hour days breathing gritty dust and fumes from explosives. They faced tremendous odds of illness and injury, if not death, every time they went down in "the hole." They had few choices and no rights as workers until the Union movement came along; then they finally had a voice, and their defiant voice and violent actions were heard and written about across the country in 1891-1892.

The Irish, especially, joined the union in great numbers and became its main leaders partly because they spoke English better than many of the recent immigrants. Many had also experienced the exploitation and inhumane working conditions in the old country, and they had come to America with high, idealistic expectations of equality and justice. Therefore, when they met the arrogant disregard for their well-being and lack of fair treatment by some of the mine owners in the Coeur d' Alenes, their outrage sparked one of the most violent episodes in the history of the west.

Much has been written about the issues and events during that turbulent time, and in this story descriptions of the union and mine owners' activities and violent events are as accurately portrayed as possible. The bull pen really happened and the conditions and events there are recorded by reliable witnesses. Nonfiction published materials consulted by the author are listed in the back.

The following people mentioned in the book did really live and were involved in the tragic events of the time:

Adam Aulbach: Owner, editor of various newspapers in the area including the Idaho Sun, Wallace Free Press and Wallace Press

Judge James H. Beatty: U. S. District Court

Edward (Ed) Boyce: President of the Miner's Union and later President of the Western Federation of Miners

V. M. Clement: Manager of Bunker Hill Mine

Sheriff Richard A. Cunningham: Shoshone County Sheriff

General James Curtis: Idaho National Guard

A. M. Esler: Owner of the San Francisco Mine near Gem

Levi (Al) Hutton: Train engineer. Ran the "Dynamite express."

May Arkwright Hutton: Boarding house operator, wife of "Al" Hutton."

Father Keyzer: Was appointed by the bishop in November, 1891, to serve Wallace, Wardner, Burke, Mullan and Murray on alternate Sundays.

Thomas O'Brian: President of the Central Miner's Union

W. A. Stewart: Editor/owner of the Mullan Mirror Newspaper

Norman B. Willey: Idaho Governor 1890-1893

What was it like for the women and children of the men involved in the struggle? Little is recorded of their day to day life. The fictional McCarthy family and their friends could have lived during that time. Like families everywhere, they were caught up in the events of the time and with their own demons. The character of Jack Bailey, however, is patterned after the real Charles A. Siringo (aka C. Leon Allison) and his role in the events are very close to what actually happened.

Writing about an historical time is like piecing together a crazy quilt. Most of the pieces are old and well worn. Which pieces do you choose to use and where do you place them in relation to each other? What kind of stitches binds them together? I chose to stitch a story from the point of view of the union workers, the common people, hoping to put a human face on one of the great tragedies of the early west.

Pat Cary Peek

~~~ ACKNOWLEDGMENTS ~~~

I thank my lucky stars for museums, libraries, historians and all the people who love a good story and keep the old tales and priceless old pictures alive. They preserve, categorize, catalog and lovingly care for the items, papers and photographs that hold our history. Julie Monroe, Dave Remington and staff at the University of Idaho Library Archives were extremely helpful. Jane Davey, archives assistant at the Eastern Washington State Historical Society, Marcia Biotti and Bob Dunsmore at the Staff House Museum in Kellogg, Idaho, Debbie Gibbler at the Kellogg Public Library, Chuck Peterson at the Wardner Museum in Wardner, Idaho, Shauna Hillman at Indelible Tidbits in Wallace, Idaho, and Jim Mc Reynolds of the Wallace District Mining Museum in Wallace, Idaho, all willingly gave their time and expertise.

Mabel and Sig Vogt, Potlatch, Idaho, kindly loaned me background material. My dear friends, Sara Holup and Cindy Magnuson, read the manuscript and gave me sound advice. Sara also generously loaned me the picture of her grandmother, Alta Johnson Shelles, to grace the cover of the book. Robin Magnuson also read it and gave me many thoughtful suggestions which improved the flow of the story.

I thank each of these people for contributing their time and knowledge to this project. A special thanks also goes to my nephew, Steve Tone, for his help with my website, and my dear niece, Shirley Hornstein, for her advice and encouragement. Finally I'm eternally grateful to my very first reader, my husband James Peek, for his patience, support and advice all along the line.

Milo Gulch, 1889. Wardner Junction, foreground; Kellogg, center;
and Wardner above. Haystack Peak background to right.
Special Collections and Archives, University of Idaho Library, 8-X729

CHAPTER ONE

Wardner, Idaho – July, 1891

There is pow'r, there is pow'r
In a band of workingmen,
When they stand hand in hand,
That's a pow'r, that's a pow'r
That must rule in every land—-
One Industrial Union Grand.
          To the tune of Power in the Blood
          Joe Hill, Little Red Songbook

The whistle of the locomotive sliced the sleepy summer afternoon like a razor. Colleen stopped in her tracks and listened as Granny came up beside her. They listened as the wild, mournful call of the train echoed from the mountains and in the deep canyons up the river. A new sound in this country, it spoke the music of far away places, like Portland, Seattle and Spokane.

Colleen's eyes sparkled with excitement as the two of them stood on the dusty road and listened until the last echo faded away. "Wouldn't it be grand to just get on that train and go all the way to Spokane Falls?" she said to the old woman. She spoke the word "Spokane" with awe. The city over the mountains to the southwest was alive with wonders only found in dreams a few years before.

"One of these days you'll do it, child," the old woman said as she took her arm. "Work hard and be patient."

Colleen shook her head and scowled. "I am working! Seems like that's all I do is work. How much patience am I supposed to have? Did you know I started cleaning Mrs. Taylor's house just last week? I have sixteen dollars saved up so far."

"Then all you need is patience!" Granny said brightly. "Now come on, honey. We want to get a good seat. The parade's due to start directly." The old woman understood. She knew the feel of a restless heart, remembered the yearning as if it were yesterday, the dream of life that was just around the corner, out of reach and unknown, but beckoning, like the tune of a song at the edge of hearing.

They came to Main Street and moved out of the way as a wagon pulled by two draft horses rumbled by at a good clip. It was filled with a family of eight, all dressed in their Sunday clothes, eyes bright with anticipation. The mother and two little girls hung onto their bonnets with one hand and each other with the other as the wagon bumped and swayed on the rough road. Three boys clung to the sides, not minding the dust, while the father and older boy drove the team.

A cloud of dust was left in their wake and after they were past Colleen brushed off her dress with disgust. "You'd think people would use the brains God gave them and slow down in town!"

They hurried down the rutted road to the main street, past buggies, wagons, horses and dozens of people on foot to a spot in front of the H. L. Day General Store. Granny, a tiny shriveled up woman, carried a bucket which she turned upside down for a seat at the edge of the street. Once she was perched there like a bright eyed bird, she looked around. "Looks like the whole town's here!" she chirped.

Colleen smiled down at her grandma. She loved the old lady like a kite loves the wind. Like a stiff cheerful breeze, granny buoyed her up and moved her spirits forward. "Yes, ma'am," she answered, looking around. She pointed to a large American flag draped from the tramway cable that hung above the street. "Don't our flag look just glorious?"

"It surely does. You live in the state of Idaho now, child, a part of the great United States of America, from sea to shining sea. Do you realize it was only one year ago today that the Territory became the forty-third star? Mighty big changes are stirring in the wind." She turned her attention back to the street, then muttered to herself, "Not all of them good, I'm thinkin'."

Patriotism ran high in the crowd as the sound of drums and bugles echoed up the narrow valley and the marchers got ready for the parade. Colleen glanced excitedly around at the crowd. Over a thousand people lived in the little settlements along Milo Creek, and it seemed like most of them were here, along the parade route standing in the bright sunshine.

Colleen bent over to whisper in Granny's ear. "Look at Mrs. Estes over there. Don't she look like the cat's meow! I heard she don't wear a thing unless it's ready made from Boston. And just look at that hat! I swear it looks like those birds are alive perched up there!"

Granny glanced across the street at a stylishly dressed woman, the mill manager's wife, and chuckled. The hat was made of black velvet with three taffeta rosettes and a plume of three feathers curving out to one side. Nesting on the front were two small black parrots.

"It do, for a fact. I think those critters could just fly down to those bony shoulders and nibble her tough old leathery ear!"

"Well, I wouldn't be surprised if something don't catch them first! I saw an eagle just this morning right up yonder above the mountain. He might just swoop down here and get himself a meal!" They laughed delightedly.

Colleen surveyed the scene around the little town of Wardner as she waited for the parade. Mountains rose thousands of feet in every direction above the false-fronted wooden framed buildings. The tall, steep-sided precipices, once covered with fir, cedar, hemlock and pine, reached to the sky on both sides of the narrow canyon. Near the town most of the timber was gone, cut to build houses and buildings of the settlement and for the huge timbers in the silver mines. In the winter, the sun's rays barely reached the town, hunkered down as it was between the mountains, but now in the heady summer time, it was hot by midmorning.

Colleen waved at a friend then suddenly noticed a stranger in the crowd. She caught her breath. Probably a little older than herself she figured, maybe even twenty, he wore a black cap pushed to the back of his head and rusty red hair curled out from under it as if he'd spent all morning with a curling iron. He wore a store-bought red plaid shirt and he stood a good head taller than the people around him. As she studied him he turned and caught her eye. He flashed a broad smile and his brown eyes danced like he'd just discovered gold in the bottom of his pan. Colleen responded with a tremulous smile and quickly turned away, embarrassed at having been caught staring.

Then the parade came up the hill and music flowed between the high mountains like a cheerful flood. The Fighting Fourth Military Band had come all the way from Ft. Sherman on Lake Coeur d' Alene, then the GAR civil war veterans, the Odd Fellows and Knights of Pythias followed. Finally the troops of miners filled the street. They marched with military precision; their heavy boots hit the bare ground in unison. Every

Miner's union in the region was represented. The large Wardner Union was followed by the Gem, Burke and Osborne Union members who proudly represented their groups.

"Oh! Susanna, oh don't you cry for me!" The music swirled between the unpainted frame houses and bubbled up the steep mountainsides. *"I'm goin' to Louisiana with my banjo on my knee!"* It caught the people in the tide and before long weary spirits lifted, tired toes tapped and cranky babies cocked their heads and stopped fussing. *"Rained all night the day I left the weather it was dry. Sun so hot I froze to death. Susanna don't you cry!"*

Colleen craned her neck to see the miners. "There he is!" she said excitedly. "There's Sam! Can you see him, Granny?"

"Yes, I declare your little brother looks right smart!"

"Takes after the rest of the family!"

Granny wasn't listening. She frowned and shook her head as her grandson found them in the crowd and waved their way. "I just wish to the Lord that he'd not be so noticeable though. Marching with the Union and all. Wish he'd just keep quiet about being a member like a lot of the men."

"Now Granny, you know that's not like Sam! He's got to be the first and the best and usually the loudest wherever he goes."

"Reckon you're right there," the old woman said with more than a touch of pride. "He's not afraid of the devil himself."

As the band continued up the street, it started the old Civil War favorite:

"I'm a Yankee Doodle dandy. Yankee Doodle do or die. A real fine nephew of my Uncle Sam. Born on the Fourth of July...."

Some of the older spectators, the Southerners, frowned with disgust at the tune. It was a Yankee ditty, and the wounds of the war were still too deep to allow them to tap their toes to that one.

After the parade went past and the flow of music became a trickle, Colleen and Granny walked with the crowd up toward the stand where the orations were to be held. As they came to the path that led back to the house, Granny stopped.

"You go on and listen to the speeches. I'll go back and help your mother with the food."

Colleen hesitated and grimaced. She knew she should go home to help. The thought of her mother chilled her spirit. If Granny was a warm breeze that buoyed her up, Clara was a cold wind. She was storm cloud and when it wasn't raining, it was threatening to. She constantly needed her oldest daughter. She kneaded her like bread dough, and Colleen felt squeezed, molded into a shape not of her choosing. The excitement of the day drained away and she bit her lip and sighed. Granny thought how much she looked like Clara when she frowned, but finally the girl shrugged her thin shoulders and brightened.

"Well, ok. Don't you reckon ma'll need me?"

"No, you go on. Clara and I'll manage just fine. You need to find your sister anyway."

"Well, I'm not going back unless I have to! I'm not hankerin' to get yelled at. Ma was so cranky this morning I'm going to stay out of her way. Trying to please her is like trying to fill up a leaky bucket. I can't do a bloomin' thing right, seems like. Nothing I do is good enough and yet she can't get along without me!"

"Now don't be too hard on your ma. There's a lot you don't know. Best not to judge the book till you've read the whole story, my dear."

Colleen narrowed her eyes and looked at her curiously. "What don't I know?" She knew Clara was sick a lot. She took medicine all the time. She knew her father, Joe, was drunk most of the time when he wasn't working, and her mother suffered for it, but she didn't need to be told that sad old news.

Granny smiled a rueful smile and shook her head. "One of these days you and me will have a long talk." She looked at her granddaughter thoughtfully, then turned and said brightly, "Not today though. Today you just put all your worries way down deep in your worry bank, lock the door and swallow the key!" She smiled up at her beautiful granddaughter and squeezed her arm. "Don't stay too long at the doings."

Colleen wrinkled her nose and grinned a sheepish grin. She couldn't stay down when Granny was there like a twinkling old star. "I won't. I've already got my box decorated for the box social. Did you see it this morning?" She was counting the hours until the dance. With all the miners here from up and down the valley it was sure to be a grand affair. Her electric blue eyes regained their sparkle as she thought of the swirl of dancers and visualized herself twirling around the floor in a magical cloud of music. Her heart beat fast with anticipation and the cloudy mood vanished.

"Yes, and I reckon it's going to be bid on by every young man in the valley."

"I hope so. Sam says the Union Fund is bound to need the money this winter."

They parted and before Colleen arrived near the speaker's platform that was draped with red, white and blue bunting, she had forgotten Granny's words about something she should know and was busy thinking about her dress for the dance that night. She had picked out the material

5

herself. It was a bright, robin's egg blue-checked and she could hardly wait to try it on.

The speaker, who was the president of the Union in Butte, Montana, had already started as she found a spot at the edge of the crowd. His voice rang out over the respectful crowd. "The companies in these parts don't believe in free enterprise except where it suits 'em! They think a free market only goes one way! They own the store; they own the boarding houses. They even own some of the saloons! You get your paycheck and they own the bank and charge you to cash it! Then you turn right around and give the rest back to them to get the things you need to live! And they're charging more than other places for the same goods." He paced the stage and glared at the audience. "You buy a gum suit and they charge you $20! That's highway robbery! The same exact suit will cost you about $11 at Butte where they do have a free market."

The men shifted their feet and shook their heads. "It's not a fair deal any way you look at it," the speaker continued. "Here in the Coeur d' Alenes you men are at their mercy. You need to stick together and it ain't just about spondulicks! It's about your lives! Not ten miles from here a man was caught in a cave in. He was killed, and the word is that the timbers they used to shore up the tunnel were half-rotten. I heard just last night about three men who died of gas poisoning. The manager cut down on the operation of the ventilating fans to save money. The money is made on your backs, but you can break your backs and they shove you aside. They take care of their investors; they don't give a hoot about you!"

One of the young men standing near Colleen grumbled to his friend, "He don't say that us single men have to live in the boarding house owned by the mine. That's what gripes me more than anything. It's a cold, old wreck of a building and the food is lousy, but if we want to work for them we got no choice. We live there and pay them our seven dollars a week."

His friend laughed. "Yeh, and they spout off about 'free enterprise.' There's other hotels and boarding houses with good food but it don't do us no good."

After the speaker sat down, the mayor of the town got up to speak. He ended by saying: "Here's to our country! And to the day we celebrate our freedom! Our country, dedicated to freedom by the blood of her fathers. Her constitution inhibits no liberty consistent with truth and offers to the oppressed of every land a home!"

The crowd clapped, cheered, and said, "Hear hear! To the land of the free and the home of the brave!" But the holiday mood that had swept the crowd with the band's lively music earlier was subdued now, and when

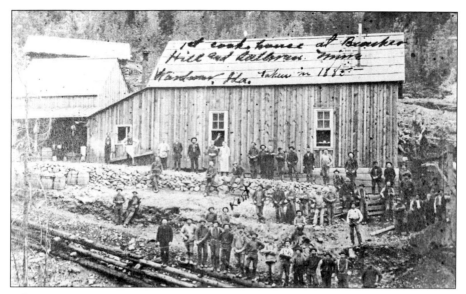

Single men who worked at Bunker Hill were required to room and board
at houses owned by the company.
Special Collections and Archives, University of Idaho Library, 5-070-1

The drilling contest, an exciting event at the Fourth of July celebration.
Note the supply of drill rods.
Staff House Museum, Kellogg, Idaho

CR&N (Coeur d' Alene Railway & Navigation) engine No. 2 at Wallace decorated for the Fourth of July. Engineer Levi Hutton on the far right.
Northwest Museum of Arts and Culture/Eastern Washington State Historical Society,
L2003.14.784, Hutton Collection, Spokane, Washington

the mayor finished many of the men shuffled silently toward the saloon to try and recapture some of the cheer they'd felt earlier in the day.

Colleen left the group and wandered up to the street where the contests were held. On the way, her twelve-year-old sister, Polly, caught up with her. "I thought you would never get here!" she said. She looked up to her older sister like a second string player studies the star pitcher. Beautiful and smart, Colleen had all the answers in Polly's mind. Whatever her big sister said must be right. They went over to watch the rock-drilling contest. Hand drilling holes in the rock of the mine to hold the blasting powder took knowledge, skill and precision, and experienced drillers were respected by everyone.

The area where the contest was held had a rope stretched around a large square to keep the crowd back from the action. There was a judge, two referees and two timekeepers to make sure all the rules were followed. Two huge granite rocks had been placed behind the rope and each team of contestants was to drill for exactly fifteen minutes. When time was called, the length of the hole drilled was measured and the men who drilled the deepest hole won.

As they got closer Colleen noticed that the stranger she'd spotted in the crowd before was watching the event from the other side. She smiled at him, then turned her attention to the contest.

In this event the men were "double-jack drilling." Just as the drillers did every day and night in the smoky, dark, humid stopes underground, the competitors did now in the brilliant light of day surrounded by spectators.

Two brawny men stepped up to compete for the fifty dollar prize. Shirtless, their muscles rippled in the sun as they looked around at the crowd and wiped their hands on their pants, ready for the signal to start. One man, the striker, wielded an eight-pound sledgehammer. His partner's job was to step in after each stroke, turn the drill a fraction of an inch, and get out of the way before the next stroke. A second's hesitation or misjudgment could mean smashed hands, broken wrists and arms or worse. Top speed for wielding the hammer was said to be up to fifty strokes a minute. After each minute or so the pair changed places, the striker became the turner and the turner wielded the hammer.

At the signal, the striker of the team raised the hammer and slammed the drill with all his might. The ring of metal on metal and metal on rock echoed up the canyon. Again and again he hit the drill and each time his partner darted in, turned the drill and dodged back out. It was amazing to watch the split-second precision of the team. Sweat glistened on their backs and ran down their faces but there was no time to wipe it off. It was like an intricate dance, and the speed, agility and strength of the men was awesome to behold.

With each blow the steel drill gradually disappeared into the rock. After fifteen minutes, time was called and the men stood back, wiped their faces and waited as the hole was measured and the next team came forward.

After three more teams competed, the judge announced the winners. "And we have here the winners of the double-jack drilling...." He paused dramatically, "the tremendous third team, Mr. Tim Riley and Willy Ford, with a score of thirty-three inches! Good work, boys! Don't spend it all in one place!"

"Isn't that man that was on the first team Sam's friend?" Polly whispered to her sister.

"I think he works on Sam's shift but I don't know his name. Do you see the man in the red shirt over there?" Colleen asked, nodding toward the stranger she'd noticed before.

"Uh-huh. Do you know him?"

"No, I don't think I've ever seen him around here before."

"Me neither," Polly answered. Then she looked at her and showed her dimples. "He's sure a looker, ain't he though?" Colleen rolled her eyes and blushed. She poked her sister in the ribs and giggled.

Just then the next event was called and the stranger looked their way. Colleen grabbed Polly by the elbow. "Come on let's go over yonder and watch the three-legged race. Sam said he's going to enter." As she turned she could feel the stranger's gaze on her back like warm sunshine on a winter day.

The girls hurried on to the place where the race was held. They got there just as the runners passed the finish line and their brother and his friend Herbert hopped over. Sam's right leg and Herbert's left leg were tied together in a gunny sack. They had come in second.

"Dang it, Herbert!" Sam said laughing as they tried to untangle themselves. "If you hadn't of got the sack all cattywhompers at the start we would've won!"

Herbert laughed, pushed him and they both fell over in the grass. "Just go ahead, blame it on me if it makes you feel any better!"

The girls came over. "Don't worry about it, Herbert," Colleen said shaking her head and laughing as they approached. "You know Sam hates to lose at anything." Then she glanced at the sun, a fiery globe poised above the mountains, and looked at her brother. "Come on home with us, Sam. It's almost dinner time." Soon the three of them walked through the town and up the hill home.

After dinner, the whole family got ready for the dance. Clara had scraped up enough money to order dress goods from the catalog so that Colleen could have a new dress. She had just got it cut out when she'd had one of her spells and Granny had finished most of it.

"Now come in here and try this on," her mother called from the other room.

Colleen, busy heating the curling iron on the oil lamp in order to curl her sister Annalee's hair, answered. "I'll be there directly, Ma, let me do these last few sausage curls first."

Eight-year-old Annalee bounced with excitement as Colleen took a strand of her blond hair. "Hold still, pumpkin!" her sister instructed. "Or else I may just curl your nose instead!" Annalee giggled and tried her best to be still. Just like Polly, she adored her sister and studied her every move in order to be just like her. She was the darling of the family and took advantage of it when she could.

Colleen finally finished the ringlets, put the iron back on the table and went to try on the dress. She picked it up, smiled and held it against her lithe frame as her two little sisters oohed and ahhed. She loved the smell and feel of the new fabric. It was just the color of her eyes, and had ¾ length leg-of-mutton sleeves, a tailored, tight fitting shirtwaist with a scooped neck and a full skirt that fell to her ankles.

She went into the bedroom, slipped it on and buttoned the tiny buttons down the front. It fit perfectly and she returned to the kitchen to twirl in front of her mother and sisters.

"It's the prettiest dress I've ever had, Ma! I love it!"

Clara was an excellent seamstress. She had a knack for sewing that was almost uncanny. She could look at a picture in the catalog and produce a shirt or a dress just like it. She made her own patterns and when she did embroidery, it looked like a work of art. Her stitches were so small they were almost invisible. On the dress, however, they were a little larger than usual and more uneven. Her oldest daughter never noticed the difference.

Colleen put her hand on her mother's shoulder. "Thank you!" She longed to hug her like she did her little sisters, but she always held back. She knew her mother didn't like to be touched.

Clara nodded as she moved away from her daughter's hand. "Well, at your age you should be doing the sewing yourself! A proper lady should know how to sew and mend at least!" she retorted sternly. "You're lucky Granny was able to work on it yesterday," but then she smiled a slight smile, pleased at her work and happy her daughter had forgotten their earlier tiff. Smiling was not easy for the older woman. Her mouth struggled to show pleasure, just as her spirit struggled to find any shred of joy in life.

Colleen often remembered a remark she'd overheard a neighbor make behind her mother's back. "I swear, I think a smile would crack her face!" Her daughter was irate at the cruel remark at the time, but it did seem that her mother's mouth, like her mood, tended down. If she saw one buttercup in February she wondered irritably where the others were.

"I know, Mama," Colleen said brightly, striving to maintain her cheer. "But I'm just no good at sewing. I'd rather slop the hogs, churn the butter or cut the wood than stitch, stitch, stitch with a little teensy needle and thread. It gives me a headache just to think about it."

"We don't have any hogs to slop!" Annalee announced.

"I know, smarty pants!"

"If you just had more patience it'd help, and you know what they say, 'a woman who knows the ways of a needle won't never go hungry'!"

Colleen frowned and shook her head. "I just never have the time!"

"Well, if you didn't wander off up to the woods every chance you get you would have the time." Her mother's voice rose to the familiar whine, but then her tired eyes softened and she shook her head. "But I don't mind doin' it," she said dreamily. "I like to sew and crochet almost better'n anything. A needle is like a magic wand, I can take thread, yarn or a piece of cloth and see it take shape into a dress, a shirt or socks that'll last for years. The cloth stays where I put it, and it stays done, not like moppin' the floor that you know will need to be mopped again in a day or two, nor cookin' food which disappears almost before it's proper cooked."

"Of course," she continued with her typical negative twist, "One pull of a single thread and a whole week's work can come undone!" Colleen shrugged her shoulders irritably and looked out of the window.

Her mother came out of her reverie, embarrassed at her sentiment. "Now go on and get out of it so that I can add the rick rack around the neck and sleeves and do the hem. Then it's done."

Colleen went back to the bedroom to take off the dress, but before she did she looked at herself in the small mirror above her mother's dressing table. People said she was pretty, and she often inspected herself in the mirror like a detective trying to find the evidence. "Pretty is as pretty does," Granny always cautioned, and tonight she was going to "do" like a princess.

Her long dark hair fell to her shoulders and she pulled a ringlet forward to fall across her forehead. She was fair-skinned and had a small nose and generous mouth. A light sprinkling of freckles graced her nose in spite of valiant efforts to erase them with a mixture of lemon juice, glycerin and powdered borax applied to the offending marks morning and night. Her eyes, brilliant blue, wide apart and fringed with dark lashes, contrasted with her dark hair. Granny said she had the look of "lace curtain Irish" because of the combination of blue eyes and dark hair, but then Granny made each one of her grandchildren feel unique.

Later on the family sat down to dinner then walked down the hill to the main part of town. Houses filled the narrow valley from what was called Wardner Junction by the Coeur d' Alene River, the railroad and the famous Mullan Road, to the top of the canyon where the mine was located more than a mile away.

George and Cora McCarthy, Colleen's grandparents, lived on the first road above Main Street and Clara, Joe and the four children lived on the highest of the three roads that ran parallel to the main street on the east side above the town.

Colleen's family stopped and picked up George and Cora and they continued downtown. As they walked along the road, Polly sneezed from the dust in the air. Granny promptly said "skachoowich!"

"What did you say granny?" Annalee asked.

"Skachoowich! I'm telling the witches to go away and leave Polly alone!"

"I've never heard that before."

"Well, sure. It's from the old country. In Ireland they think that when you sneeze it's a sign that witches are about."

Annalee looked up at Granny with wide eyes. She gave that some thought. "Well, then, on Halloween I'm going to sneeze and sneeze!" They all laughed, and even Clara smiled at her youngest.

They met others along the way and soon came to the large wood frame structure that served as the Union Hall. Colleen carried her box for the box social carefully. She had spent hours decorating the shoebox. First she'd covered the box with tissue paper, making sure the lid was covered separately so it could be opened without spoiling the wrapper. She'd mixed a paste of flour and water to make glue and cut dozens of small pink roses out of tissue paper. She'd then pressed each one over the eraser of a pencil, dipped the top in the glue, pressed the glued part to the box and then carefully removed the pencil. When the sides of the box were covered in tiny flowers, she fashioned a large pink bow and secured it to the top.

Inside the box was dinner for two. It had baked beans, corndodgers with butter and honey, cole slaw and two large pieces of apple pie.

When they got to the hall, Annalee went with Colleen to stealthily put her box in the cloakroom while the rest of the family waited.

"How come we have to sneak in here?" Annalee asked.

"Because we can't let anybody see whose box it is. The boys have to guess whose box is whose."

"Who do you think will get yours?"

"Well I sure hope it ain't some no account like Elmer Estes that got mine last Christmas. I thought I'd gag on my food, trying to shove it down so's I could get back to the dance. He's a few bricks short of a load even if his pa is one of the bosses."

They joined the family at the door. A man with a patch over one eye took tickets. Joe paid for them and they entered into the large room and looked around. The men joined a group nearby while Clara and the girls looked to find a seat. "Let's sit over here, Ma, on these hay bales!" Polly said. They started over, but Clara stopped and shook her head as they got near the seats. She frowned, shuddered and looked across the hall.

"What's the matter Ma? Don't you want to sit here?" Polly said. Colleen stopped and looked back at her mother. She hoped she wasn't going to have one of her spells.

Clara hesitated. The pungent odor of the hay made her feel nauseous and she had a vague feeling of anxiety, but she couldn't put her finger on the reason. She smiled at her daughter. "I'm OK but let's go over there and sit in those chairs. My back gets tired with nothing to rest it on." So the four of them crossed the room and sat along the far wall.

The fiddlers tuned up with the strains of the Virginia Reel and they watched as several couples walked out onto the floor and formed lines opposite each other.

Sam came over and bowed to his little sister. "Would you care to cut a rug, my lady?" Annalee giggled, hopped up and they walked to the floor to find a line that needed one more couple. Her head, covered with ringlets, barely reached past her big brother's belt and she beamed up at him as if he hung the moon. Colleen watched them proudly as they disappeared into the crowd; then she looked around, hoping to see the handsome stranger, but he wasn't there as far as she could tell.

Colleen danced with several young men; then Sam came back and said, "Come on Sis, let's see what we can do." She followed him out as the band started a schottische. "Oh dang it! I don't know how to do that!" he said, stopping to turn back to the chairs.

"Sure you can. Nothing to it. Now you just follow me. One two three, hop, one two three, hop, one hop, two hop, three hop, four hop." She laughed as he stumbled and stepped on her toe, then laughed and stumbled and stepped again.

"Oh, sorry. I just washed my feet and I can't do a thing with 'em!" he said, shaking his head in mock horror.

"Don't worry, Sammy. I walk on them too!" she answered, laughing. Soon they were almost in time with the music and her cheeks were pink with the exertion. As they hopped and twirled around the room she glanced at the door and there he was, standing near the table that held the punch in the throng of people. After the music stopped, Sam went to find his friends and Colleen went back to sit beside Polly. "There's that man we saw at the drilling contest," Polly said, pointing toward the door.

Colleen grabbed her finger and looked the other way. "For heaven's sake, don't point!" she whispered with alarm. "I know. I saw him while we were out on the floor. Is he looking this way?"

"He's coming over to this side. I think he's going to ask you to dance!" Polly said. Colleen stole a look and sure enough he was making his way through the crowd toward them. Then the music started and their neighbor Billy suddenly stood in front of her with his hand out. "You're in fine fettle this evening, Miss Colleen," he said with mock formality as he held out his hand. "Would you care to dance?"

Colleen smiled and hesitated for a second. "Oh, hello, Billy," she said brightly, looking over his shoulder at the other man. It was very poor manners to refuse a partner; so she nodded yes, and with much chagrin followed him to the floor.

After the dance was over, she hurried back to Polly and stole a glance toward the stranger, then studiously looked the other way.

Suddenly he was standing directly in front of her. She looked up and smiled.

"May I have the next dance?" he asked with a twinkle in his eye. "Faith, I'm thinking a man has to get in line around here!" Colleen blushed and nodded. Her heart beat like a drill on solid rock as she jumped up, almost tripping on her own feet in haste, and followed him out to the floor as the music started.

"Excusing my feet, I'm hoping you are!" he said with a lilt in his voice. "They have a mind of their own, they do, and don't always go where I tell them to!"

Colleen laughed. "You're new here, aren't you?"

"Aye, my uncle and I arrived about a week ago. My name's Ryan Kelly."

"Irish?" she asked, as if he could be German with a name like that.

"And how in the world would you be knowing that?" he answered with an even more pronounced brogue.

She laughed. "Me too, I'm Colleen McCarthy." They danced two more dances before it was time for the auction and by that time she knew he was from Pennsylvania where he'd worked in the coal mines.

Close to midnight the music stopped as everyone gathered around the stage to bid on the box lunches. Colleen's was the fifth one and she stood nervously off to one side trying not to give away that it was hers. "Yours is the prettiest box here!" Annalee whispered to her.

"Shhhh!" her sister hissed. When her box was held up, the bidding was lively

"Five cents!" a young man with a beard called out.

"A dime!" a friend she knew from school countered.

"Two bits!" Billy yelled, looking right at her as if he knew it was her box. Colleen looked around for Ryan. He stood and watched from the edge of the crowd. She caught his eye and smiled but he made no move to join the bidding.

"Forty cents!" The man with the beard yelled. Forty cents was higher than any box had raised so far and Colleen was proud of the job of decoration she'd done.

"Four bits!" The boy from school answered. Nobody wanted to go higher; so the box was handed down and Colleen came up to claim the box and her dinner partner. Disappointed, but trying bravely not to show it, she followed him to the back of the room. "He's not a bad lad," she thought to herself. "It could be worse." They watched until all the boxes were auctioned off and Colleen noticed that Ryan never bid on any of them.

After eating, the music started up and soon she was in a whirl of sound and movement. She searched for Ryan each time she returned to her seat but he must have slipped out after the auction. She had hoped he would ask to walk her home.

CHAPTER TWO

August 1891

Would you have freedom from wage slavery?
Then join the grand industrial band;
Would you from mis'ry and hunger be free?
Then come! Do your share, like a man.
            Joe Hill
            Little Red Songbook

For the next two weeks Colleen couldn't get her mind off of Ryan Kelly. She watched for him everywhere and found any excuse she could to get out of the house in the evenings just in case she'd see him. Then early one Friday morning she walked out the door of the post office after picking up the mail. He suddenly materialized by her side.

"Good morning," he said smiling. "It's early you are this fine day!"

She stopped dead in her tracks, suddenly tongue-tied, and wished she'd worn a better dress today instead of the faded one she had on. Her cheeks were bright pink as she tried to adjust to the fact that he was actually talking to her. "Uhh, well, hello! Mama likes me to get the mail right away. A letter from home really perks her up." She took a deep breath, recovered her senses and smiled up into his intense brown eyes. She put the mail in the pocket of her dress and racked her brain for something else to say to keep him there.

He saved her the trouble and asked, "Mind if I walk with you?"

"Not at all." They turned the corner and saw a burro with some kids on his back. Colleen nodded toward them. "Do you know who owns that little burro?"

"No, can't say that I do."

"Well, he's about the richest man in the whole valley. That's Noah Kellogg's burro. He says that little jackass discovered the mine."

"You mean the Bunker Hill and Sullivan?"

"Yes." They continued to walk as she told him the story. "It was about six years ago, they say, and Noah was a gold prospector, poor as a church mouse. He was down and out, but he talked some business men into giving him a grubstake and he went up in the mountains looking for gold. After weeks, he'd used up the supplies and didn't find anything.

He finally came up here, Milo Gulch, and made camp not far from here. He was just about to give up. He went to sleep one night and in the morning his jackass was gone. He had a habit of running off and old Noah was spittin' mad. He'd just about had it with that stupid critter."

"That's not too unusual. I've heard they are ornery beasts."

"I think you're right! Well, the story goes that he was madder than a wet hen and just about ready to shoot that jackass. He trudged up the mountain, looking for him and finally heard him bray. Then he spotted him way up on the side of the mountain, just staring at something across the way that had his attention. His ears were trained forward and he

Noah Kellogg's burro was a major attraction in Wardner since he was credited with the discovery of the Bunker Hill Mine.
Special Collections and Archives, University of Idaho Library, 8-X548

never moved. Noah climbed up to him and realized that the jackass was standing on a mineralized vein of pure silver and he was staring at an outcropping of galena across the canyon. It reflected the sun like a mirror."

They were almost halfway to Colleen's house by the time she finished.

"Wow! That is interesting," Ryan said. "Then is old Noah the owner now?"

"No, he sold the rights, but I hear he has plenty of money to last his life."

The talk soon turned to themselves and Ryan told her about how he'd come to America. "I was born in the old country, my family came over from County Cork when I was ten years old. My pa said this is the land where if you work hard and keep away from the bottle any man can be a success, you're just as good as the next bloke. No lords or earls here that you have to tip your hat to like back home."

Colleen laughed. "I never thought of that!"

"Ma hated to leave her family and the old ways, but Pa wore her down, and I'm glad he did. How about you?"

"Oh, my father's family came over right after he was born, about forty years ago, and mama's family goes way back to early times in Illinois," Colleen said.

"Oh yes, then he came during 'an droch-Shaol,' you know, the bad times ...." He was quiet for several seconds, then continued. "My family still talks about the hunger and the death during the great potato famine. Mama says she saw dead people lying along the road, their mouths green from eating the weeds.... They'll never forget it. We lost a lot of our family... my grandma, uncles and aunts...." He sighed, then, to change the subject, asked, "Have you lived here in the Coeur d' Alenes long?"

"Not very long. We came here on the train when I was going on sixteen. Grandpa George came out to the Territory first. He worked on the railroad; then when that was finished he got a job here at the Bunker Hill. After a couple of years we all came out on the train, Grandma, Pa, Mama and us kids. Then mama's younger brother Alfred and his wife Mattie came out."

"They live here too, then?"

"No, Uncle Alfred is a business man. He has a drugstore down in Wallace."

When they got to the door she invited him in to meet her mother and sisters. The kitchen was hot, but her mother had a fire in the cook stove to heat the sad irons, since it was ironing day.

"Mama, I'd like you to meet Ryan Kelly. He's just recently come here from Pennsylvania." Ryan stood shyly near the door with his hands in his pockets, then inched farther into the kitchen.

Clara put the iron on its stand, wiped her brow with her sleeve and met him in the middle of the kitchen where she shook his outstretched hand. "I'm pleased to meet you. Are you staying at the boarding house?"

"Yes, ma'am," he answered, grinning broadly. He looked at the girls who stood together, staring at him like he'd come from another planet. "And who might these people be, pray tell?"

"These are my sisters, Polly and Annalee."

He shook each of their hands solemnly. "Mighty pleased to make your acquaintance." After a few more minutes of polite talk about the weather he took his leave.

After he left, Polly squealed, "He's so handsome!"

Clara nodded her approval. "He seems like a very nice boy."

"He is, Ma," Colleen said dreamily. "He works up at the mine and he wants to call on me next Wednesday for the lyceum lecture. Abigail Scott Duniway is going to speak."

Her mother frowned. "You don't need any of them high falutin' ideas that she spreads around. First thing I know you'll be wearin' bloomers and ridin' on one of them fancy bi-cycles! You just watch yourself, young lady." Colleen started to answer her back with a sharp retort, but just then they heard Sam come up on the porch. He hung his hard hat with the candle holder on a nail and burst into the kitchen.

He put his lunch bucket, a lard pail with a wire handle, on the table. After ten grueling hours on the graveyard shift, his face was dark with the dust and smoke of the silver mine, but beneath the grime it glowed with his usual good humor. His wide smile showed a row of even white teeth and his clear blue eyes sparkled with life. Lean and muscular, he wore leather hob-nailed boots, sooty bib overalls and a wool shirt. His arrival lifted the mood of the kitchen like a hot cup of coffee mellows a frigid winter morning.

"Well, the fat's in the fire now," he said excitedly as he got the kettle from the stove and filled the wash pan. "The company gave us the so-called vote, you know on the hospital. I just knew there'd be some trick when they said the miners could decide."

"You voted to have your dollar a month go to the new miner's hospital I hope," his mother said.

He laughed bitterly. "No, ma, I tore the damn ballot to shreds and stomped the pieces on the floor, just like most of the others did."

Clara winced. "Don't curse, Sammy, please!"

His sister turned from the stove. "What did you do that for?"

"They let us vote all right, but our hospital wasn't even on the ballot. The choices were to have no doctor care at all and they'd let us keep our dollar, ain't they generous now? Or the great Bunker Hill and Sullivan Company would furnish ground and lumber for a hospital here at Milo. The Union would have to pay for all the other expenses, though, wouldn't you know, and we'd have no say in running it. The other choice was to keep on with the miserable doctor care that they give us here. We ain't putting up with it. That bumbling old drunk they have now don't even know how to set an arm. You seen Mr. Miller lately?"

"Yes, his arm is a mess, all crooked and never will be right. Everybody knows the union can give our sick and wounded better care for our money," Clara answered.

"I'd rather carry a hurt man eight miles to Wallace on my back," he continued, "than to have him mangled a second time by the quack up here." He washed his hands and face in the wash pan and dried with the towel made from a flour sack that hung on a nail near the stove.

He poured himself a cup of coffee, added sugar and cream and got a cold biscuit from the top of the stove; then split the biscuit in a bowl and poured the coffee over it, making what people called a "soakie." He continued to talk as he ate. "The company claims it costs them $1 a month from every man there to run their service. If that's really true then they shouldn't object to letting us take the money and do it ourselves."

Colleen looked at him and shook her head. "You can bet your bottom dollar they're keeping some of that money. With twelve hundred men working there that's a lot of greenbacks. You'd better be careful, Sam, Old Four Eyes will send you packing!"

"They can't do a thing if we all stick together. Trouble is some of the Poles and Dagos and others who just got off the boat don't have good English. They go along 'cause they don't understand, and they're so desperate for work, but those of us who know what's happening have got to make sure they do. The company's not going to pull the wool over our eyes!"

He continued, talking with his mouth full, his words tumbling over each other like stones in the creek, pausing only to take large bites of the biscuit. "Now that the union's here and at the Gem, Mullan, Burke, and all the other miners in this whole country have got together, we're even stronger. The Miners Union of the Coeur d'Alenes is going to be a new force to be reckoned with!" he said with a grin.

"What did your pa do?" Clara asked.

"The same. Almost all the union men threw the ballot down. Surface men voted for the one at Milo. You should have seen the boss! His fat face was puffed up like a grouse on a drumming log. Red as a beet, too." He laughed. "It was right comical." His sister joined in, but she knew it was no laughing matter.

Clara just looked at him sadly. "Well, mark my words," she cautioned with a scowl. "The capitalists won't give up so easy. They've got the money on their side, they won't give an inch to the workers if they can help it."

Sam had followed his father and grandfather into the mines a few months before when he'd turned sixteen. He'd quickly progressed from a low paying mucker's job to work as an underground driller for $3.50 a day. Ten hours a day, six days a week, he wielded a double jack sledge-hammer to drive a drill rod into the rock wall of the stope, the area that was to be blasted. Several of these holes were made, dynamite was inserted to blow up large sections of rock which was hauled out by shovelers, placed in the buckets on the tramway and sent down the mountain to be processed for the silver.

Clara and the girls adored Sam. His mother especially depended on him. Whereas she could see very little light in the world, he seemed to carry around his own candles. He lit up his space and everyone else's with his charm and cheerful disposition. Life was just a wonderful adventure to him and he managed somehow to skim through unscathed between his father's wrath and his mother's black depressions.

When Sam and his father walked up the hill to see what was happening the next morning after the "vote," the union men from both the day and the night shift were huddled outside. Their strident voices punctuated the still mountain silence and Sam could tell they were mad.

"Looks like the company men, those freeloaders, voted the way the owners wanted all right," one of them told them as they approached. "One hundred and twenty-three voted and one hundred and eight voted to build the Company Hospital here at Milo."

"I'm not giving my money to pay for a company hospital! I don't care what they do! I don't trust 'em," one old man said decisively. "Them bigwigs had their chance to do a decent job and all they done is look out for the stockholders. They don't give a God damn about us." The others nodded.

"Looks like we'll pay them to build a hospital here all right," Sam's friend Herbert Wiles told him sadly. Herbert was a year older than Sam but was shorter and more wiry, with a crooked grin and boundless energy. Like Sam, he liked his work and never thought of doing anything else, except hunting and fishing of course, in his off time. Mining was what his family did.

Sam looked at him with amazement, appalled at the defeat that showed in the slump of his shoulders and the resignation in his voice. "That ain't right," he said. "They can't do that! That was not a proper vote and they know it!"

His father Joe, standing quietly nearby, laughed a bitter laugh and spat on the ground with enough force to quell a forest fire. "They can do anything they want, son, they've got all the power."

"Go on in there and read the notice," Herbert said. "It's right inside the door."

They walked inside the change house where each man had a peg to hang his surface clothes when he prepared to go underground. The room was damp with the smell of sweat, wood smoke, wet wool and drying socks. Each miner's hat was also on the peg and his boots were lined up neatly underneath. They went to the bulletin board near the door and read the following:

> *Notice to Employees: By the vote taken this day, the ticket headed "Wardner Hospital" was carried by a majority of 93. Accordingly $1 per month will be retained from each employee's pay for the benefit of the Wardner Hospital. As previously notified, any and all employees who do not wish $1 per month retained for this purpose are not only at liberty, BUT ARE REQUESTED to call at the company's office for their time.*
>
> *V. M. Clement, Manager*

"So we do it their way or we're out of a job?" Sam whispered to his father.

"Sure as hell," Joe answered. "Nothing we can do." He was ready to give in on the issue. He was a tired bitter old man and didn't really expect things to get better for himself or his family, but Sam had fire in his eyes as they stomped back outside.

The knot of men had grown in size when they joined them. More than a hundred voices rumbled and growled as they discussed what to do. Like a swarm of angry hornets, they buzzed around near the entrance to the mine and their voices rose as the injustice of the manager's response registered.

"What are we going to do now? Give in?" Sam said as he looked from one to the other of his fellow workers with fists clenched. He could feel the tension in the air and was ready to go in and clean up on the bosses and the other workers who had sold them out by voting with the owners.

"Every one of the other mine owners in this whole valley has agreed to support our hospital," a man with three fingers missing on his right hand put in. He coughed with the familiar dry, hacking cough that was rampant among all the miners. The others waited patiently until he finally cleared phlegm from his throat in order to speak. "It's only this blood sucking outfit that wants to keep control of our life even when we're sick, hurt or half dead. It ain't right!"

"Not on your life am I going to knuckle under," one of the newer men barked.

"Are you ready to be out of work?" his friend nearby asked him. "Maybe you have a rich grand daddy somewhere but I sure as hell don't!"

"It's not like we're demanding more money," one of the older men grumbled. "We just want to take care of our sick and wounded."

"Did you hear about the explosion over at the Last Chance yesterday?"

"No, what happened?"

"They don't know how it happened, but the powder blew up and killed the driller. They said nothing touched the caps and the candles were on the wall a safe distance away, but he's dead just the same."

They were all quiet for a moment, then the talk of the hospital continued. "Well, I for one ain't about to call at the office for my pay like a whipped dog. I ain't giving my dollar for their damn hospital neither," the new man said.

Then another new man, a strong union supporter from Butte, got everyone's attention. His voice dominated the others and they soon fell silent. It was as if a wave had gone through the crowd. He was a big Swede who was well respected by everyone. He had been silent up until now. "We don't have to take it!" he yelled. "I say we walk!"

"Yes! We walk!" The words rumbled through the crowd like a steam roller, gaining momentum. "We walk, WE WALK!" They picked up their lunch buckets and swarmed in one body down the hill to town.

SHUTDOWN! Three hundred men were suddenly on strike. Not all of them union members but not enough non-union workers were left after the walkout to keep the operation running. Without the mine, the mill down the canyon was soon out of ore, so it closed also within a few days. The noisy mill machinery that gobbled up tons of rock and spit out the worthless ore from the silver suddenly stood silent adding sixty-five to the number of men who hung around the saloons, worked in the garden or took their kids fishing in the middle of the day.

"They can't run their operation without us, and they're losing money every day," Sam told Herbert happily as they went out behind the privy to dig for worms to go fishing. "It can't last for long."

"I don't mind a week or so off myself," Herbert answered with his crooked grin. "A few days of sunshine is just what we need! We may be wage slaves, but we're free men today!" In the North Idaho panhandle, summers are like a blessing, beautiful beyond belief. Cool, crisp nights give way to sunny days with temperatures in the 80's and 90's. Warm breezes waft down from the high rugged peaks bringing the heady smell of cedar, fir and hemlock. Tiny crystal-clear streams gurgle around mossy stones to make larger creeks as they rush down the steep rocky cliffs to join rivers filled with trout.

Colleen escaped the house as often as she could and tried to stay out of the way of her Pa. He hated to see her reading, and when he caught her at it he always found something for her to do. "Always got your nose in a book!" he sneered. "That's where you get all them smart alecky ideas. Clara! Can't you find something useful for this girl to do?"

Joe McCarthy was a man who hated his work but didn't know how to rest. He spread his bitterness around like tar on a leaky roof. The tension in the air when he was home was palpable, and now with the strike, he had more time to drink. He slept late in the mornings, maybe cut a little wood, then hightailed it downtown. He sat on the bench outside the Silver Pick Saloon with his friends, grumbling about the fate of the world and the sorriness of the human race until it was time to go home for the noon meal. After dinner he went back to the saloon to start the serious drinking of the day.

The Silver Pick was one of the few saloons not owned by the company. The two-story framed building on Main Street had a false front and a swinging door. The first floor had several gambling tables and a pot-bellied iron stove in one corner. An ornate, oak bar with a mirror in the back took up the entire back wall. Its owner, a man whose family all worked in the mines, didn't dare openly support the union, but his heart was with the laborers and they knew it.

On most days after dishes were washed and the kitchen cleaned, Colleen walked up the hill and into the forest. Today as she gained altitude she found the last of the summer flowers; purple asters, goldenrod and yarrow. She studied the forest floor like an open book for the secrets it held. One of her teachers had encouraged the students to learn the names of plants. Colleen was fascinated that each and every plant had a name and those names were actually written down, in books. She kept the scrapbook of pressed flowers she'd made then in a little wooden box she called her treasure chest. She remembered coming home from school when they'd first started collecting plants and announcing to Clara "We learned about BOTANY today!" Just then Annalee, who was about six years old, came into the kitchen.

"What didn't you buy?" she asked.

Colleen and Clara looked at her, puzzled. "I didn't say I bought anything," Colleen said.

"Yes, you did, you said you hadn't bought any!'

They laughed. "Oh, you silly nincompoop!" Colleen said, still giggling. "I said BOTANY. It's when you are a scientist and you study all about plants."

She often stopped in an opening where she could see the valley far below and the huge mill. This was her secret place, a place to escape the crowded house, to gaze and dream. The mill was a huge four-story rough board building where the ore was pulverized, washed and agitated to separate the silver bearing rock from the lighter waste rock. Today she sat on a large outcropping and picked three asters to place in the buttonhole of her blouse. She couldn't stay long since she knew there was churning and ironing to do before late morning when Ryan was coming to take her up Milo Gulch to pick huckleberries.

The Irishman had come to call several times since the Fourth of July and she was captivated by his quick humor and steady disposition. He never seemed the least bit upset about anything. Most of all he listened to her and seemed absolutely fascinated by everything she said. She told him of her plans to teach school in the fall and her dream of going to college in Spokane to learn about Botany. He teased her about becoming a "spinster school marm" but she could tell he admired her ambition. She counted the days between their meetings and when she was with him it was as if she were in a different world, a world balanced between tranquility and great exciting possibilities. She wondered if this was love.

When she returned to the house she went into the bedroom to check on her mother. Clara was having one of her spells. She was propped up in the bed and leaned against the iron bedstead as she thumbed absently through the A. C. Roebuck Co. catalog. She dreamed of buying a sewing machine.

"Can I get you anything, ma?" Colleen interrupted her reverie.

"No, dear. I took another dose of laudanum just a while back," Clara said with a sigh. "You get busy with the ironing, and you'll need to get dinner ready for pa before you leave. I just feel so weak…."

"Ok, ma. I'll get it done before I go." Colleen shut the door softly as Clara went back to studying the catalog.

Colleen rushed through her work. The day was going to be hot and she packed a bag with sandwiches, cookies and a jar of iced tea for their dinner. Right before he was to arrive, she got the ice pick and removed several large chunks of ice from the block in the icebox. She put them into the fruit jar of tea, secured the lid tightly and wrapped it in a flour sack to keep it cold. She placed it carefully in the bag, took the lunch and her wide brimmed hat and waited on the front porch.

While she waited, Sam came home. He had a copy of the *American Industrial Liberator* newspaper which he'd borrowed from a friend. Workers in unions across the U. S. read its pages. It was known as the "conscience of the Irish American working class." He sat down on a stump of wood beside her chair and opened the paper, then looked at his sister. He noticed the extra buckets beside the lunch bag. "Going huckleberry picking?"

"Yes, Ryan is coming. He's bringing me a horse from the stables and we're going to ride," she said, her eyes shining. Since Ryan worked days and Sam worked the night shift, he hadn't really gotten acquainted with his sister's suitor.

"Now what did you say he's doing at the mine?"

"He's mucking right now, but he thinks he might be drilling before too long. Have you heard any word about the strike, when it might be over?"

"I don't think it will be long now. We have a meeting tonight...." Just then Ryan rode up on a high spirited roan horse. He led a chestnut filly outfitted with a side-saddle for Colleen. He got off, tied the horses to a nearby fence post and came up to the porch.

He grinned, said a warm hello to Colleen and turned to Sam. "Howdy, Sam. It's catching a lot of fish you are from what I hear from your sister," he said as he took a seat on a bench nearby.

"Yep. Got four nice trout last week. All you have to do is think fish and they fly to your line. You need any fish?"

"Staying at the company boarding house I am. I'll ask the cook." Colleen just beamed and said nothing. She was anxious for her brother to get to know Ryan. They were so much alike, she knew they would be good friends.

"You going to the meeting at the Union Hall tonight?" Sam asked.

Ryan frowned and shook his head. "No, I reckon not," he said reluctantly. "I'm not a member."

"Well, we can sure fix that in a hurry. We need all the members we can get."

"I'm not partial to Unions," Ryan said, his jaw tightening slightly. "America is a free country. We don't really need socialism. Every man should be able to work where and when he wants." Colleen looked from one to the other. She knew Sam's strong feelings about the Union. It was like a religion to him and to her father as it was to many of the men she knew. Her brother's good-natured face went dark. He grimaced as if he had a sharp pain in his stomach.

Sam got up and went to the door, then turned to face the older man. He had a fire in his eyes that Colleen had never noticed before, even when he was furious with his father, which was not often.

"I'd caution you to change your mind about that," he said grimly. "We sure as shootin' don't need no more sponges around these parts!"

Ryan looked at him calmly, he didn't want to argue with Colleen's younger brother.

He smiled a small sad smile and nodded. "Sure and I'll be thinking on that," he said quietly as Sam turned to stomp into the house. "Are you ready to go, Colleen?"

They placed the dinner in Ryan's saddlebag and he helped her up into her saddle. She was disturbed by the words that passed between Ryan and her brother but quickly put them out of her mind. The day was beautiful and the strike would soon be over, then it wouldn't matter who was union and who was not.

She was right on the first premise. One evening a few days later, Ryan picked up a paper on the table at the boarding house. He scanned the August 22nd edition of The Mullan Tribune:

> "Work has resumed at the Bunker Hill and Sullivan this morning after a strike of two weeks. Everyone is rejoicing at Wardner over the favorable termination of the strike. Both sides made concessions though it is said the settlement is slightly more favorable to the miners. All underground men are to receive $3.50 per day and the men appropriate as they please the hospital fees."

When Sam and the other union men heard the news, they were ecstatic. "It's clear sailing now!" Herbert called out to Sam as he waited for him to join him to walk up the hill as they went to work that first day.

Sam, swinging his lunch bucket and hat, caught up with him and slapped him on the back. He laughed his infectious laugh and answered. "I think the powers that be have got the message all right. They backed down before when they tried to cut our wages and now they see that we can't be pushed around on the hospital either. It's about time the working stiffs got some backbone. We won't be slaves for the damn shareholders no more!"

ᨀᨀ CHAPTER THREE ᨀᨀ

September, October, 1891

Remember then, the six-hour day
Must be our first demand;
For miners from our ranks each day
From death receive a call;
The miner's "con" you soon will see
Will lose its deadly pall,
And we'll make this camp a grand old spot
For the workers, one and all.
              James J. Ferriter
              Little Red Songbook

L ife resumed after the strike. The dusty roads of August were sprinkled with welcome September rains and the cottonwoods along the creeks began their annual transformation to bright yellow.

Grandpa George and Grandma Cora's house was directly under the tramway. Night and day, the townspeople heard the sound of the tram cars, each carrying up to 800 pounds of ore, grinding, bumping and scraping their loads along the cables seventy to eighty feet above the houses. Another cable brought the empty cars swiftly back up the mountain to be loaded again. The sounds were constant background noise to the sounds of the town.

Granny was so used to the rumble, rattle and groan of the tons of ore speeding along the cable high above their house, that she hardly noticed it.

One day she was home alone, as usual. George no longer worked regularly since he was sick with miner's consumption, but he spent hours down at the Silver Pick. She had a roaring fire in the cook stove and she stood at a rough wooden table near the dry sink where she kneaded bread dough. She called it "light bread" as opposed to corn bread or fry bread. Her wrinkled arthritic hands snapped and popped the dough with energetic rhythm, throwing the smooth dough on a clean flour sack dishtowel, folding it with one swift motion, then repeating the process. She worked automatically as she daydreamed.

After several minutes, she stopped to tuck a strand of white hair behind her ear and suddenly heard a loud CRACK! She stopped, then a loud BOOM shook the house. The quiet of the day was shattered as the cable carrying a tram car full of ore snapped. Her heart leaped, but before she could move from the spot where she stood to see what was happening, more than a ton of rocks crashed through the ceiling like boulders from hell.

The little kitchen was smashed and granny's body was crushed beneath the rocks like a fragile piece of paper. She never knew what hit her. People rushed out into the road when they heard the noise. They looked up in the sky above their heads and the tramway car dangled from the severed cable like a broken cup on a string, its contents of lead-silver ore piled in a heap where Granny's kitchen had been.

Clara was filling the water bucket at the pump behind her house farther up the hill when she heard the crash and ran down to join the others at the scene. As she approached, she saw the dangling ore car directly over her in-laws' small house.

"It's Mrs. McCarthy," someone told her as she came closer. Her face paled as she looked with disbelief at the pile of rocks.

"She's under there?" she said lamely her voice quivering; then the color drained from her face and she slumped to the ground.

"Somebody get some water over here. She's fainted!" Her neighbor Hilda rushed to her side and when the world came once again into focus she watched numbly as women and a few men dug frantically at the pile of rocks. The larger ones had to be dragged by mule from the mangled body. Clara sat on the hard ground, watching the activity as if it were a nightmare. She thought about her parents-in-law, George and Cora. What she thought she could not voice, but she wished with every breath that she took as she stared at the pile of rubble that old man McCarthy had been in the kitchen and met the rain from hell instead of his dear wife.

Chapter Three

For the next few days the talk at the saloon was of the accident. "It was just a freak occurrence," one of the storekeepers insisted.

"Like hell it was," said a union miner. "I heard that one of the men told the boss that cable was frayed. The company is out to make as much money as it can. Cables cost money. They should have checked it out but that would have slowed down the operation." He laughed a bitter laugh. "Wouldn't want to cut down on the dividends for the investors, now would we?"

"You're damned right," someone else joined in. "Just two weeks ago a man was killed when a rope broke at the Union mine. He fell 95 feet onto solid rock."

"My cousin was bad hurt just yesterday from a cave in. They didn't use enough cribbing timbers to shore up the manway chute. It's murder as far as I'm concerned."

They buried Granny the next day. Her husband George, their son Joe, Clara and the four children stood at the edge of the hole as they lowered the simple pine box coffin into the ground. Colleen didn't cry, but she felt as if her heart would break. The pain in her breast was sharp, as if a knife had been thrust between her ribs, and she knew for the first time what "heart ache" really meant. The old woman was her confidant, her friend and her inspiration.

After the coffin was shut, the priest made the sign of the cross over the grave, and the prayers were said, the people drifted silently away. That afternoon they quietly assembled back at the house, arriving by foot, wagon and horseback bearing gifts of cakes, pies, fried chicken, potato salad, pickled beets and corn bread. They all lived with specters of that ghastly trio, death, illness and injury, and they mourned their losses together and went on. They knew the sad routine all too well. Usually the danger was in the deep shafts in the bowels of the earth, however. They weren't prepared for this, an innocent old woman struck down in her own kitchen.

The day after the funeral Joe went back to the mine and Clara and Colleen went back to washing, carrying water, cleaning, cooking and all the other daily chores. That night Joe came home late, which was not unusual. Clara could tell she was in for it, just by the way he wore his cap pushed back on his head, but little did she know just exactly what she was in for. He threw the hat and lunch pail down near the door. "Well, what are you looking at?" he growled.

"I'm not looking at anything," she answered quietly as she stooped to pick up the hat and pail. She slowly put the hat on a hook near the door then took the pail over to the table. She knew she should stay out of his way as much as possible, that when he'd spent three hours at the saloon he was probably looking for a fight.

He glared at her. "Ain't no sin to have a tipple or two when a man's done with an honest days work!" he mumbled.

"No, I kept your dinner warm," she said as she put the plate in front of him and filled it with venison steak and potatoes. She knew if she could get him to eat and go to sleep things would be all right, but he was in a quarrelsome mood.

He ate a little then pushed the plate aside as if it was poison she was trying to feed him, and stood up shakily. "I'm going over to see Pa. He can come over here and live with us now he don't have Ma to tend to him."

She looked at him in disbelief. "We have no room for the old man," she said softly. "Where on God's green earth would we put him?"

"Always room in my house for my own flesh and blood. Sam can sleep on the cot here in the kitchen."

She stood up and faced him. She felt sick, and her heart thumped inside her breast like a sledgehammer as the full import of what he said sunk in. She hugged her thin arms to her body to keep from trembling. "No, I won't have the man in my house!" she cried, then covered her mouth in fear. She knew better than to talk back even when he was sober, much less when he was stumbling drunk.

"Sure you will, and I'd like to remind you whose house this is, woman!" he yelled. He stepped toward her threateningly with fists clenched, and she cringed against the wall, trying to make herself as small as possible. Then he turned abruptly and went out the door. She threw herself on the bed and sobbed as if her heart would break. Several minutes later, when all her tears were out and she felt as hollow as a fruit jar and just as breakable, she got up, washed her face and went into the kitchen to clean up the dishes. It wouldn't do to have the children see her this way.

The house was unpainted, rough-hewn boards with a small porch on the front. The front door from the porch led to the sitting room. To the right of the sitting room was the kitchen and off the kitchen was a tiny bedroom where Clara and her husband slept. Above the bedroom was a loft area where the three girls slept on a corn husk mattress on the floor. They climbed up to their "roost" as they called it on a ladder nailed to the wall near the cook stove. Sam slept on a day bed in the sitting room in the winter but now in summer he had his bed out on the porch.

Colleen came in the front door and into the kitchen. She looked at her mother closely. "What's the matter, Ma? Pa give you trouble? I saw him coming so I slipped over to Sally's place." Sally O'Sullivan was her best friend. She lived on the first street above Main Street with her mother, Maggie, who was a widow, and her little brother Tommy.

"He's going to bring his father over here to live. For me to take care of."

"Well, it can't be that bad, can it? I can help. He's likely not to last long as sick as he is. Miner's con is going to get the old coot."

Her mother looked at her in despair, "I'd sooner have a snake at my table. But I'll say no more of it," she said shrilly, then slammed the door behind her on the way to the outhouse. She knew there was no way she could refuse the sick old man, and neither her children nor the community would understand. Anger had accumulated in the depths of her soul like rust on the tramway cable, and year by year it frayed her mind and hardened her heart. Every day the weight of it dragged her down. She wished with all her might that it had been her life that was crushed beneath the ore. She took an extra dose of laudanum and went to bed early.

They moved the old man into the tiny house two days later. He ensconced himself in their most comfortable chair and proceeded to take advantage of his good fortune in having such an able, if not cheerful, waitress and nurse.

After dinner a few days later he squinted up at her with a toothless grin when she brought his coffee. His eyes, scratched from years of exposure to the gritty dust of the mine, watered constantly. "Thank you kindly, maam," he said as he spit in the can next to his chair. Tobacco dribbled down from the corner of his mouth and he either didn't feel it or didn't care. Clara turned back to the kitchen without answering, disgust and revulsion on her face.

Colleen sat at the table. She frowned at her mother. "Grandpa is trying to be nice, Ma, seems like you could be a little kind to him."

"I'm doing my duty," Clara snapped as she gave her a look that could wither most people like early frost on tomato plants. It never daunted Colleen. She shrugged her shoulders and started clearing the table. Her mother's dark moods and animosity, especially toward her grandfather, were mysteries she chose not to contemplate. She began clearing the table and looked at the ornate pieces of silverware as she picked them up. Rogers Brothers Victoria pattern, it was her mother's most precious possession and their one luxury.

Clara and her brother Alfred had been part of a stable, loving family in their early years until tragedy turned their lives upside down. When

Clara polished the silver, as she did often, she remembered her mother's words:

> *"Now my darling, when I am gone, I want you to have this lovely silver. You will need to keep it polished, but it will last for several lifetimes. And I want you to use it. Don't put it in a drawer to be forgotten." Clara, age eight at the time, nodded obediently and ran out to play, never dreaming that their lives would soon be changed forever. Her father was killed in the Civil War and her mother would follow him three months later. She died of "autointoxication from stasis" or slowdown of passage in the bowels, according to the doctor, even though she had used "Jamison's eager colon cleanser" for months. The doctor said her condition was complicated by nervous exhaustion.*

Now Clara's only comfort was her God and the promise of a life in the hereafter. "Lord knows," she often thought, "there's nothing much in this world worth hoping for."

She clung to the promise of salvation like a drowning woman clings to a rope. She looked to the priest for solace while Joe and most of the other men looked to the saloon. Colleen sometimes thought the men had the better idea, at least they seemed to have fun.

Clara tried today, as she often did, to get her daughter to attend Mass. "Now Colleen, come with me to Mass tonight after supper. There's a new priest and he's preaching at early candlelight. It'll do you good,"

Colleen lifted the stove lid and put another piece of wood in before she turned and frowned at her mother. She shook her head. "I can't see that Jesus has done you much good, Ma," she said. Clara's face fell. Her beautiful daughter's words were thorns that could pierce her heart. She shrugged her thin shoulders and sighed as she sat down at the table. She had the same dark hair as the girl, and the blue eyes, but she was a bigger boned woman than her daughter and thirty-six years of mean living, birthing seven children and the bitter grief and disappointment of losing three had taken its toll. Now she had the old man on top of everything else.

Her eyes had dark circles under them and her hand shook as she poured herself a cup of coffee. "Colleen McCarthy," she said with little hope of making an impression on the head-strong girl, "that's blasphemy, even if it is true, and you don't know the half of it. So shut your mouth before the Lord strikes you down dead!"

The girl looked at her with irritation tempered with a touch of contrition. "I'm sorry Ma. I got no right to make cracks. But I don't know why you put up with the way pa does. Women have RIGHTS you know. I've heard tell that more than likely someday we'll even get the vote!"

Clara shrugged her shoulders and snorted. "Humphh! And just what good do you think that'll do?" Just then Polly came in with her knitting. Polly had a round face and was built more like her father, stocky and sturdy, but her disposition was like Granny's. Steady and dependable, she loved to sew, embroider and was learning how to knit. She often helped Clara with sewing projects and spent hours looking at pattern books with her. "Mama, can you help me here? I must have dropped some stitches a couple of rows back."

Clara looked at her second daughter with a smile. This was something she could fix.

"Bring your chair over here by the window so we can see what we're doing." Colleen looked fondly at her mother and sister, sitting by the window, their heads together, one dark and the other light, concentrating on the task at hand, then she slipped out the door to take a walk.

* * * *

Sam's pay helped the family to keep afloat, and Colleen helped by housekeeping for neighbors when they were ill or had a newborn, but the jobs were few and far between. Most people in the area were as poor as they were. She had worked for Mrs. Estes doing cleaning and laundry until the strike, when the manager's wife told her she wasn't needed anymore. Colleen surmised that Sam's activism in the union had something to do with it. She kept the money she'd earned in a tobacco can in her dresser drawer, hoarding the few dollars as if they were diamonds.

She came home one day from town and went to her dresser to see exactly how much she had left. When she took the lid off of the can she couldn't believe her eyes. It was empty.

"Ma," she called into the kitchen. "What happened to the money I was saving? I had sixteen dollars in here and it's gone!" Her mother came into the room. Her shoulders sagged and she looked at the girl with hopeless eyes but said nothing.

"Pa took it didn't he?"

Clara nodded. "I'm sorry. I know how hard you worked for it, but there's nothin' I could do. He just went in and got it the other day. Said he needed it to pay on our bill down at the store."

Colleen glared at her mother with contempt. Anger boiled up inside her like a tide.

"That's not fair! That's stealing! More likely he spent it at the saloon!" She shook with fury at the injustice. She wanted to strike out at someone but she knew her mother was powerless, so she finally shrugged her shoulders and went outside. When her dad stumbled through the door a few hours later, she didn't dare say a word to him. She knew there was no use appealing to him. In his eyes she owed him for the roof over her head and the food she ate. He didn't owe her a damn thing.

She escaped to the woods and spent hours exploring by herself. Her friend Sally once asked her, "Ain't you afraid to go off up there in the woods alone? There's wolves and catamounts, you know. My ma won't go out of eyesight of the houses."

Colleen shook her head and smiled. She and her brother had explored the nooks and crannies of the mountains since they were children. "I reckon I'm not in any big danger," she said brightly. She wanted to explain that she had a much greater fear of her Pa when he was drunk than any wild animal out in the forest. She would never breathe a word about that, though, even to her dearest friend. It was too humiliating to admit to such shameful goings on.

"I want to study plants someday," she confided to Sally. "I want to be a botanist."

"What's that?"

"Like I said, a person who learns all about plants. You know that teacher we had in school two years ago? We learned all about it."

"I don't remember that."

"Don't you have the book of flowers we pressed? The teacher said even a woman could do it if she got the proper education."

Sally shook her head. "Well, maybe it's somewhere."

The tapestry of the deep forest, interwoven with pungent smells of woods, water and earth, soft pine needles, rich soil, mossy boulders and pristine streams, was a refuge for Colleen's private dreams. She studied how the light slanted through the green boughs late in the day. She greeted the trees, the huge ancient firs, cedars, hemlock and larch, like old friends and inspected each wildflower and each track in the soft earth as others would a fine painting. Free of the tensions in the little house, she crept quietly for miles along deer paths alert for the rustle of a grouse, rabbit, coyote or bobcat. Once she came around a huge outcropping and was almost nose to nose with a black bear. She backed off briefly around the rock until she could hear the crash of brush as he escaped, then she continued on her way.

These sightings of deer, elk or bear were always reported to Sam and the family. Colleen never carried a gun, but they relied on wild meat for the larder, and her pa and brother liked to keep track of the game for future hunts.

She often walked for miles up swift-flowing Milo Creek past the mine and the steel pier that carried the tram line and on up Haystack Peak above Wardner. A spring here gurgled out of the cliffs and filled a small pool with crystal clear water before it tumbled down the mountain through lichen-draped firs and around mossy banks. Huge boulders were scattered near the pool below the ridge, and if she climbed to the top of the tallest one she could see the smoke from the houses a mile below. Bald eagles sailed on the wind currents above her head and red tailed hawks circled and gave their rusty cry when they spotted her below. She spent stolen moments at her secret spot, stretched out on a flat boulder, dreaming and planning the future. First she would get a teaching job, then save her money to go to college.

With the long summer behind them now, she relished the days of glorious autumn when the nights dipped down to freezing. After the hot and dusty summer, the fall rains washed the land clean, and frosty nights painted the trees and bushes in brilliant reds, yellows and golds. The rich dark green conifers only accentuated the blazing glory of yellow aspens and cottonwoods along the creeks and rivers. Fiery red maple dotted the sides of the draws and in the gulches up the narrow canyons ninebark leaves curled into tiny fists of orange and sumac burst into brilliant red.

High up on the mountainsides, among other giants, the larch gradually showed its face as its needles changed from the green of its neighbors to a feathery light gold. In the spring and summer the mountains were all a uniform darkness, but as September gave way to October the larch gradually became visible as if conjured up by magic. They were like hundreds of bright candle flames lit one by one on the dark mountain slopes and matched the aspens down below for pure gold.

*   *   *   *

Colleen mourned her granny and thought of the dear old woman often as she rambled through the forest. It was Granny who had first taught her to identify many of the medicinal plants and wildflowers long before she learned the word "botany." She could hardly bear to walk along the street where Granny's house had stood. The pile of rocks was still there although the precious lumber had been carted away to build new buildings.

One day she did walk by the pile of rubble and stood staring for several minutes in a deep reverie. She felt totally alone, empty and deserted. Sadness settled over her like a frayed gray blanket. The day was gloomy as well, with huge black clouds looming over the mountains threatening rain. As she stood quietly, though, it was as if Granny was suddenly there, right beside her. She remembered the two of them walking to town one day as they so often did. They met Lily Thompson, one of Granny's friends. Lily had one arm that was useless, just shriveled up, and she carried it close to her body. She also had a limp and used a cane. Lily hailed them from across the road with a wave and a big smile and they crossed over to visit for a few minutes.

After they left her and continued on, Granny said, "You know Lily's husband was killed last month. Crushed in a rock slide at the Last Chance. She has six little ones to clothe and feed, but you'd never know she had a care!"

"How does she do it, Granny? Keep going so cheerful and all?"

"What can she do?" She stopped in her tracks and looked hard at her granddaughter. "The Lord gives us each day, child. Just this day, and whatever happens it's still our day to do with."

"I don't think I could stand it."

The old woman looked at her sternly. "Oh, yes. You could. You just put one foot in front of the other and keep on keeping on." Colleen frowned, thought of Clara, and it was as if Granny read her mind. "Now don't you go being hard on your Mama. She does the best she can."

"But Mama is healthy...."

"Someday you'll understand. There's different kinds of wounds, dear, different hurts. Some you can see, like poor Lily's arm, and some you can't. It's the wounds of the soul that are hardest to mend." As Colleen stood there, alone, by the pile of rocks, a great peace enveloped her.

She thought a lot about Ryan Kelly. He was smart and it seemed he knew about everything. He read books and newspapers and told her about things happening in New York and Ireland. He liked music and could play the banjo and sing, but his lighthearted demeanor and charming personality hid a serious, contemplative nature. He was the first in his family to finish high school in Pennsylvania, and he told her how he wanted to go to college. He had gone to work in the coal mines with his brothers, his father and uncles as a temporary measure. But then his father had died the next year from consumption and he and his two brothers were left with their mother and younger sister.

When one of his uncles decided to go out west to seek his fortune, or if not fortune at least adventure, he asked his nephews to go along. Ryan was the only one to say yes. He was all for it and he started packing that same night. Like many of his friends, he had dreamed of the west for years and read everything he could find about the wide-open spaces and gold mines of Montana, Idaho and California. He'd read Joaquin Miller's book "Songs of the Sierras" and had devoured a little book called "The Resources and Attractions of Idaho Territory." In the latter he underlined the words; *It is ascertained that Idaho, in spite of her isolation and her numerous discouragements, has produced in precious metals since the discoveries of gold in 1860, the enormous sum of $90,000,000."*

"The iron horse is plowing its way into every corner of the west," his uncle Sean Kelly told him. "And now that Idaho has become a state, the whole country is wide open. The sky's the limit, my boy! We'll get in on the ground floor!" Sean was more like a brother than an uncle. He was only eight years older than Ryan. Ryan's mother was the oldest child and Sean was next to the youngest in a family of ten. Sean, like Ryan, was tall and well built, but he was darker and more quiet. The two had been close friends their entire lives.

They landed in Wardner, got a room at the boarding house and were soon employed at the mine. Ryan wrote his mother:

Dear Ma:

The country here is really beautiful. Like pictures you've seen of Switzerland. The mountains are astounding! They rear up for miles all the way into Montana. I've gone out hunting a few times and a person could eat good just on the fish in the rivers.

You asked me about the work here. It's work, that's about all I can say. It's not any better than the coal mines back there, the same dirty, dark and damp holes in the ground. The only difference is that in the silver mine we don't work in such cramped spaces. I don't know how Pa stood it all those years. I feel like I'm going down to hell when they lower us down. The dynamite we use makes silver mining real touchy, even worse than the coal mines if that's possible. Four men were killed at the Black Bear Mine last Wednesday. An explosion filled up the mouth of the tunnel with dirt and shut off the air supply. I aim to get out of the mines as soon as I make enough money, but don't worry about me. Real careful, I am, and the men on my crew are steady. They listen to the rock, they say it talks to you and as long as it's talking everything is alright. When the popping and grinding stops and it gets real quiet we're supposed to get out pronto cause that's when it's going to crash.

You know how I'm always whistling? Feeling jumpy I was when I first started, and commenced to whistle. The other men jumped all over me! Seems whistling is bad luck. Supposed to drive out the good luck spirits, it is.

We have a pet mouse down in one of the tunnels. His name is Henry. We know which one he is because one of the men painted his tail. They say that's another way to tell if the rock's going to give, if the mice scatter.

That's all for now,

Your son, Ryan

The young Irishman especially hated going down in the cage. He always felt like he was being buried alive. The "cage" was a platform with sides and a partial roof similar to an elevator in size and dropped at up to 1,200 feet per minute. It was held with a thick wire cable powered by compressed air attached to the top. The hoistman up on top worked the cables that moved the cage and directed the system of warning bells to move men and equipment. Their lives were in his hands.

Apprehension settled over Ryan like drilling dust every day when he arrived at the change room. The room, where the workmen kept their clothes, was in a small wooden building next to the mine, with a horse shoe over the door for good luck.

Today Ryan put on his underground clothes, which had dried from the day before, and hung up his surface clothes. Then he donned his boots and was given his allotted three candles and matches to last for his shift. The candles were precious and he guarded his carefully.

As he left the change room, he passed Sam and the other men from the night shift on their way out. He said "Hello, Sam," but Colleen's brother just nodded curtly and went on. Ryan noticed one of the men he passed had a hand that was curled like a claw and held toward his body at an odd angle. "Cramps," he thought to himself. He'd never gotten them, but knew it was important to eat the salt tablets provided and to stop repetitive movements at the first sign of a headache.

He chewed his lip and suddenly grew quiet as he and the other men on his shift walked into the open cage. The warning bell sounded and they began the jerky descent into the black bowels of the earth. The cable whirred and the cage thumped and thudded as it hit the guiding timbers on the fast trip down. They plunged into the dark shaft as the smell of damp ground, rotting timbers, powder smoke and stale air enveloped them. He tightened his grip on the iron bars of the cage and

Each man was allotted three candles for his shift
before he went down to the stope.
Historic Wallace Preservation Society, p.16962, Wallace, Idaho

The smell of damp ground, rotting timbers, powder smoke and stale air
surrounded them as they ate their dinner by the light of their candles.
Historic Wallace Preservation Society, p.16962, Wallace, Idaho

watched the shadows of their candles flicker on the damp rocks. It seemed as if the walls were moving toward them and he had a sinking feeling in the pit of his stomach.

The Bunker Hill was known as a "dry mine," and it was, compared to others, but water dripped on top of the cage and on their heads just the same. Small rocks tumbled down on top of them and bounced off their hard hats like hail. Sometimes a large boulder became dislodged and crashed down the shaft as well. Then Ryan's heart pounded and he covered his head with his hands as he cringed and held on for dear life with the others.

Now the blackness was absolute except for the candles they carried and the lights as they passed "rooms," large caverns at every two hundred feet where men worked. The tiny candles on the hats of the miners there flickered in the blackness like fireflies as the cage flew past.

Suddenly the cable came loose. The cage dropped abruptly and Ryan was terrified. He had left his Catholic faith back in Pennsylvania, but he started saying "Holy Mary, mother of God, pray for us sinners now ..." and crossing himself as fast as he could. The man whose hand was on the automatic brake was quick, however. It was only a matter of seconds that the cage was out of control. He jerked the handle of the brake on the cage, called a "dog," and the sharp teeth of the brake bit into the wooden timbers alongside the shaft and the cage stopped abruptly. When the cable was secure, they continued.

The farther down they went, the warmer it was, often over a hundred degrees. Whether it was winter or summer up on top made little difference down below.

They finally arrived at the central "station," where mining supplies, water barrels and extra gear was kept. They exited the cage, and Ryan breathed a sigh of relief as they walked past the mules that pulled the carts of muck to the hoist. Then they went on to the stope where he was to work that day.

Once under way, he wielded his shovel and kept pace with the best of them. Mucking was the toughest job underground. After the drillers set the dynamite and blasted the rock, it was the mucker's job to shovel the raw ore into the ore cars so it could be hauled to the surface.

Ryan looked forward to the day when he could start drilling, but even more he dreamed of getting out of the mines. Each night when he emerged from the depths of the mine after ten hot dirty hours of labor, he felt like he'd been resurrected; and that particular night after such a close call, he was exuberant just to see the sky and feel fresh air in his lungs. He felt like a butterfly emerging from a cocoon and he didn't know how he could face going back, but he did.

Colleen and Ryan made a handsome pair, but after Sam's discussion with Ryan about membership in the Union he seldom came over to the house. Sam had informed their father of Ryan's refusal to be a part of the union.

On Halloween night Sally had a party. It was to be a taffy pull and Colleen had agreed to meet Ryan there. She was excited and hurried through her work that evening in order to get ready. She wore one of her best dresses, had her hair pulled back in a coil at the back of her neck and had lightly dusted her cheeks with pink tinted powder. As she came down the ladder and headed for the kitchen to get the molasses cookies she was bringing, her pa stopped her. He'd been down at the Silver Pick most of the afternoon and he was spoiling for a fight.

"Where you going all dolled up like some kind of hurdy gurdy girl?"

"Just down to Sally's place," she said quietly, ducking her head and heading for the kitchen. "She's having a bunch of us over to make taffy."

He screwed up his mouth and mimicked her, "Just down to Sally's place." Then he growled. "I bet that Ryan fella, the scab, will be there too." Colleen nodded and turned to leave.

"Wait just a minute, young lady. I didn't hear you. You answer me!" She looked at him with smoldering disgust.

"Yes, Pa," she said through clenched teeth. "He's coming."

"Then you just get your fancy duds off. You ain't going nowhere. You ain't hanging around with them kind." Colleen looked at her mother, who stood nearby watching nervously, but she said nothing.

"But, Pa …."

"Don't you give me any back talk," he yelled as he advanced toward her. "You hear me? Now get up yonder and change your clothes, and while you're at it, scrub the paint off your face."

Colleen did as she was told. She meekly went up to the loft, but she was growing up and getting bolder; she wasn't going to give up quite so easily, she wasn't going to lie trembling under her covers with her hands over her ears trying to block out the rasp of his voice as she had as a little girl. She rustled around as if she were getting undressed, then waited quietly. Like the rabbit who knows the ways of the coyote, she knew his pattern. She knew that if he didn't start in on her mother, he would be snoring in less than an hour, at which point she would tiptoe down the ladder and out the door.

All was silent down below except for the occasional consumptive cough of her grandfather in the parlor. Colleen always had a book to retreat to. Like a magic curtain for the mind, it waited for her to slip between its covers and emerge in another world at a moment's notice. She sat by the tiny window at the end of the attic room where light from the setting sun still filtered, and opened her current book, *The House of Seven Gables*, which she'd borrowed from a friend. Soon she was in New England at the old mansion on Pencheon Street where old Matthew Maule was executed for the crime of witchcraft. After about an hour she closed the book and came very quietly down the ladder.

Her mother was in the parlor darning socks and her two sisters played checkers at the kitchen table. They whispered "gotcha!" very softly when they captured a man. Gramps snored in his bed in the corner, and Pa was stretched out on the bed in the next room. The goal of everyone in the house was to keep from waking him up. Colleen went to the kitchen to get the cookies, put on her coat, opened the door softly and started out. Her mother put down her darning and followed her out to the porch. She quietly shut the door behind her. She wrung her hands on her apron and looked at her daughter. "Now Colleen, don't do this," she whispered. "You know what he said. He'll tan your hide if he finds out."

"I'm going, Ma. I don't care, and he more than likely won't never know unless you tell him!"

Clara shrugged her thin shoulders and sighed. "I don't reckon I'll say anything," she said wearily as she turned and went back into the house.

The girl walked down the muddy dark street toward town. A light swirl of snow began to fall, the first real snow of the season, but she could still see the stars high above the mountains. It felt good to be outside and she couldn't wait to see Ryan again. *I don't care if Pa does find out,* she thought defiantly as she made her way. *I'm pretty near grown and he can't stop me any more!* As she got near Sally's house she saw a figure coming toward her through the snow.

"It's waiting for you I've been!" Ryan called as he came closer. "We all were wondering what happened to you, and I just thought I'd come and see. I knew I should call for you proper like, at your house." He got in step with her and she looked up at his handsome face. Snowflakes settled on the bill of his cap and his eyelashes.

She smiled and shook her head. "I just had some chores to do," she fibbed, then decided she owed him a little more truth. "And you know it's better if I meet you somewhere else," she added quickly. "My pa's in a terrible temper and there's no sense getting him riled." As they approached Sally's door he put his hand on her arm. It was the first time she'd felt his touch, and her heart beat like a woodpecker on a dead tree. She turned to face him and waited.

He looked into her eyes. "Sure and that's just what I've been thinking. Now you can tell me, Colleen," he said earnestly. "Your Pa don't want me courting you because I'm not a Union Man, that's right, ain't it?"

She nodded dejectedly. "That's right. And it seems so silly," she answered. "Sam and Pa are so caught up in that Union they can't see anything else." Then she added in a rush "I don't see why you can't just join?"

He shook his head and frowned. "I'm not believing in unions much. Pay here is a lot more than we got back home. There we got two dollars if we were lucky!" He turned to knock at the door. Then he looked at her with his engaging grin. "Now don't you worry about it," he said lightly. "My dear Mama always says things have a way of working out."

Sally opened the door and they were swept into the warm kitchen, which smelled of candy, popcorn and cider. Billy, Colleen's neighbor and admirer, was there as well as four or five others. After greeting them warmly, Sally rushed back to the stove to continue stirring the candy. She was a plain girl, big boned like her mother, with brown hair and blue eyes, but she always had a kind word and a smile and she never lacked for beaus.

Her cheeks were flushed from the heat and she wore a large white apron over her dress. "Billy, come over here and stir this for awhile," she said. "I need to get some refreshments for these two."

"Glad to oblige," Billy answered as he took the spoon and began to move it back and forth.

Sally watched for a minute, then shook her head and laughed. She came back and took the spoon from him. "No, no. You have to really stir it. Go around and scrape the bottom, like this," she said impatiently as she vigorously stirred and scraped the dense candy. "Now you try it," she commanded. By this time everyone was laughing.

"Bill, I don't know if you can handle this candy making or not," Ryan said chuckling as he took off his coat. "Just think of it as mucking a pile of sugar and you'll get the hang of it!" Laughter rocked the little kitchen and Maggie, sitting in the other room with her knitting, looked up and smiled.

Several of Sally's and Colleen's friends from school were there and a couple of younger boys who were Sally's brother Tommy's friends. "What's Sam doing tonight? I thought he might come too," Tommy asked Colleen.

"I'm afraid he's up to no good. He's roaming around town with some of his rowdy friends. You know old Mr. Jackson, who lives on the street down below us?"

"Yes, we can't get near his yard without him bawling us out!"

"Well, I have a feeling Mr. Jackson's sugar shack is going to be tipped over into the creek! I just hope he's not sitting on the throne when it happens!" They laughed at the thought.

Sally brought out some apple jack. "We've got some of Ma's hard cider for the fellows and punch here for the girls." Later in the evening Colleen took a few sips of Ryan's apple jack.

Sally was aghast. "Colleen, how can you stand that stuff?"

"It's quite delicious," she answered giggling. "I just may have some more later on."

Ryan had brought his banjo and took it out to play. He smiled at Colleen as he began picking a few chords and soon all the chatter stopped and they gathered round. "Here's a song I learned as a kid in the old country," he said. "It's a catchy little ditty about a highwayman. Sure and most of you might know Brennan on the Moor."

"Oh, I know that," Colleen said. "Granny used to sing it to us when we were just babes."

Soon Ryan's clear, strong, deep voice filled the little house and Maggie came in from the other room to listen as he sang with his Irish lilt:

It's of a fearless highwayman a story I'll tell:
His name was Willy Brennan and in Ireland he did dwell.
Twas on the Limerick Mountains he commenced his wild career,
Where many a wealthy gentleman before him shook with fear.

A few of the audience joined in to sing the chorus, and Colleen's voice was one of the strongest. Her eyes sparkled and she sang with gusto:

Brennan on the moor, Brennan on the moor,
Bold and yet undaunted stood young Brennan on the moor.

Then Ryan took up the next verse as people clapped time to the music.

A brace of loaded pistols he carried night and day,
He never robbed a poor man upon the King's Highway.

46

But what he'd taken from the rich, like Turpin and Black Bess,
He always did divide it with the widow in distress!

Now Billy and couple of the others who were not Irish and didn't know the song, joined in for the chorus as well, with Colleen leading them.

Brennan on the moor. Brennan on the moor.
Bold and yet undaunted stood young Brennan on the moor.

Ryan sang several more verses, then stopped to catch his breath and have a drink. He looked at Sally and raised his glass. "Outstanding cider, this is," he said with a grin. "Now I'm thinking you know this one." He said to the group as he adjusted the banjo and took another swig. "It's Drill ye Tarriers Drill."

Every morning at seven o'clock
There were twenty tarriers a working at the rock
And the boss comes along and he says kape still,
And come down heavy on the cast iron drill.
And drill ye tarriers drill!

Then several joined in for the chorus.

Drill, ye tarriers, drill!
It's work all day for sugar in your tay;
Down behind the railway.
And drill, ye tarriers drill,
And blast! And fire!

Then Ryan took the lead again for the verses:

Now our new foreman was Jean McCann,
By God, he was a blame mean man;
Last week a premature blast went off,
And a mile in the air went big Jim Goff.

Next time payday comes around
Jim Goff a dollar short was found;
When he asked "What for?" Came this reply,
"Yer docked for the time you was up in the sky."

When the verses were over, Billy looked at Ryan quizzically. "What are tarriers anyway?"

Ryan laughed and shook his head in disbelief. "You mean you never heard of who built all these fine railroads? Sure and I'm certain Colleen here can tell you." He nodded to Colleen and winked.

Colleen blushed and told Billy, "It was the poor Irish who worked on the blasting gang to build the bed for the railroad tracks."

Other songs were sung and they played games like "Clap in, clap out." The girls sat in a circle and all the boys left the room. A girl called out the name of one of the fellows for her partner and he was called in. He looked carefully at each girl, then sat beside the one he thought had picked him. If he was right, he got to stay, if wrong he was "clapped out" and banished back outside. The game continued until all had partners.

About ten the party broke up and Ryan walked Colleen home. He took her hand as they left the boardwalk and came to the rough road going up the hill. She let him hold her mittened hand and her heart beat so hard she thought she'd faint from his touch.

When they got to her porch she looked up at him and smiled. "It was a lovely party, wasn't it?" she whispered. He nodded and kept her hand for a moment longer as he looked into her eyes as if she were the most wonderful thing on earth.

"A jolly good time it was," he replied smiling. For a second she thought he was going to kiss her, but he just squeezed her hand and let it go.

"I'll be seeing you soon, Colleen," he said, "Lord willing and the creek don't rise."

She laughed and said "I hope so," and he turned and walked down the road. Colleen stood on the porch for a few minutes watching him as he disappeared into the night. It was only then that she remembered Pa and what could be in store for her.

She opened the door and went in quietly. Then she saw him sitting by the stove smoking his pipe. Her heart gave a lurch, but she recovered quickly, said, "Howdy Pa," and moved resolutely toward the ladder to her room.

"Wait just a minute!" he bellowed. "You come sneaking in here like some alley cat! I've a mind to whup you good!" He walked to the wall by the water bucket where he kept the razor strap. Colleen stopped and waited. Her mother came out of the bedroom in her nightgown.

"Joseph, please. You can't do this," she said approaching him. "The girl's pretty near to grown!" She put her hand on his arm. He shoved it away.

"The hell I can't! And you go siding with her you'll get the same! I told her to stay home and she went right against me!" Colleen looked at them. Tears welled in her eyes but she was determined not to cry. She hated the groveling that it took to placate him almost more than the threat of a beating.

She stood up straight and looked defiantly into his face. She was out of his reach and intended to stay that way. "I just went over to Sally's house. I wasn't alone with anybody. There's no harm in that."

"No harm, you say? Long as you're under my roof, you'll do as I say!"

Colleen's knees were shaking but she shook her head and looked him straight in the eye defiantly. "That's not fair!"

"I'll show you what's fair! Don't you talk back to me!" he said as he changed direction and picked up a stick of wood from the wood box behind the stove. He advanced toward her and she backed off. She watched him for a second, her heart beating like a hammer against her chest, then turned and made a dash for the ladder. Red faced and furious, he let the wood fly, but his aim was off and it hit the table nearby. The coal oil lamp on the table fell and the glass chimney crashed into a hundred pieces.

Colleen didn't look back, but climbed the ladder quickly, expecting any second to be hit by another piece of wood or called back, but her parents were quiet. She quickly undressed and put on her nightgown in the dark. Her sisters were awake, staring up at the ceiling with wide eyes, but they were as quiet as mice for several minutes. Colleen crawled into bed with them and hugged Polly, who slept in the middle.

When they finally heard Pa go into the bedroom, Polly whispered to her older sister with awe in her voice, "Pa was mad as a wet hen when he woke up and found out you'd gone. What was that crashing noise?"

Colleen laughed and answered her little sister with a bravado she didn't really feel.

"Just an old stick of wood! He couldn't hit the broad side of a barn if his life depended on it! It broke the chimney on Ma's beautiful lamp though. She's going to be just sick about that."

"It's lucky you didn't get a beating!"

"Yeah," Annalee whispered from the other side. "I'm scared, Colleen," she said starting to cry.

"Now you just quit that, Annalee, you hear me? Pa ain't bad when he's not drunk," she said. "You know he don't do much but rant and rave. Polly, move over here and I'll get in the middle." Polly crawled over her and she scooted to the middle. She hugged the little girl.

"I defied him, sugar," she whispered. "You just be good and you got nothing to worry about." After the girls were asleep she lay wide awake, thinking and worrying. She was old enough to be on her own. After hours in the darkness she finally made up her mind on a plan and gave in to restless sleep.

CHAPTER FOUR

October, November 1891

It is we who plowed the prairies; built the cities where they trade.
Dug the mines and built the workshops; endless miles of railroad laid.
Now we stand, outcast and starving, 'mid the wonders we have made;
But the Union makes us strong.

Ralph H. Chaplin
Little Red Songbook

Early the next morning before the family stirred, Colleen dressed quickly, then quietly took a small bag from the storage box beside her bed. She put her nightclothes in the bag, then added an extra dress, underwear, toothbrush, hairbrush and comb. Then she inched softly down the ladder to the kitchen, avoiding the rungs that made noise. She paused in the dark kitchen to put on her coat, hat and mittens then glanced at the clock on the shelf near the stove. It said seven. She let herself out the door, went to the outhouse then started down the hill toward Wardner Junction. She had five dollars she'd saved from doing chores for a neighbor and she planned to take the stage from the Junction to Wallace. It was slower than the train, and she had to wait awhile at the stage stop, but it was less money.

Soon Clara got up and made a fire, first in the cook stove and then in the heater in the sitting room. Then she put the coffeepot on the stove. She went into the bedroom and got the chamber pot from under the bed where Joe was still sleeping. As she headed toward the door to empty the pot, Polly and Annalee crept down the stairs. Clara glanced up to the attic. "Colleen," she called. "You need to get up now. Today is washday you know and you need to cook the breakfast so I can get an early start!" The two sisters looked at each other. "What's the matter?" Clara asked.

"Colleen's done gone," Polly said as she handed her mother the note they'd found on the stool by the bed; then she looked around the kitchen. "Did you see my sampler I was working on yesterday?" Clara, busy opening the note, just nodded toward a chair nearby, and Polly picked up her work. It was a large square piece of muslin with roses and ivy stamped around the edges and the words "Home Sweet Home" in the middle.

Clara stared at the note in her hand and the two girls watched her face as she read:

"Don't worry about me, Ma, I'm going to Wallace to see about work. I knew if I asked you, you would say no like before but I heard they're fixing to put on a new school marm and I think I have a chance."

Clara sat down and put her head in her hands. "How could she do this?" she mumbled to herself. "She knows how much I need her around here!"

Then Joe came into the room all sleepy eyed and groggy. "Do what?" he asked quietly. He was always humble and polite the morning after a rampage.

"Colleen's gone. She went to Wallace by herself."

Joe frowned and shook his head. "Good riddance is what I say," he growled. "One less mouth to feed!" Clara sat down on the kitchen chair and hugged herself as if to keep everything together, as if her thin body might just fly into a million pieces if she let it go.

He looked at her briefly and then turned his attention to the floor. "Don't worry your head about it. She'll be back here with her tail between her legs in no time. You just wait and see. You have any coffee over there?" Clara got up and poured his coffee then proceeded to stir up some biscuits.

"Now my dear," he said. "I know you've had your eye on some piece goods over at the merc. You and me just might go see about it come Saturday."

Clara looked at him and nodded. "That would be right nice, Joe." No more was said as Clara rolled and cut the biscuits and put them in the oven.

Sam came in from the night shift before the bread was done. The aroma of baking biscuits and coffee permeated the little kitchen. While he took off his coat, his sisters filled him in on the news. "That girl!" he said, shaking his head. "I swear she's got more gumption than a man."

His mother looked at him and smiled a wan, sad smile. "I reckon she'll be all right," she said nervously. "She will surely go to my brother."

His father scowled and looked at his son. "It ain't becoming in a woman to be willful. She'll come to no good end, you mark my words!" Clara opened her mouth, started to respond, but caught herself in time. He knew he had been at fault last night and she knew that he knew. Now for a few days she could count on a sincere, quiet, mild mannered husband who kept the wood box full. She blamed Colleen more than she blamed him. If her daughter had minded him, if she wasn't so headstrong, he wouldn't have been forced to lose his temper.

After breakfast, Joe went to work, Sam went to bed and the girls went to school. Sam slept up in the loft in his sister's bed when he was on night shift in the winter.

Later on Clara needed baking powder, and since Colleen wasn't there, she decided to walk to town. It was a nice day, chilly but warm in the sun. She got as far as Main Street when suddenly she was so overcome with fatigue that she could barely keep her head up. She moved in slow motion, as if she were swimming against a heavy current. She was overcome with a dark sadness like a heavy curtain over her mind. She stopped for a moment, pondered what it was she was going to town for and sighed. She shook her head and struggled to continue, then finally gave up, turned around and went back to the house.

Her father-in-law was up sitting in the kitchen waiting for his breakfast when she got back. She managed to fry some eggs for him, then went to the bedroom, lay down on the bed and pulled a quilt over her head.

Hours went by. The fire in the wood stove died down and the ashes in the cook stove in the kitchen were cool that afternoon when Sam got up around two. He went to the bedroom door and called his mother. "Ma, you all right?" he asked.

She roused from her fitful sleep. "Son, is that you?"

"Yes, ma. You get up now. The girls will be home soon."

"That's fine, son. You make the fire and I'll be up directly," she answered groggily as she pulled the covers tighter around her head. When Polly and Annalee burst through the door Sam had a fire crackling in the stove and water boiling for tea.

"Ma's having one of her spells," he told them. "Go in and see if you can rouse her."

* * * *

53

Colleen arrived in Wallace in the late afternoon. She hadn't seen the town since the big fire the year before, which had burned most of the wooden buildings, but it was rebuilt within months and again throbbed with life. It was similar to Wardner in size and boasted, in addition to the railroad, five doctors, ten lawyers, a brewery, twenty-eight saloons, a theater, a bank, a drugstore, a new Episcopal church, eight restaurants and six hotels besides three lodging houses, a blacksmith, laundry and livery stables, not to mention the "pleasure houses." Colleen was most excited, however, about telephones and electric lights, things that had not made their appearance in Wardner. She had heard that a few people here had the new inventions.

She knew she'd be welcome to stay at her uncle's home on the hill-side above town, but she didn't feel like telling him about her troubles, and she knew his wife, Aunt Mattie, would pry and wheedle until she spilled everything. Her mother's brother and his wife had little use for her pa anyway, and the less they knew the better. She went instead to Mrs. Parker's house which was just off of Bank Street. Mrs. Parker, a widow, did sewing for everyone in Wallace. She was Sally's grandma and Colleen had stayed there with Sally's family two summers ago.

The widow, an upstanding citizen of the town, was considered well off. People said her late husband had invested in one of the mines in the valley and done quite well when it was sold to a large company. She had the latest model Burdick treadle sewing machine and fine uphol-stered sofas and arm chairs in her parlor. She had a fancy new icebox and water was piped right into her kitchen. But the thing Colleen loved about visiting Mrs. Parker was her books. She had two large bookcases full of books and she was generous about loaning them out.

Colleen walked from the stage stop along Sixth Street and turned on Bank. She stopped at the corner to inspect the impressive pyramid of ore samples the town fathers had erected there. There were chunks of ore from almost every mine in the district, tangible testaments to the wealth of one of the richest mining districts in the world.

Colleen arrived at the substantial two-story house with wrap around porch and gingerbread trim. She went up the steps, knocked on the door and waited. Finally the door opened, but instead of Sally's grandma, a young woman a little older than herself stood inside. Colleen was con-fused. She thought perhaps she'd gotten the wrong house. The girl was beautiful and wore a pink satin dress that fit over her slim figure as if it were painted on. On her feet were black patent leather shoes that had five buttons up the front. Colleen stared at this apparition and finally mumbled, "I was looking for Mrs. Parker."

The girl smiled and put her hand on her hip. "Well, darlin' you got the right house but the wrong woman! Come on in." She opened the door widely and motioned for Colleen to come in. She inched hesitantly inside the door and wished she hadn't come here.

"Now just take a chair over there. Miz Parker will be back quicker than you can blink your eye. She just went over to the dry goods for some needles. You getting some sewing done?"

"No, I'm sort of a friend," Colleen answered shyly.

"I'm Ruby. Glad to meet you, Sort of a Friend!"

The younger girl giggled. "My name's Colleen. I come down from Wardner today."

"All by yourself?"

"Yes, but I have an uncle who lives here. Maybe you know him, Mr. Buchanan, he owns the drug store down near the livery stable."

"I can't say that I've ever met him. I don't believe he's one of our regulars though." Colleen looked at her blankly. "Well what are you looking to do here?" Ruby continued.

"I'm hoping to get a job at the school. I've got a letter of recommendation from my teachers and I heard they recently lost their teacher." Just then Mrs. Parker came in the door. She was a small, white haired woman with an abrupt, no nonsense way of speaking. She began talking a mile a minute as she set down her package and began to take off her coat.

"I swear that Michael Brown is as slow as molasses! Took him ten minutes to find one little package of needles!" Then she noticed Colleen. "Why Colleen McCarthy! Bless my soul! What wind brought you here? Is Sally with you?"

"No, maam. I'm just here by myself. I was wondering if I could stay with you for a few days."

"There's always a bed in my house for you, girl! Just let me finish up with Ruby here and we'll rustle us up some dinner. In the meantime you can put the kettle on and help yourself to the cookies there by the stove. Made them just this morning, I must have had a notion I'd be getting company!" Relieved at the welcome, Colleen did as she was instructed. As she was filling the teakettle from the cold water tap, she heard a faint ticking sound directly above her head. She looked up and there was a light bulb hanging from a black cord on the ceiling. She was amazed. It went on as if by magic. The bulb glowed with a soft light and she watched it for several seconds, mesmerized.

Soon Ruby left and Mrs. Parker came into the kitchen. "You have electricity!" Colleen said excitedly. "I've never seen it work before! How can it come on all by itself?"

The old lady chuckled. "Yes, it's real nice. We got a water wheel on the creek that makes the power. It turns on from the power plant at 4 o'clock in the afternoon and back off at 7 o'clock in the morning. I just have the one light in the kitchen here. Costs me $1.50 every month for one light, but it does make it handy in the winter, especially, not to have to light a lamp all the time." She went to the stove and poured boiling water into the teapot.

"Did you get Ruby's dress finished?"

"No, this was just a fitting. I have to hem it up yet."

"It's beautiful, and I haven't never in my born days seen such fancy shoes as she was wearing!"

"Yes," the older woman said as she sighed and sat down at the table. "She's a lovely girl, but not the kind for a good Christian girl to be seen talking to. I'm sorry you happened to come in just now." Colleen's eyes widened.

"You mean ..." she faltered, not knowing how to say the words, "she's one of those... those fallen women?"

"Yes," Mrs. Parker whispered as if the neighbors might hear. "I do sewing for Miss Bessie's girls. They pay me well, but you don't tell a soul about it, you hear? If my other customers find out they'd never set foot in my house again!"

Colleen loved secrets, and she laughed. "Don't worry. I won't breathe a word," she answered. "I thought she was rather nice!"

"Huh!" the old woman snorted. "Now what are you doing here today, may I ask?"

"I heard they were looking for a teacher and hoped to apply."

"Why, yes, dear. I think they are. The new one we had was only here for a month before they had to ask her to leave. Word was that she was riding around in broad daylight with some Dago kid! The school board couldn't have that."

Colleen nodded. The next day she went to the man's office who was chairman of the school board and asked about the job.

"Well, young lady," he said good naturedly. "You're just a mite too late. We gave the job to Mr. Brown's daughter just last week, but if you'd be so kind, fill out this form here and we'll keep you in mind. Miss Liza has the boys buzzing around like bees to honey. She just might take a notion to get married, and then we'd need a fine girl like yourself." He looked her up and down, then added. "Course, I'm afraid you be a mite too pretty as well. You'd not likely last long, soon as the young men get a gander at you."

56

Colleen blushed, took the form, sat down at a desk nearby and filled it out. Then she handed it to him and turned to the door. "I would like the job just the same if you'd keep me in mind."

On the way back down Cedar Street she ran into Ruby. "Well, did you find out about the job?" she asked.

"Yes, but they already hired somebody," Colleen answered, her voice faltering.

"Well, never you mind," the older girl said sympathetically. "Come on up to my place and have a cup of tea." She nodded to the stairs beside the door of the Oasis Saloon.

"Oh, I don't think I'd better," Colleen said with a nervous giggle.

Ruby shook her head and laughed. "Now what is there to be afraid of? I swear I don't bite," then she added wickedly, "at least not so's I leave much of a mark!" Colleen wasn't sure what she meant by that, but she laughed also. She was curious about this bold, beautiful girl and the house of sin where she lived and worked.

"I reckon a cup of tea won't hurt," she said shyly, and followed the older girl up the stairs.

The stairs that led up to the second floor had a buzzer on the third stair from the top so the madam always knew when someone was there. When the two girls got to the top they came to a heavy door with a small peep hole at eye level. They knocked and the small window in the top of the door slid open. A bloodshot eye appeared in the slot and the door swung open. Colleen knew she shouldn't be there, but curiosity overcame fear as she followed Ruby inside and the door was shut behind her. The owner of the establishment herself had let them in.

"This is Miss Bessie," Ruby said. The woman gave her a smile. She had a gold tooth right in front of her mouth and she was dressed in a green robe that was none too clean. Rings adorned both her hands and she gestured for the girls to go down the hall.

"Come in, girl," she said heartily as she looked Colleen up and down approvingly. After the examination given by the school board chairman and now this, Colleen felt like she was on display at a side show. Miss Bessie was always looking for new girls, not that a local girl could work here, but she would send her to Spokane or Walla Walla and get someone from there to come here.

Colleen blushed at the woman's gaze and backed toward the door. She decided this was really a bad idea, and she wished with all her heart she'd never come. She saw four big locks on the door they'd just come through.

Ruby noticed her apprehension and giggled. "This is Colleen, Ma," she said as she grabbed her new friend's hand. "All the girls call Miss Bessie, Ma" she explained to Colleen, then turned back to Bessie. "She's a friend of mine. We're going to have some tea." Bessie scowled and went back to the sitting room.

"Don't mind her," Ruby said. "She don't like us getting too cozy with the town folks. Bad for business, she says. But I get plumb tired of these girls here sometimes!"

Colleen looked up and down the narrow, dark hall. At the right end was the door where Bessie had disappeared. "Do you want to see my room?" Ruby asked.

"Sure," Colleen answered dubiously. The hall to the left was lined with doors on both sides and they opened one about halfway down on the right. It was a tiny room with a double bed, dresser with a mirror and a commode with a large pitcher of water and a bowl. An oil lamp with a beautiful rose colored base and a chimney with a rose etched in the glass stood on the dresser. Hanging on the wooden frame of the mirror was a beautiful hat with silk flowers on the brim. Two more lavish hats with feathers hung on the flowered, wallpaper wall. Nice, fashionable clothes were flung carelessly on the bed and draped over the two chairs.

"This is where I sleep and also where I entertain the gentlemen," Ruby said, looking at her new-found friend slyly. Colleen nodded and looked around, impressed that she should have a room of such luxury. She thought she knew what Ruby meant about "entertaining gentlemen," but her knowledge was vague.

The two girls went back down the hall to the small kitchen where Ruby prepared tea. Colleen was fascinated by her hands. They were as soft and white as a baby's cheek and her nails were long and perfect. "Never has to use a scrub board, carry in wood in the biting cold or stand for hours washing a pile of dishes," Colleen thought enviously.

They talked for an hour and Ruby told Colleen about growing up near Portland, Oregon. An only child, her parents had died in the flu epidemic when she was twelve and she'd been sent to live with an uncle. "He took liberties with me from the first night I was there," she said matter of factly. "He would whip me good for hardly no reason, too. I had to do all the wash, the cooking and cleaning. I ran away when I was fifteen and got started working the next year after that."

"Ain't it hard, though," Colleen said haltingly, "with just anybody who comes in?"

"That's what the peep hole is for. If Ma sees the man is drunk or if he is dirty she won't let him in. Ma's really good about that. It's sure better than the last place I worked, in the cribs in Portland. If there's some-body we don't like we can say no, too, and let some other girl take him." She glanced nervously at the door. "Course, we don't dare say that very often or we'd be out on the street."

The younger girl nodded. The wheels were turning inside her head as she assimilated this new information of the world. She thought of her mother's role in marriage and this girl's strange life. She sighed, shrugged her shoulders and said, "Seems like a woman don't have it easy any which way. Ma scrubs and cleans and cooks and cuts wood and nurses the sick, and at night when she's plumb wore to a frazzle she darns and mends, that is when she isn't sick and in the bed."

"She don't get paid no six or eight dollars a day or more either, I'll vow!" Ruby said disparagingly.

"No, Pa gives her what money he thinks she needs." Then Colleen felt guilty about her outrageous comments comparing her mother's life to a life of Godless sin and eventual hell fire and damnation. "Pa ain't so bad when he's sober though," she added. "He buys her nice things when he can, and he works hard." She looked at her new-found friend and ventured quietly, "Then I reckon, too, Ma is respectable."

Ruby's face fell at this remark. She looked down at her lovely soft hands and raised wide blue eyes to meet Colleen's. She stiffened and shrugged her shoulders. "I know I ain't respectable," she said belliger-ently. "And mostly I don't care. Respect never put food in my belly nor clothes on my back. I pretty near starved when I took off from my uncle's. I had nobody."

"I'm sorry. I never should have said that," Colleen said apologeti-cally.

"It don't matter," she whispered, her eyes darting again to the door. "I'm saving my money. I've got more than three hundred dollars put away, and someday I'm going to get me a millinery shop." She grinned as she added, "Then you'll see Miss Respectable. Now you'd better get out of here. It's almost three, and I'm supposed to be getting ready for work."

"Maybe I'll come to see you again," Colleen said.

"Yes, please do. It's so seldom I can talk to a person like you, a regular girl. Come tomorrow. After that I get two weeks off and I'm going to Portland on the train."

The next day Colleen slipped away and walked down Cedar Street, hoping to see Ruby. She was afraid to walk up the stairs and knock on the door, but her new friend saw her from the window and came out to meet her. After initial greetings, they walked a short way in silence, then Colleen ventured, "So you make hats?"

"Yes, my mother taught me how to sew and she loved beautiful hats. I've made them for a lot of the girls."

"The ones I saw in your room were really splendid. Where do you get the materials?"

"I order them from the catalog mostly, but when I go to Portland I'll buy things there." Her eyes darted up and down the street. "I'm thinking we should go back to my house. It won't do for people to see you with me." She laughed. "If you're set on being a school marm, that is."

They turned around and went up the stairs to the sitting room of the house. They talked and talked, each one anxious to learn more about the other's world. Colleen told her about Ryan and Sam and the problems with her mother. Finally she bid her goodbye and hurried down the stairs.

Just as she came out on the street, she saw Sam on the other side. He immediately saw her as well.

Clara had insisted that Sam go to Wallace to get Colleen on the day she left, but he couldn't go that soon. Today he'd borrowed a horse from a friend and ridden along the Mullan Road to the town. It was a crisp cold day with not a cloud in the sky and he was happy for the diversion from union activities and work.

When he arrived in town, he went to their uncle's place first. Uncle Alfred was at home for the noon meal and the couple greeted their nephew warmly. "Come in, come in, son," he said. "We haven't seen you for a coon's age!"

Sam asked if Colleen was there and was surprised when they said she wasn't. "You mean you haven't seen her?" he asked incredulously.

"Neither hide nor hair, son. You sure she come here?" His uncle, a tall thin man with a long drooping moustache, looked the part of a successful businessman, with a stiffly starched blue striped shirt with stiff white linen detachable collar and cuffs, and wool trousers. From a buttonhole of his custom tailored vest a gold chain led to his watch pocket which held a gold engraved watch. He took it out now to check the time since he was due back at the store.

Sam shook his head and frowned. "I'm not sure of much when it comes to Colleen! But maybe she went over to visit Sally's granny. I know they stayed with her before. She probably didn't want to put you folks out."

"Put us out?" his aunt said with a sniff. "Blood is thicker than water, I vow. What on God's green earth was she thinking of? Your sister should have come directly here!" Mattie was a large woman with arms almost as big as her husband's legs. She wore a long cotton print dress with an apron tied around her waist like a ribbon around a barrel. Her dark hair was pulled up to the top of her head in a tight chignon but her mouth was her most prominent feature, constantly in motion, and when she laughed, which was often, her whole body shook.

Sam could tell she wasn't really put out with Colleen. Not much bothered her. "Well, if you don't mind, ma'am," he said with his most engaging grin, "I'd sure be beholden to you for some victuals and a bed this evening!" His aunt brightened immediately and hustled toward the kitchen like a portly hen with a new chick.

"We'd be glad to have you, Sam," his uncle answered. "I'm needed back at the store now, but I'll see you this evening."

"And why do you think your sister took off all by herself?" his aunt inquired later as she and Sam sat down at the table. He shrugged. He knew why his sister didn't come to visit their aunt. She could talk a person's leg off in no time flat. And she was nosy. Not only meddlesome and nosy but smart enough to put bits of information together to find out stuff. In spite of this, he was fond of both of them. These two were their only family for thousands of miles. They had no children of their own and he knew they would do anything for his sisters and himself.

"I reckon she just took a notion. You know how high strung she is, just like Ma, but don't tell her I said so," he said laughing. Mattie rolled her eyes and nodded.

Sam left his horse there and walked back to town. It wasn't hard to track Colleen down. Mrs. Parker told him she was downtown and he headed that way.

Now he stopped dead in his tracks when he saw her coming out of the stairwell next to the saloon across the street. Music from the Victrola inside the Saloon filled the air, and he had to yell to be heard. "Colleen!" he called. He started to dash across just as a fancy cabriolet carriage and four horses wheeled around the corner. It barely missed him and he waited for it to pass before continuing.

Colleen waited for him to come across. "Good afternoon!" she said brightly. "What are you doing here?"

"Me?" he said as he looked at her quizzically and motioned to the building behind her. "What were you doing in there?"

Colleen laughed. "Having tea."

"You know what that place is?"

She adopted the bored look of an older sister tolerating the kid brother. "Of course. I didn't just fall off the turnip wagon you know. And anyhow, how would you know what it is?"

Sam laughed. "The men talk. I've never been to one of these pleasure houses, but," he added defiantly, "I might someday. It's different for men. You know pa would kill you if he knew you set foot in that sinful place."

"I'd be more afraid of Ma. I swear she'd take to her bed for the rest of her life!" They laughed together as they walked along the boardwalk. Colleen was pleased to see her brother.

Sam grew serious. "That's what I come to tell you, Sis, Ma's been real bad since you left, worse than ever. Polly's been doing most of the cooking. You've got to come home. The girls miss you terrible and I know Pa will be all right."

They walked toward the depot. Colleen shook her head. "I don't think so, Sam. I know she needs me but next time Pa starts in on me it will just be worse."

"There's not a thing for you to do here." He glanced back toward the saloon. "I can see you're getting in with some real bad eggs and that will come to no good end."

"Oh pshaw!" she answered brightly. "That girl just needs a friend and I can't see no harm in visiting her."

"Well, it don't matter anyway I'm thinking. The truth is we need you there at home and Pa will be all right. You just have to mind him and quit seeing Ryan. That's all there is to it."

Colleen set her jaw and looked at her brother through eyes that were mere slits. "That's not fair. He's a wonderful person, everybody says so; everybody that is but you and Pa!"

"You don't seem to understand. This is like a war. Sooner or later we'll have another strike. It will be bad again, probably worse than before, and he's on the other side. He's going to be putting our men out of work, taking food off the table of our friends and family all because he don't want to pay the little bit of dues to belong to the union. I don't call that wonderful. He's a scab!" He spit the word out. "A scab's nothing but a two legged pimple that festers and spills its disgusting pus on organized labor."

Colleen looked at her brother with disgust. "Don't be nasty, Sam." She sat down on a bench in front of the depot and he sat down beside her. With sagging shoulders, she looked at her brother. Close to tears by now, her voice broke. "Let's just leave Ryan out of this. Thanks to you and Pa, I doubt if I'll be seeing much of him anyway. You're the one that don't understand. It's not Ryan and it's not just Pa, either. I need to find work. If I can just make some money maybe I can go to school. Is that so selfish?"

Sam, sorry to see his sister upset, touched her shoulder. "No, it's not selfish. I know it's not easy for you, Sis, and we all depend on you more than we should, but right now is a bad time to leave the girls."

Colleen was torn. She knew she would have a better chance of working here where she wasn't known as Sam's sister, but she also knew her sisters needed her and she couldn't bear the thought of Polly taking on all the responsibility that she'd had. That was what finally convinced her. With a heavy heart, the next day she reluctantly agreed to ride back home with her brother. She felt she had little choice since she had no employment. She did, however, borrow several books from Mrs. Parker to read in her spare moments. She wrapped them in layers of paper before packing them carefully in her small valise. She thanked her friend, walked over to her uncle's and visited with her aunt for a few minutes before she and Sam started home. They took turns, riding and walking, back along the Mullan road.

Soon after they arrived back home, Grandpa George died. They buried him with little fanfare, and Clara was not present at the simple ceremony. She was at home in bed with a headache.

* * * *

That fall the Bunker Hill Mine shut down, and about four hundred miners were out of work. This time it was a decision by the owners because of trouble over water rights. The Last Chance Mine claimed the larger company was usurping their water supply. One week later the matter was settled, and work resumed, but the fear and uncertainty of life at Wardner for the McCarthys and other workers continued.

The unions gained strength and numbers through the help of the powerful Miners Union of Butte, Montana. During the struggle for the hospital they had formed a federation of all the unions in the district, known as the "Miner's Union of the Coeur d'Alenes." The mine owners got worried and decided to fight fire with fire. They decided they needed to organize as well. So the "Mine Owners Association" was formed with the largest companies, the Bunker Hill and Sullivan, Helena-Frisco and Gem leading the way. A part of each company's gross output was to go into a fund to crush the union. When the workers heard about this they realized that they were in for an open battle.

* * * *

October days were beautiful, warming at midday and cooling down to freezing at night. Colleen walked up the mountain one afternoon. She worried about her mother and went over in her mind how she could get work. She also worried about Sam and his involvement with the union. She knew he was right, trouble was just around the corner and he was in the midst of it. She decided to go into town and ask around for a job.

Suddenly she heard high-pitched cries high above her head. She looked up at the blue sky and watched two large V-shaped skeins of geese on their way south for the winter. She stood in the road and watched and listened to the lonesome sounds as the geese called to one another, telling stories of their travels, where they'd been and where they were going. She watched until the cries dimmed to quiet and the birds were tiny spots in the endless blue above the mountains. A longing came over her that was almost palpable. She wanted to soar through the crisp air and exchange stories with the geese. She wanted to fly across the mountains; the air was so light and buoyant she almost felt as if she could. Instead she sighed and continued sedately back home.

November turned from yellow-gold to bronze-brown. The tamarack trees on the mountain slopes dropped their brilliant yellow needles, and cold winds blasted through the canyons taking leaves and lovely autumn with them. Colleen had little time to roam the woods up Milo Creek. In addition to the chores of cooking, cleaning and laundry, there was the last of the canning and preserving to do for the winter ahead. Clara often got her and Polly started, then drifted away before the job was finished, trusting the girls to finish up.

Their mother was pale and wan. She often sat in the wooden rocker by the small front window staring out as if expecting salvation to come up the dirt road and carry her away. Colleen tried hard to understand. She knew a good Catholic girl should honor her parents and obey, but she secretly resented the constant pull of responsibility, lack of privacy and constant work. She looked at her rough, red hands and thought of Ruby's soft white skin. She thought of the fine clothes and nice room Ruby had and wondered briefly if going to heaven instead of the other place was worth it, then shook her head in horror at the idea.

"What's wrong ma?" she asked her mother one day after she finished canning twenty-five jars of venison. Her mother sat in the chair, her hands folded still in her lap, rocking back and forth silently. "Do you hurt some place?" Colleen continued.

Her mother finally turned slowly her way. Her face was haggard and drawn. "No, child. I'm fine, just a mite tired. I feel as if I can barely move. I think I'll just go in and lie down for a little while." She looked at her daughter with large sad eyes. "Would you go down to the drugstore and get me some more of my medicine? I'm almost out."

Polly was sitting nearby, looking at the catalog. After her mother left she called to her sister who was getting ready to leave. "Have you seen these electric belt things in the catalog here?"

"What?" her sister came back into the room as she put on her coat.

"Maybe Mama needs something like this. It's the latest thing to improve your health, an electric belt that runs on some kind of battery. It says here it's 'for nervous exhaustion, poor circulation, female weakness, sick headaches,' all those things that Mama has."

"I don't think so," Colleen said shaking her head and laughing.

"It says 'the constant soothing alternating electric current is ever at work touching the weak spots. It will cure you and save doctor bills.'"

"Well, even if it would work, can you imagine Mama putting on something like that?" Colleen said. Polly giggled at the picture. She could see Clara draped with the belt in the picture, jiggling away toward health and well-being.

"Now if it was granny," Colleen continued, "she'd try it in a second!" She shook her head and smiled as she went to the door. "I'll be back in a little bit. Keep the fire going."

She quietly closed the door behind her and hurried out to the frozen, rutted road. It was a beautiful sunny day, crisp and clear as a bell. The mountains had a slight dusting of snow and the air was tinged with the sweet smell of wood smoke, along with the usual smoke and dust from the mill.

With every step she took from the little house her spirits rose. She planned to stop by Sally's house. She didn't get a chance very often to see her friends and catch up on the news. She hadn't heard anything from Ryan since the party.

She knocked at Sally's door and her mother answered. She was a big, robust woman who had never been sick a day in her life.

"Well, look what the cat dragged in!" she said heartily. "What a surprise. How have you been, dear? We heard you took a trip over to Wallace." Colleen came in and took off her coat. Her spirits rose with the sight of her friends and the aroma of coffee and sweet jam that permeated the little room. She sat down at the small kitchen table. It was covered with a starched white muslin tablecloth with embroidered flowers around the border.

"Oh, we're just fine. Yes, I was looking into a teaching job but they already had somebody," she answered quickly, then changed the subject. "Looks like you've been busy just like the rest of us," she said looking over the rows of canned goods on the counter.

"Would you like a piece of bread with some of this choke cherry jam? Sally and me just made it this morning and it's still warm."

"Oh, that sounds divine," Colleen said.

"I'll get some tea," Sally said, "or would you rather have coffee?"

"Tea sounds wonderful." Sally poured the tea into their best china cups and sat down across from her friend. Her mother got biscuits from the warming oven above the cook stove and placed them on small plates. They split open the hot biscuits and spread butter on each side, then added the thick tart-sweet jam. They talked of how much canning they had finished, and of their friends. Sally picked up the latest Godey's Ladies Book from the table.

"Let me show you the quilt pattern in here. It's the most beautiful thing I've think I've ever seen! It's the Dresden Plate. Have you seen it before? Mama and I are going to do it as soon as we get the right cloth. We're going to piece it in all shades of blue with white."

"That will be really pretty."

"What kind of hand work are you working on now?" Maggie asked.

Colleen laughed and shook her head, always embarrassed to admit her lack of skill and interest. "Not much of anything. I swear, I don't know where the time goes. Mama's been doing some tatting lately. It's very pretty. She's made some nice collars and cuffs for one of her dresses."

At last she asked the question she'd had on her mind. "Do you see anything of Ryan Kelly?"

"Not much to speak of," Sally said hesitantly.

"Well, he's still in town, ain't he?"

"Yes, he's still over at the boarding house …."

"Is he seeing anybody? Come on Sally, tell me the truth."

Sally sighed. "Well I heard that Martha Cummings, the new manager's daughter, had a hay ride the other night and he went. I think he's courting her."

Colleen scowled, "That won't last long," she said derisively. "Martha has a new beau every month!"

Sally and her mother laughed. "You're right about that," Sally said. "She changes beaus like we change our socks!"

66

⤳ CHAPTER FIVE ⤳

December, 1891- March, 1892

Scorn to take the crumbs they drop us;
All is ours by right!
Onward, men! All hell can't stop us!
Crush the parasite!

Down with Greed and Exploitation;
Tyranny must fall!
Hail to Toil's Emancipation;
Labor shall be all.
                    Written in Leavenworth Penitentiary
                    By Ralph L. Chaplin

The days grew shorter and gradually, day by day, glorious fall turned inexorably to winter. Winters can be ferocious in the North Idaho Mountains. Snow swirls down from wind swept peaks and often covers the land for four or five months. It stays on the ground in shady spots in the deep canyons and on the high slopes for two or three additional months. Temperatures drop to the teens or below zero, and the short dark days of winter are darker still in the shadows of the mountains. Even on sunny days, the sun only reaches the bottom of the canyons for a couple of hours at midday. Often clouds and fog obscure the sky for weeks on end and the sun disappears entirely as if snatched away from the earth by a vengeful God.

The casual snowflakes that lazily drifted down to the village in Milo Gulch in October transformed into serious snow by the end of November. Previously muddy roads and yards sparkled clean and bright. The ground was covered in a thick blanket of white by mid December, and a body would be unable to touch bare ground until April.

By late December, three feet of snow covered the ground and the branches of the firs and cedars drooped with their coat of winter ermine. On Christmas Eve the sky cleared and the winter sun bathed the world with slanted rays of gold.

After dark, Colleen, Sam and the two girls went down to the depot at Wardner Junction to sing carols. First they walked into town to see the store windows, bright with candles and gas lights. The girls looked longingly into the brilliantly lit window of Levi's Drugstore. The showcase had fancy writing paper of all colors, and pens. Also several plush toilet cases were opened and displayed, each with a fancy comb, brush and manicure set arrayed on a background of pink puffed satin.

Then they continued down the road past the town and black night enveloped them. Colleen held Annalee's hand and gazed overhead. The sky was ablaze with a blanket of stars tacked to the canyon rims with blue black mountains. They continued on down the hill to the depot.

The depot was bustling with activity. Wagons pulled by teams of horses and mules were lined up nearby to unload incoming freight, and people milled about the station, talking and laughing.

Colleen soon found Sally, Tommy, Herbert and other young people from up and down the canyon to sing carols and meet the train as it pulled into the station from Spokane.

The Washington and Idaho Railroad was one of several companies that recently had unrolled silver tracks, like strings from a ball of twine, across the plains, over the Rockies and into north Idaho opening up the rugged mountain wilderness. It had only been completed two years before and was still a marvelous wonder to the residents of the canyons.

The eastbound train left Spokane at 4:00 p. m. and arrived in Wallace at 10:15 p. m. It stopped in Wardner before that. A crowd usually turned out to meet it just to see who was coming and who was going. Christmastime was an especially festive occasion. It was a thrill to see the huge black locomotive emerge from the cold like some imaginary monster and chug to a stop at the little depot. Hearts beat a little faster as the brakes squealed and steam formed gigantic clouds in the frigid air. Then the people spilled out, dressed in furs, muffs, heavy coats and sturdy boots, laden with packages, bundles and bags of every size and description, eyes bright with anticipation of the holiday ahead.

Their breath made little clouds of steam as Colleen and the crowd of young people stood to one side and their clear voices greeted the emerging passengers with the strains of "It Came Upon the Midnight Clear," "Hark the Herald Angels Sing," and "Jingle Bells." They ended, as always, with "Oh, Little Town of Bethlehem" before happily trailing back up the mountain toward home.

Clara had been feeling better the last few days, and that night the family prepared to go to the Christmas Eve dance. Animosities were put on hold in the community for the most part, as young and old, miners and citizens, shop keepers and mine managers would all be there. People came from up and down the canyons, some from as far away as Wallace, Burke and Mullan. A special train was to leave Wallace at seven that evening to bring revelers to the hall at Wardner for the festivities. It would pull out to return to Wallace with its cargo of tired and exhausted dancers at six the next morning.

The hall was decorated for the event. Pungent swaths of pine and fir hung along the walls with bright red bows and silver balls. In one corner a huge pot-bellied stove crackled with a new-made fire and in the opposite corner, farthest from the stove, stood a huge Douglas Fir tree, its branches laden with strings of popcorn, colored glass globes, candy canes and hundreds of small tapers, all aglow. Along the wall, to the right of the door, was the kitchen with a long counter where the food would be served at midnight.

Children of all ages scampered about, and as the evening wore on, the babies and toddlers would drop off to sleep, one by one, on the hay bales, benches or chairs. At the end of the evening, the older children, sleepy-eyed and exhausted, would each receive a candy cane.

Colleen wore her hair up in a pompadour with a beautiful white ribbon in it which contrasted with her dark hair. Her dress was crepe with a braid along the neckline. It had a red velvet yoke and high neck. She wore a large red velvet bow on her left shoulder, and she couldn't wait for the music to begin.

A small wooden organ, painted with black enamel and gold trim, loaned for the event by one of the townspeople and brought by wagon, stood in one corner. Two fiddlers and a banjo player tuned up to join the organ, and music soon filled the room. Then the caller jumped to the stage. He was an Irishman with a melodious voice that could be heard all the way down the street. He started off with a lively square dance, and Kathleen and Herbert squared off to the call:

Choose your partner, form a ring,
Figure eight and a double L swing.
First swing six and then swing eight,
Swing 'em like swinging on a gate.
Ducks in the river, going to the ford,
Coffee in a little rag, sugar in a gourd.
Swing 'em once and let 'em go,
All hands left and do-ce-do.
You swing me and I'll swing you,
And we'll all go to heaven in the same old shoe.

Colleen danced every dance until her feet were sore. She danced with one man of about thirty who was missing his left hand. She held gingerly on to his metal hook and tried to make conversation. The evening, however, was a disappointment. Ryan wasn't there. She searched the crowd as she twirled around the floor, half listening to the chat of her partners. She'd seen him only twice since she came back from Wallace and that was briefly as she walked along the street. She knew he was staying away in order not to cause her trouble. She wanted to tell him trouble was a small price to pay; she wanted to boldly march to the door of the boarding house and ask for him, but she didn't dare. Even she wasn't that audacious! She thought of him constantly and dreamed of the two of them together. His face was the last thing she thought of at night, and after she fell asleep her thoughts turned to dreams. She didn't dare mention his name to her family, however, even to her sisters.

After the dance, they all walked back up the hill along the snowy road. The night was cold, and a sharp wind blew from the west. After they got to the house, and Joe and the younger girls were in bed, Clara, Sam and Colleen decorated a small tree.

On Christmas morning, Annalee's eyes sparkled with anticipation as they all took down their stockings, which were hung above the window, since there was no mantle. An orange, candy and nuts were in each one. Then they turned to the tree. Since Annalee still half-believed in Santa, they all oohed and ahhed over the gifts he'd left. Colleen unwrapped a scarf and new mittens and the two girls each received a new stocking cap. Sam got new socks and gloves.

They finally turned to the gifts from their Uncle Alfred and Aunt Mattie. Annalee squealed with delight when she opened her package and saw a beautiful Majestic doll. "Look!" she exclaimed. "Her arms and legs move! And her eyes open and shut! It's like magic, like she's really alive!"

Joe scowled and shook his head at his wife. He didn't approve of Clara's brother sending such lavish gifts, but there was little he could do about it.

Colleen received a beautiful inlaid comb and brush set, and Polly was thrilled with material for a new dress in a bright red pattern. Sam was happy to find a hunting knife in a fine leather case in his package.

Clara and Joe did not exchange gifts. Money was tight, and anyway, they believed that Christmas was for children.

That night Sam had promised to take Polly and Annalee sledding. "Come on, Sis," he said to Colleen. "Come with us. No use moping around here like some moony-eyed sick cow. You need to get out of the house. It will do you good."

"I'm getting too old for such stuff."

"Oh, hogwash!" he said vehemently. "I think Sally's going to come. She's not too dignified to have a little fun!" Finally she agreed and they bundled up in their long underwear, sweaters, coats, stocking caps and heavy mittens.

As they made their way up the road, Annalee sniffed. She dug into her pockets but came up empty handed. "Sam, have you got a snot rag?"

"Annalee!" Polly said sharply. "That's not a nice word for a lady. You should say 'handkerchief.'" The little girl giggled as Sam pulled a square cloth torn from an old shirt out of his pocket and handed it to his sister.

"I'm not a lady yet, besides, it's not a handkerchief. It's a rag!"

"Well, then, say 'nose rag!'" Annalee wiped her nose and with a shrug of her thin shoulders and an impish grin, handed the rag back to her brother.

After they left the lights of the town, Colleen gazed up in awe at the sky. The moon was full, and it reflected from the snow like a spotlight. The wind had blown the dust and smoke from the mill away and it was a crystal clear, cold night with stars that beamed with uncanny brightness. They sparkled high above their heads like lanterns lighting the way to heaven and Colleen's spirit lifted. Who could possibly be down on a glorious night like this? It was times like this that she knew there must be a God, a kind and just spirit, a brilliant and magnanimous force in the universe.

"Make a wish," Polly said as she stopped beside her.

"Ok," her sister said. "You have to make one too."

"Ok, but it probably won't work because we aren't looking at the first star we've seen!" They stood and closed their eyes tightly with their faces to the sky as Sam and Annalee pulled their sled on ahead.

Star light, star bright
First Star I've seen tonight
I wish I may, I wish I might
Have this wish I wish tonight!

As the crunch crunch of Sam's and Annalee's boots and the swoosh of the sled disappeared into the white stillness, silence enveloped the two girls. Suddenly a great horned owl hooted somewhere up in the trees nearby. His call, like a telegraph message from the universe, intoned one long, two shorts and another long.

"What did you wish for?" Polly finally whispered, reluctant to break the spell.

"I can't tell you or it won't come true!" Colleen replied.

Polly giggled. "You don't have to tell me. I know anyway!"

"Little Miss Smarty Pants. You just think you know." Colleen took off running to catch up with the others and Polly followed close behind.

They met Sally, Tommy, Herbert and Billy on the road. Sally had a large bobsled that could hold four people, and Billy had a sled as well. They all pulled the sleds up the hill toward the mine. As they gained altitude, they could see the twinkling lights of Wardner; Kellogg farther down the gulch, and in the far distance, a faint glowing haze that was the settlement of Wardner Junction.

They came to the leveled off area where the trams were loaded and wagons turned around. A short distance from there they had a bobsled run all the way down to near the Junction almost a mile below. Earlier in the day Sam and Herbert had laid wood and kindling to make fires along the way. They lit the one at the top and the dry wood crackled and popped as it sent sparks up toward the dark trees and into the cold night sky.

"I'll go first," Herbert said as he pulled one of the smaller sleds to the run. "I'll stop and light the bonfires along the way and wait for you at the bottom."

"I'll go with you," Tommy said. They sat down and Sam gave them a push. They swooshed down the first hummock and around a corner out of sight. The others waited for a few minutes; then Sam, Colleen, Polly and Annalee got ready to go on the bobsled. Sam was in front, the younger girls in the middle and Colleen in the back. Colleen wrapped her arms around her sister's waist as Billy pushed them off. A rush of cold air whipped their faces as they gained speed on the steep slope. The dark trees flew by, faster and faster. Colleen felt as if she were flying as they careened down the mountain in the darkness. Annalee squealed with delight. The run leveled off slightly as they approached the bonfire that was near town and they slowed a little. They saw two figures in the shadows near the fire.

They were covered with snow and one tugged at the sled in the snow-drift. They waved as the bobsled got closer. "Hey! Got room for one more?" Herbert yelled, laughing as they barreled down alongside him. "We took a spill!"

"See you at the bottom!" Sam yelled back as they continued their headlong journey into space. Colleen's heart pounded and her breath came in gasps when they finally got to the bottom. Annalee's eyes sparkled like the stars overhead as they unwound themselves and got off the sled.

"That was fun!" Polly said, laughing, "And we didn't spill once all the way down!" Her nose and cheeks were rosy as they went over to the pile of brush and sticks that Sam lit. They huddled around the fire as the flames leapt up and curled around the small twigs as they waited for the others to come down the mountain. Colleen gazed into the fire and dreamed. The night was magical, like a story in a book, and all she needed to make it perfect was for Ryan to appear, but she knew it wouldn't happen. She looked at her brother who stood on the other side of the fire from her with their two sisters on each side of him. The glow of the blaze lit his face and reflected in his eyes. He was right, she thought, it was good for her to get her nose out of her book and come out. He was so often right, she thought, but he wasn't right about Ryan.

Herbert and Tommy soon joined them, then Billy and Sally careened down the mountain next, screaming with delight, breaking the silence. They crashed into a snowbank a few hundred yards from the fire. Laughing, they untangled themselves from the sled and walked the rest of the way, pulling the sled. Finally they joined Colleen and the others around the fire.

Soon they all trudged back up the hill to make the wild ride again. After two more runs, they finally settled down around the fire at the bottom. Tired and happy, they watched the flames and all was silent.

Even Annalee was quiet as the snowy world enveloped them, but then she couldn't stand it any more. "Let's tell stories!" she piped up. "Sam, tell the one about why the moon can't always be big like it is tonight!"

"Well, all right," her brother said. "This is an old story that Granny said came from Ireland. Her granny used to tell it to her when she was a little girl about your age."

"It all started with a war up in heaven. In the beginning the devil was one of God's angels. In fact, he was the highest of all the angels. And God had a parlor up there in heaven, and he told the angels they were never to look in there."

"Why couldn't they go there?"

"Because that's where God kept a picture of the glorious virgin who wasn't to come to the world for two thousand years! Anyway, Lucifer went and looked. God was very angry so he punished him and all the things that took his side. In those times everything could talk, the sun, the moon, the stars, even the ocean, and they all took sides. The sun was on God's side so he stayed the same, but the moon sided with Lucifer so he was reduced to just a thread, then back to and fro to full size again. The sea backed Lucifer too, and until then it was steady, but God had to punish him so he goes back and forth, six hours ebbing and six hours flowing and striking himself on the rocks."

"What happened to the other angels?"

"The bad angels were banished from heaven, and no thicker snow has ever fallen to earth than that time when all the angels were leaving heaven."

"But some of the angels were left up there, right?" Sam got up and poked the fire as he continued.

"One of the angels begged God not to empty heaven, so he said, 'as it is now, let it remain,' so some of the angels are forever between heaven and earth and they fly in the sky in gusts of wind. That's what we see when it snows."

Colleen looked over at her little sister, and her eyes were drooping. "I think it's after some people's bedtime. We need to get home and get into some warm clothes." They all reluctantly left the fire and started down the hill, exhausted and happy. They left the fires to go out on their own in the snow and the coals winked and flickered like candles on the mountain for hours. Years later, Colleen would look back on this night as one of the most beautiful of her life.

The day after Christmas was a regular work day, so Sam got up late and reported for the night shift in the afternoon as usual. He was in the stope two levels down when the boss brought in a new device. He called everyone to the station. "You see this here, boys," he said as the ringing of the hammers stopped and they crowded near. Water dripped from above their heads and the only light was from their headlamps. Shadows bounced from the moist rock ceiling as they tried to see what he had.

Sam, near the front, got a good look at the device. "It's a machine drill," the manager said. "Yes, sir, this here little piece can do the work of five men. We'll have to be making some changes in your jobs." Sam at first didn't realize the implication of the man's words, but while the boss demonstrated the drill, it hit him like the now old-fashioned sledge hammer hit the drill rod. He was low man on the totem pole and he would not be the one in five that would operate the new machine. "We'll be needing more shovelers now to keep up with the output of the new drill," the boss explained. Sam knew that meant a cut in pay to $3.00 a day.

When he got home from work that morning he told the family over breakfast. "It's not so bad for me, living here at home, but it ain't right for the men trying to feed a family," he said glumly.

His father helped himself to more gravy and biscuits and growled. "You're just a kid, how would you like to give twenty years of your life, sacrifice your health and all to the damn company, then be knocked down to mucking?"

The unrest among the workers increased as winter wore on. Grumbling and rumors whirled through the settlements along the river and swept down the canyons like the stinging winds. A few of the workers and most of the storekeepers were loyal to the company, but resentment festered among the men like a sore that wouldn't heal.

After automation arrived with the machine drill, the owners got a real boost in production and miners were thrown for another loop that would push them toward violence.

It was not the miners that made the next move, however. Three months after the Mine Owners' Association was formed, on January 16th, 1892, the owners shut down every mine in the region. Twelve hundred men were locked out in the dead of winter. The feelings of outrage were especially virulent at the Bunker Hill Mine at Wardner.

It was partly the attitude and hard headed stubbornness of one of the managers, Mr. William Schmidt, that made the situation especially volatile there.

Schmidt, a German Protestant, stood near the entrance to the mine on the day of the lockout. Behind him on a post was the following sign: *"Don't get hurt. There are twenty men waiting for your job."* He was despised by every union man in the valley and his disdain for the common workers, and especially the Irish Catholics, was evident in his face and his voice. He drew himself up to his full patrician height and sniffed his Protestant nose as he looked over the crowd of scruffy workers. His voice fairly dripped with arrogance and superiority as he addressed his employees.

"You men know we wouldn't close down if it wasn't absolutely necessary," he began. The men shifted their heavy boots and looked sideways at each other as the man continued. "Here at Bunker Hill we have all we can do to break even. You know that the ore from this mine needs more processing than most. Now the railroad has raised the rates of transport again and the price we get for silver has slipped. We can't afford to continue to pay all underground workers $3.50 a day. Think it over, a little lower pay for a few of you is better than no work at all," he concluded as he stepped down from the ore car he was standing on.

The miners shuffled silently away. They didn't have to think. Some of them had predicted this would happen as soon as the Owners' Association was formed.

Sam walked down the hill with Herbert, Billy, and a new man, Jack Bailey, who sported a large bushy black moustache. Barely five feet eight and a hundred thirty pounds, he wasn't a big man, but somehow he walked with authority. A Texan of Irish-Italian descent and forty-four years old, he exuded a steely-eyed toughness that the younger men admired. The Colt 45 that he always carried on his hip didn't hurt either. He had started to work at the mine last fall after the strike and had immediately joined the union. He was smart and articulate, a natural born leader who got along well with everyone. Sam and the others listened when he spoke. Within a month he had been elected secretary of the union.

"It won't be easy," Bailey said. "I think we're in for a long battle."

"They're out to break our backs," Herbert put in. "Those other reasons for the shutdown are nothing but a smokescreen! The god damn blood sucking company is out to gut the union!"

"It's a war all right," Bailey put in, "but how long can we hold out? New scabs are coming in every day."

"We'll hold out till hell freezes over!" Sam said grimly. Herbert laughed and looked up at the snow laden mountains and the icy stumps where trees had stood along the road. "That may not be too long at that, old buddy!" he said, trying to lighten things up.

But Sam was not in the mood to laugh at their predicament. "It's us against the millionaires," he said. "We're fighting for our lives, for bread on the table and shoes on our feet. They're fighting for their jewels and their mansions in Spokane."

Billy looked at the ground. His family was more destitute than most. His mother had been sick last summer and fall, so there were few jars of canned goods in their cellar. Their cupboards, if not bare, were sparse. "I can't see how we can hold out for long," he said dejectedly. "We're hardly filling our bellies right now, even with me and Pa both working ten hours a day and six days a week." He was scared; they all were if the truth were known.

If any of the miners believed it was economic necessity that shut down the mines, they soon knew, or thought they knew, otherwise. Word circulated in the saloons and barbershops that the fat cats were rolling in dough, and the union leaders had the figures to prove it. Huge dividends of over $30,000 a month were paid out to wealthy shareholders who had never seen the Idaho mountains. Even the skeptics now believed that the excuse of high freight rates was just a ruse to try and force the unions out of the region.

Lead as well as silver streamed from the earth, and the profits as well as the raw material poured back east as fast as it was produced. The largest producer was the Bunker Hill and Sullivan Mine. They produced more and they gave more to their stockholders for the capital invested. Because of the machine drill, the shovelers were driven harder than before to keep up, and wages were much lower in relation to output.

Sam and Joe went to a meeting at the union hall attended by miners from all over the region. Fear and outrage permeated the crowd of several hundred. It was one thing to be out of work in the balmy days of summer, quite another to be without income during the long frigid winter.

The miners assembled in the large union hall, the same place where the dance was held before, but now the Christmas feelings of peace and goodwill were forgotten. The smells of sweat, wet wool, wood smoke and tobacco filled the air. The stove had a roaring fire, and with the crush of bodies, Sam was soon plenty warm. He took off his cap and gloves and stuffed them in his pockets. Joe did the same as song books were passed among the workers.

Five men jumped to the stage along with a fiddler and he tuned up. Many of the older miners were members of the Knights of Labor movement and they sang one of their fight songs:

> *I'll sing of an order that lately has done*
> *Some wonderful things in our land;*

Together they pull and great battles have won
A popular hard working band.
Their numbers are legion, great strength they possess,
They strike good and strong for their rights;
From the North to the South, from the East to the West,
God speed each assembly of Knights.

The audience joined in with loud, booming voices and stamping feet. The rafters shook as Sam and Herbert, along with all the others, raised their fists as they bellowed out the words to the refrain:

Then conquer we must,
Our cause it is just,
What power the uplifted hand;
Let each Labor Knight
Be brave in the fight,
Remember, united we stand!

The leaders sang several verses, then ended with the following:

Then fight on undaunted, you brave working men,
Down the vampires who oppress the poor;
You use noble weapons, the tongue and the pen,
Successful you'll be, I am sure.
With hope for your watchword and truth for your shield
Prosperity for your pathway lights,
Then let labor make proud capital yield,
God speed each assembly of Knights!

After several more songs were sung, the assembly raised their fists, stamped their feet and shouted, "United we stand! United we stand!"

Soon Thomas O'Brian, President of the Central Miner's Union, got everyone's attention. "Now men, we have to stick together. They want us to panic, and that's not about to happen. Not as long as I've got breath in my body!"

"Hear! Hear!" someone responded.

O'Brian continued. "We'll send word tomorrow to the unions across the country. They have pledged their support just as we've pledged ours to them."

After the meeting the men filed out into the cold afternoon. A stiff wind blew ice crystals and snow from a fir tree along the street, and Sam hurriedly put his cap and gloves on as they walked. Jack Bailey walked next to him. "It's a war between the millionaire capitalists and us!" he proclaimed. Sam looked at him and nodded in agreement as they hurried toward the Silver Pick. "They've tried before to cut our pay to

$2.50 a day and it didn't work then and it won't work now!" Bailey continued.

Joe, who walked on Sam's other side spoke up. "They are hoping to starve us into submission!"

"They may just accomplish that noble goal," a thin young man with a limp said sarcastically. "I know I don't have any money saved to buy groceries. In a few weeks time I'll be begging!"

But the miners hadn't counted on their union friends across the west. Within two weeks provisions started rolling in. It wasn't fancy, and there wasn't much variety, but no worker's family would starve. The major mining centers from Butte to Helena, from Denver to Virginia City sent carloads of flour, sugar, potatoes and other staples to the valley. Miners from all over the west also taxed themselves in order to send cash assistance to the Coeur d'Alenes.

The union workers in the valley shivered into January after the shutdown and on into an unforgiving February, when the sun barely peeked over the mountains before it sank down again like a sputtering old candle behind a grimy window pane. Freight cars loaded with supplies rolled in from every direction to support the effort. Sam drove a wagon to the train station to transport the boxes of food. On the side of one train was a banner that said: "From the working men of Spokane to their brothers in the Coeur d' Alenes!" More than $400 worth of food was delivered every day.

Colleen worked at the commissary to unload and help organize the food.

Sam stopped beside her as he carried in a box. "Did you hear that we got some food from clear down in California yesterday?"

"Yes, I heard that. They said it was from Eureka, California. I swear I don't know what we'd have done without all this."

"We wouldn't have been able to hold out like we have, that's for sure. This is a war, Sis," he said, smiling broadly as if he were at a picnic. He poked her and added as he walked past, "And we are the troops!"

"I don't feel much like a troop. I just feel pooped!" Colleen retorted as she stopped and stretched her back.

Fuel for cooking and heating was a major problem. It took a lot of wood to heat the drafty cabins of thousands of families when the temperature hovered between 10 and 20 degrees and plunged to zero in between times. In the years since the valley was settled most of the trees near the settlements had been cut. It was necessary to go farther up the draws and on the mountains to find wood, and cutting, as well as hauling it, was difficult work in the winter.

The miners waited patiently for the next move from the enemy. The Irish, having brought their strong belief in fighting for their rights from the mines of the old country, were ready for the battle.

Joe McCarthy didn't talk much about the situation. He took advantage of the freedom from the mine to maintain a level of alcohol that blotted out most every other worry. Many of the other miners did the same. Long hours of breathing gritty dust and hard backbreaking labor as well as the inevitable accidents and injuries, took their toll on the mind as well as the body. Joe was a broken man at age 40 and he was fairly typical of many miners who would be so crippled up they couldn't work by their late forties.

Clara waited on him hand and foot, and when she was down in bed and couldn't rouse herself to bring him his coffee and serve him his meals, Colleen and Polly did it for her. The girls kept out of their father's way otherwise and Colleen stayed home most of the time. Since she couldn't see Ryan, she felt little need to socialize.

Sam was out and about the community constantly. He talked to other miners and paid attention to the talk about what the company was up to. He read the *Coeur d'Alene Miner,* and they all speculated upon what the eventual outcome would be. They were of one mind on one thing. They would not weaken; they would not be starved out. The community as well as the McCarthy family waited and watched and hoped for an equitable settlement week after cold and miserable week.

The snow piled up, then melted back only to be frozen into place to provide a basis for new snow. The wind swirled down through the deep canyons sculpting the new snow into curls and waves of glistening white.

It was a major expedition to make a trip to the outhouse, and Sam had to shovel the path from the kitchen door to the privy almost every day. The path was a narrow, icy trail between walls of snow over three feet high, and once a person reached the two holed toilet you can bet they didn't stay to read the Roebuck Catalog that they found there for long. It was a shocking wake-up call in the early mornings when Colleen left her warm bed in the attic, climbed down the ladder, put on her coat and opened the door to a blast of frigid air as she headed to the outhouse.

They threw an old rug over the hand pump in the yard at night to keep it from freezing, but when the temperature dipped below zero, it froze anyway, and they had to prime it with warm water. Often, when they got up in the morning, the water bucket in the kitchen had a coat of ice.

Clara usually got up first to make the fire and start the coffee, but some days Colleen got up to find the fire unmade and her mother sitting in her rocker near the window, hands idle in her lap and mending nearby as she stared out vacantly. Lately her stitches were more uneven when she sewed, and she seldom picked up her knitting.

One blustery cold winter day near the end of February, Colleen got up to find the house cold and her mother there by the window, her knitting, a pair of socks she was making for Sam, lay in her lap.

Colleen put a quilt around her mother's shoulders. "Mama, aren't you cold?"

"Yes, I'm cold. But I can't seem to get this yarn to do a thing right! It's a mess. Where is Polly?" Just then Polly came into the room.

"What is it, Mama?"

"Come here and help me fix this." Polly pulled a chair up close to her mother and patiently untangled the yarn.

Colleen, thankful for her sister, hurried into the kitchen to make the fire and set the kettle on to heat. Later that day she walked up the gulch with Sam and Billy. The sun was low in the sky, just above the mountains, and it sent filtered rays of light through the frigid winter forest. A gentle wind sighed and ruffled the tops of the conifers a hundred feet above their heads. The temperature overnight had dipped to 15 and each blade of grass was etched with heavy frost. Each twig and branch of the serviceberry and ocean spray bushes sparkled with white lace. The bundles of needles on the pine tree branches stood out stiffly, like halos stitched around the faces of next year's cones. They glistened and sparkled in the winter sun. As the sun warmed the branches, the ice crystals dropped through the heavy boughs, tinkling like tiny bells.

They looked for a good tree to cut for firewood. The snow was soft underfoot and melting off the trees. They talked about the shutdown and how much longer it could last.

"I heard the railroad is going to lower the rates," Billy said.

"If they do, the company will have to open," Sam responded as they approached a stand of fir trees. "They can't hold out forever. They are losing money every day."

"Well, I wish something would happen," Colleen said. "I'm getting so tired of beans I could scream. I hate washing them, I hate cooking them and I can't stand eating them!"

"At least it keeps your belly from talking to itself," Billy put in. "I can't believe all the supplies that the unions have sent in." They continued across the unstable snow. Colleen made a game of keeping her feet on the crust. She tested each step before putting her full weight down, but every few steps one boot would sink down into a hole, throwing her body off kilter like a drunken miner on Saturday night. Her cheeks, rosy red from the cold, burned and she kept her handkerchief handy to dab at her dripping nose, but she felt she could walk forever. It was good to escape the house.

On the fifteenth of March the company announced they were ready to open. A group of miners clustered around a sign nailed to a post near the post office. The sky was pewter gray and clouds obscured the tops of the mountains. A light cold rain sputtered and spit. Water dripped from Sam's cap as he came up to the group and nodded to Billy and some of his friends.

"What does it say?" someone asked. Many of the workers couldn't read, or were so new to the country that they couldn't read English. Sam stepped up and read the notice out loud:

> *"Due to the fact that the railroad has agreed to lower its rates, the Bunker Hill and Sullivan Mine announces it is opening next Monday morning. All previous workers are asked to come to a meeting this Friday and to report for work next Monday."*

"Hot dog!" Billy yelled as he did a little dance in the muddy street. This was the news they'd been waiting for. The euphoria lasted for a day, until Mr. Schmidt had the meeting on Friday.

Sam stood near the front of a crowd of over two hundred hopeful and happy miners....

Schmidt cleared his throat, "We are happy to announce the mill and mine will reopen on Monday morning," he said to the crowd. Several men shouted "hooray!" They grinned as they looked around at their friends, but Sam noticed Ed Boyce, president of the local union, and as he made his way to the front he wasn't smiling.

"And the pay is the same as before?" Boyce asked as he came to the front and faced Schmidt. The crowd suddenly grew silent as they strained to hear. Soon the joy drained from their weary faces like snow from a ravaged hillside.

The boss looked the crowd over before he spoke. At last he narrowed his eyes, shifted feet, sighed and answered. "I'm afraid that's not possible, men. Carmen and shovelers will be paid $3.00 a day now. The company can't afford to pay them $3.50 like before and keep the mine operating." The miners stood for a moment in disbelief. After all this time, the owners still thought they could divide them.

Sam shook his head and stomped away with the others. "Offer? That's no more of an offer than the man in the moon," a man nearby who had an eye patch on one eye said. "That's a damn slap in the face." Sam looked at him and nodded.

Jack Bailey joined them. "What do you think, Sam?" he asked.

"He's right. It's a slap in the face. No way am I going to go back for that." He had gotten better acquainted with Bailey and heard from Joe that he was a good sort. The new man often showed up at the Silver Pick, and more than once had bought drinks for the regulars. Sam was glad they had him and the other union leaders.

They went to the union hall that evening to a meeting to discuss it. Over a hundred men crowded together in the stuffy room. The air reeked with the odor of cigars, pipes and cigarettes as well as smoke from the oil lamps and stove. Stale beer, damp clothes and unwashed bodies added to the mix.

It smelled normal to Sam as he joined a group of friends near the stove. One of the workers was an older man, nicknamed Skillet, who often played poker with Joe and his friends at the saloon. He had no family and Sam knew him because he'd been sent by his mother to deliver food to the old man's shanty when he was sick with the flue. He claimed to have acquired his nickname after his ex-wife slammed him aside the head with a frying pan and he lost his hearing, but no one knew his real name or where he came from. He was a good-hearted sort, though, and Sam had been his buddy ever since he'd recovered from his illness.

"They are trying to break us!' Skillet said.

"I heard that Schmidt said he'd never hire another union worker," another man put in.

"All the other mines are paying more. Why do we deserve any less?"

"They think because the Bunker Hill is a dry mine we don't need as much pay. Don't have to buy the wet clothes!'

"That's a stupid, cockeyed reason if I ever heard it," Sam said. "It's just an excuse. They want to drive us out of this whole country."

Then a man near the stove sighed and shook his head. He was one of the older men, maybe forty-five, and he reached up and adjusted his cap as he cleared his throat. He had three fingers missing from his hand. His voice was barely audible. "I don't know about you fellers, but I'm thinking a half a loaf is better than none. My misses is at the end of her rope with this darn business. I say we go back and hope things get better in a few months."

The crowd turned to him. A couple of them nodded slightly, waiting to see the reaction. Most were appalled at the thought. "Are you crazy?" one of them said. "After going this far you want to give up? That's just what those parasites want us to do."

"That's right! Never give up!" someone else yelled. Then they all joined in. "NEVER GIVE UP!"

Later that night the executive committee of the union met to make a decision about their response. It didn't take them long to decide the owners had no deal. They wrote a letter to the Owners' Association stating they "would not accept the wage scale offered by the owners. They would only return if wages were the same as before the shutdown."

The mood in the town was low. There was no celebration now, but the next day was March 17th and it couldn't be ignored, no matter how dire the future looked.

"Come on Sam," Colleen urged. "Let's go down and watch the St. Paddy's Day parade. We'll show them we Irish don't stay down for long!"

Sam grinned at his sister. "Well, you're right," he said reluctantly. Then he called to the two younger girls, "Come on, my darlings, might as well go listen to the pipes and drums. Tap a toe or two, won't we now?" They got their coats and before long the strains of "The Wearin' of the Green" and "Danny Boy" filled the valley as Professor O'Malley and his Irish band marched down Main Street along with marchers dressed in green carrying the Irish flag and banners that declared "Erin go Bragh."

The crowd was light and they easily found a place near the drugstore to watch just as the band took up the familiar tune of the Irish National Anthem. All stood at attention; the men took off their hats, and a few older folks wiped away a tear as they remembered "their sainted isle of old" and joined in the familiar refrain:

We'll sing a song, a soldier's song
With cheering rousing chorus
As round our blazing fires we throng
The starry heavens o'er us ....

The next day the seriousness of their plight settled over the houses and saloons once again. How much longer could they hold out?

A portion of the original "Glory Hole" which was the start of the Bunker Hill Mine
Special Collections and Archives, University of Idaho Library, 8-X2

The animals wore "palousers" around their necks, which was a gallon
can with a candle inside so the animal could see underground.
Staff House Museum, 88.1.0, Kellogg, Idaho

CHAPTER SIX

April, May, 1892

Workers of the world, awaken!
Break your chains, demand your rights.
All the wealth you make is taken
By exploiting parasites.
Shall you kneel in deep submission
From your cradles to your graves?
Is the height of your ambition
To be good and willing slaves?
Arise, ye prisoners of starvation!
Fight for your emancipation;
Arise, ye slaves of every nation
In one union grand.

Joe Hill

On April 5th the Owners announced that the mines were closed until June first. Membership in the union had dwindled perceptibly since the beginning of the shutdown. Many of the single men and drifters had moved on and they now had about eight hundred members compared to more than two thousand in January. Mainly the married men and permanent residents remained; Ryan Kelly was an exception.

He stayed at the boarding house in Wardner and made sure he stayed clear of the saloons and public places. Hours were spent in his tiny room reading magazines like National Geographic and the Saturday Evening Post, which were handed from room to room until they were worn out. He was sometimes able to borrow books. He had recently read "The Return of the Native" by Thomas Hardy and had read all of Mark Twain's books. He was anxious to find a copy of the most recent Twain book, "A Connecticut Yankee in King Arthur's Court."

He occasionally played cards with his uncle Sean and others. Jack Bailey lived down the hall from them, and Ryan was surprised at his friendliness considering he was a union man. Bailey sometimes joined them for a card game and never mentioned what was on all their minds.

Ryan roamed the woods for miles in every direction, savoring the wild mountains and untouched wilderness. He wrote a letter to his mother that spring:

> *Dear Ma:*
>
> *Hope you and everybody are doing good. We are just dandy even if we are not working right now and the soup at this place is hardly more than water. I think the cook just drags the dish rag through it and puts it on the stove. Not like your thick old stew at all! One of the men here shot a bear last week though. It was a big one and we've had bear steak most every night lately, which is a lot better than soup! Now you don't be fretting about us. My money is mostly gone but Uncle Sean still has some left and we think we'll get work at the mine soon.*
>
> *The union is strong here and there's a whole lot of pressure to join, but you know what Sean and I think of unions. After what we saw back there with the Molly Maguires we're steering clear. I remember what you said about me going on to school. Thinking hard on it I am and hope to work steady and save some money so I can. I plan on getting out of these holes in the ground and spend my time in the daylight before too many more months go by.*
>
> *Your gopher son.*
> *Ryan*

His uncle wasn't quite so optimistic as his nephew. He was extremely tired of waiting around for the mine to reopen, and now that spring was finally in the air he was restless to move. The tension in the town was growing, and he didn't cotton to the idea of being in the midst of the trouble that was sure to ensue.

He suggested many times that they move on to greener pastures toward the coast. "Sure as daylight, there's going to be big trouble here, sooner or later."

Ryan wouldn't consider it. "It's a gloomy devil, you are!" he told him stubbornly. "This trouble can't last forever, there's going to be good steady work here soon, and besides that, I love the country. Let's wait just a little longer." Sean suspected there was another reason for his recalcitrance, but he humored his nephew, and the weeks rolled by.

*   *   *   *

On the second week of April one could have guessed it was still mid-winter. The snow banks on the northern side of the slopes had only melted back slightly. Winter, that ferocious old crone, had barely loosened her grip on the Coeur d' Alene country. Like a capitalist's wife with her jewels and her fancy carriage, she wasn't going to let go easily. During the day the sun managed to peek out of the clouds, and water trickled down the road and made muddy puddles in the ruts where the horses and wagons traveled. Then when evening came, and the oil lamps were lit for supper, the temperature plunged down. During the night it dropped to below freezing and winter got her icy grip on the town again. The puddles and mud froze hard and the tiny new shoots on the serviceberry bushes were encased in ice. Each day was a little longer than the one before, though, and slowly, surely, the season changed.

At least the road is almost bare of snow, Colleen thought as she walked up the draw above the town. It was an overcast, damp day and far from warm, so she wore the same heavy coat she'd worn throughout the winter along with her heavy walking skirt. She climbed quickly up the rutted wagon road which was awash with snow melt and mud. Her boots sank in and squished with each step as she gradually left the canyon and the road behind and took a trail through the trees. The trail here, covered with pine needles and dark green moss, made a cushion for her feet like a lush carpet. Within twenty minutes she was high above town.

A mist filled the air and wisps of fog brought an ethereal magic to the pine, fir and cedar forest. The nearby mountainside was invisible behind the damp fog curtain, and the mist outlined the nearby pines, which stood out in bold relief. A slight breeze sighed a hundred feet above her head in the tops of the trees, a rushing sound like gentle waves on the ocean shore, but here on the ground all was still.

Mosses and lichens, plump and succulent with the moisture, were on the lower dead branches of the trees and on the trunks. She walked closer to inspect them. Dark green-brown strings, called "old man's beard" hung from the limbs and she knew that deer, elk and especially caribou depend on it for winter food. There was also blue-green suede-like lichen that had curled leaves and an olive green spongy sort with tiny cups, but her favorite was the brilliant chartreuse green plants that grew in tufts along the branches.

She walked quietly, stealthily, like a bobcat, so she could blend in with the misty spirits; she might come around a corner and see something wonderful. She remembered once, on a day such as this, she'd come to an opening and watched a mother coyote with her two pups hunting for mice in the soft light of evening.

Suddenly the sun came out through the fog. It slanted through the trees as she climbed up near a rocky outcropping, then from nowhere, fine tiny pinpoints of hail began to fall. They silently settled on the damp pine needled ground and bounced among the bright green velvet-like stars of moss on the rocks.

As she started down, she inspected a south-facing slope for the first flowers among the old snow, and then she spied them. Buttercups scattered like sparkling stars on a pine needle firmament. Soon there would be bright yellow dog toothed violets, then blue eyed grass and then ....

She thought of each flower as it would inevitably appear, and its name. Granny had told her when she was small that "When you name a thing its essence clings to your soul like the pollen of the flower clings to the bee. It becomes a part of you, and when you come upon it next spring or a dozen springs from now, and are struck once again by its beautiful perfection, you will know it and say hello!"

Colleen stooped, inspected the buttercups, and whispered "Hello there! Nice to see you again!"

As she returned back toward the town she passed a swampy area near the road filled with cat tails. She listened for the red-winged black-birds. Then she heard them; their unmistakable call echoed up and down the gulch. "Whee-oo, wheeee-ooo," they cried as they fluttered among the fluffy remains of last year's plants. They were always among the first birds of spring to arrive and they swooped and climbed in and out of the dry rushes preparing for their summer home.

Before she got back down to the houses, snow began to fall. Big, lazy flakes of snow, as soft as a baby's cheek, began to drift from the steely gray sky. It covered the bright green shoots of new grass and the waxy yellow buttercups. It nestled on the branches of elderberry and serviceberry in the draws and melted silently into the puddles on the road.

Colleen dreamed of the day when the fighting would be over and life could return to normal, but it seemed like a long way off. She fantasized that Ryan would suddenly appear at her door and they would walk together into town for a soda, but she knew in her heart that it was unlikely to happen.

The days were longer now, and as April gurgled and spit to its end, the streams fed by springs and glacial lakes in the high mountains swelled into icy torrents with the melting snow. They roared down through the narrow canyons carrying branches, mud and debris from the denuded slopes above the towns. They poured from every direction into the north and south forks of the Coeur D' Alene River and often spilled over to flood the low lying areas of the towns.

*   *   *   *

Near the end of the month Ryan learned that the company needed a few men to do maintenance at the mine. "It's dying of boredom I've been," he told his uncle. "Let's go sign up. We've got to do something."

Sean sighed and shrugged his shoulders. "Well, I guess we might as well. Word down at the saloon says that the company brought in some Pinkerton men to protect the mill and the workers."

They and two other men started work at $3.50 a shift the following day. It was tense, but quiet the first two days. On the third day as they walked up the hill toward the mill they noticed movement in the brush beside the road and stopped. Suddenly some union men walked out and blocked their way. Two of them carried guns. Then more men came out of the woods. Sam, Joe and Billy were in the backup group.

Ryan, Sean and the others stood their ground in the middle of the muddy road. They knew they were outnumbered, and they didn't see any sign of the guards up at the mill.

"Let us by," Ryan said evenly. "We've got protection." He looked around and bit his lip as he realized what was happening. He glanced at the crowd behind the leaders, noticed Sam and quickly looked away with disgust. How dare these people come and try to stop them from making a living? Anger boiled up inside him, and he clenched his fist and took a step toward the miners.

Sean grabbed his arm. "Not now, buddy," he said quietly. "Faith, and thinking I am that it ain't worth getting killed for."

One of the leaders with a gun stepped toward them. "You men know what you're doing?"

"Yes, sir. We do. Minding our own business we are, and hoping to God you'll do the same," Sean said.

"We don't want any trouble. Just want to ask you peaceable like to join the union."

"Free men we are, and we won't be needing any union," Ryan said through clenched teeth, "and you tell your goons back there to go home. We come to America because it's a free country. We've got a right to work."

"You'd better come with us and tell the people down at the union hall that, then," the leader said as he gestured down the hill. Ryan hesitated. He was outraged at the injustice, and if he had ever considered joining their damn union he made up his mind then that he'd die first. He planted his boots in the road and looked at his uncle. Sean shook his head and motioned down the hill. The four of them had no choice. They turned around and walked down the hill toward town with the guns pointed at their backs.

When they got to the union hall more than 150 union members were waiting. Once again the four men were asked to join the union.

"If you join, you will be able to get relief and go to work with the rest of us when the lockout is over," they told them. The other two men thought it over. They didn't have the stomach for a fight and they knew it. Finally they agreed. That left the Kellys, Sean and Ryan. They looked at each other and shook their heads. The Kelly clan in Ireland was always up to a good scrap and neither one was ready to back down.

"We are thinking we'll work wherever we damn well please," Sean said levelly as he crossed his arms and stared at the men.

Ryan nodded. He stood as stiff as a poker. He felt sick to his stomach, but it was a matter of principle with him now. He wasn't going to be forced into membership in any organization, not at the point of a rifle. "With Sean here, I am," he said quietly. Sweat dripped down the back of his neck as they stood waiting for the next move.

The leader of the crowd looked over the men's heads. "What shall we do with them?" he yelled at the mob. Joe and Sam stood near the middle of the crowd.

Joe was in a sour mood, having tanked up more than usual the night before. His voice was wheezy from years of breathing the gritty dust of the mines. "String up the sons of bitches!" he croaked as he looked directly at Ryan, then doubled over with a coughing fit. The vitriol that lurked just behind his eyes, the bitterness just below the surface, erupted easily. Sam looked at his father, shocked at the thought and yet not a word against the idea was voiced by him or any of the others.

Sheriff Cunningham was near the back door. He was a union supporter and had no sympathy for scabs, but he knew it was his job to keep order. He made his way to the front of the mob and faced them. "Now men, that's not going to happen!" he bellowed.

"Send them up the canyon!" someone near the back responded.

"Yes, Wardner is no place for scabs! Get rid of the scum!"

"Lucky Colleen isn't here," Sam thought as he watched six men move toward Ryan and Sean and escort them out the door. The sheriff just watched as they marched them up the road toward the edge of town, guns pointed at their backs.

"Don't be thinkin' you'll stop at Wallace, neither," one of them growled. "You ain't welcome anywhere in this valley." Ryan's heart beat like a drill in solid rock as they covered about a mile and their captors turned back toward town. They kept jogging along the road until they were out of sight of the men. Ryan seethed at the unfairness of their treatment. They had no bedrolls and no food, but Sean always managed to have money in his pocket. They walked all day, slogging through mud and snow.

They skirted past Wallace but when they got to Mullan, Sean went in to the grocery and quickly and bought some bread and canned sardines. Ryan waited outside, nervously watching the door.

Just outside the town they came upon a tiny cabin nestled in the woods. They watched as a woman appeared at the window. Ryan's eyes grew wide. "Holy Mary! I'm thinkin' that's a pie she's putting there!" he whispered. "Smells like mince meat! I'm going to borrow it!"

His uncle chuckled. "So it is, son. Sure and I never thought either one of us would end up thievin', but this here's what I would call an emergency!" As soon as the woman disappeared, Ryan crept toward the house. His mouth watered as the aroma of the fresh baked pie hit his nostrils. He was within a few feet when he froze in his tracks. A blood curdling scream came from the cabin. Then it turned into a wail and Ryan recognized a baby's cry. Good news. Now mama was sure to be busy for a few minutes. He made a dash for the windowsill, grabbed the pie and ran for the nearest cover. The tin was so hot he had to hold it with the ends of his shirt sleeves to keep from getting burned. He hid nearby and waited. The baby was still bawling its eyes out, but it was losing steam.

He went another hundred yards where Sean was waiting and they took off upstream. Ryan dipped a finger in as they ran. "Oh, boy! It is mince meat!" He declared. He wanted to stop immediately and eat it, but his uncle insisted they go farther. Finally he agreed they were far enough away and they dipped the warm sweet meat and crust out of the tin with their hands. It was the best food Ryan had ever tasted.

As night fell, Sean looked up at the sky. "No rain in sight, nor snow neither. We've got luck on our side!" When it grew too dark to see, they found a mossy hole under a huge old cedar to spend the night.

Ryan dreamed of his mother's kitchen; then suddenly Colleen was there, spooning up chicken and dumplings. He slept fitfully, then woke with a start. Stars glittered like candles through the fronds of the old tree. He shifted positions, his legs and back stiff as boards. "So this is where our great adventure into the west leads," he thought bitterly. He remembered his dream and thought of Colleen. He hadn't seen her for several weeks, but she was never far from his thoughts.

The next morning the sun streamed through the trees as they got stiffly up, drank the water they'd saved in one of the cans and continued. Snow was mostly gone in the valley, but snow on the summit of Lookout Pass had measured ten feet that winter. As they gained altitude, patches of old snow appeared. By midday they were slogging through snow up to their knees, and as the afternoon waned they approached the summit where the snow drifts were still several feet high.

Luckily there was a hard crust and they were able to follow game trails to the summit. At the top they came to a saloon built beside the railroad tracks on the border of Montana. They went in, ordered dinner and stayed the night. The next day they caught the train down to the valley and the town of Missoula.

When they got to Missoula and found a rooming house, Ryan noticed a copy of "The Coeur d' Alene Barbarian" newspaper lying on a table near the front door. He picked it up and scanned it quickly. Then he grinned when it dawned on him that one of the articles could have been about them. It was dated April 30th. "Listen to this Sean," he read out loud:

> When a horde of seventy-five men take two men anxious to work, lead them out of the state, and set them adrift because they will not join the Miners' Union, it is the carrying out of a verdict of a principle which the Miners' Union has erected as its God; a God elevated above the laws of the land ... Has the time come when our hands are tied, our tongues stuck in our throats and our manhood turned to a dung heap for lawless curs to dump their excrements of ignorance upon? Is American Independence to pack its traps and turn its liberty over to intimidation? Shame, Shame...."

Sean shook his head and chuckled. "Well, seems like some people over there across the mountains have got a little common sense and realize what's right and wrong!"

*   *   *   *

A few days after Ryan and Sean were forced out of town, Colleen walked down to Main Street. Her step was light in spite of the tension that gripped the hearts of shopkeepers and working men alike. It was a siege that seemed to have no end, and she and the other women were almost inured to the threats of more violence. Each day dawned with new worries, and fear lurked just behind the eyes of the people she greeted; but it was spring never-the-less, and today the sun sparkled over the snowy peaks above her head with the warm and gentle promise of flowers and more sunshine sure to come.

She met Sally as she came out of the dry goods store. She hadn't seen her friend for more than a week, and the two stood in the muddy road and chatted. Sally had news for Colleen but wasn't sure if she should mention it. Finally she blurted, "Did you hear about the men that were forced up the canyon last Saturday?"

"No, Sam didn't say anything; what happened?"

"He doesn't want you to worry, but Ryan and his uncle refused again to join the union. The union even offered to pay their room and board if they'd quit work and wait out the strike; but my brother said Ryan got his back up and said he'd rather die than be forced by gunpoint to join."

Colleen's face fell and the joy she'd felt in the sunshine and sparkle of the day disappeared in a heartbeat. "Was it just the two of them, then?"

"That's what I heard. There were four of the scabs together, but the other two decided to be smart and join our men."

Colleen bristled at the words. "There's nothing stupid about Ryan!" she said sharply. "If he don't believe in a thing he'll not take part in it."

Sally touched her arm. "Oh, I know," she said quickly. "I didn't mean he's not got brains. Probably more than some of our hotheads, but he ought to realize the danger he's in."

Colleen nodded and grimaced. "I tried to talk to him, but it did no good. Did they have bedrolls and food, do you know?"

"I don't know, but they'll make it across the mountains, I'm sure. It's only a three day walk across to Montana, and the weather's been good." Finally the friends parted, and Colleen hurried home. She dared not mention what she'd heard to her family. It was best not to mention the name Ryan Kelly.

The Owners' Association wasn't about to stand still for the threats to the non-union men coming in to the district. They decided it was time to get their big guns and get rid of the "criminal elements" that were upsetting their business. On May 7 federal judge James H. Beatty issued an injunction against the union prohibiting their interference in mining operations. They could be arrested for even approaching the non-union miners.

"In other words," Sam said bitterly the next day at the dinner table, "it's against the law to even try to talk to those puke faced pitiful excuses for men." Colleen looked at her plate and the two younger girls stared at their usually jovial brother with wide eyes.

His mother frowned and shook her head. "I wish you wouldn't get so mad, Sam. Try to stay away from the trouble makers."

"Your ma's right, son," his pa spoke up. "These people are just itching to see us break the law."

Sam took another biscuit and broke it open savagely as if it were the law and he planned to bust it open. He glared at his father with eyes that smoldered with defiance. Being first generation Irish, he had rebellion, resistance and protest coursing through his veins like debris on the River Shannon.

"I heard Mr. Ed Boyce talk last night. He said we're part of the United States of America now. The constitution says we have what they call 'free speech and the right of peaceful assembly,' which means we can talk to whoever we want and we can have meetings."

"It's all on paper, son. The owners have all the power and the politicians on their side. Old Beatty was put in as judge by the Bunker Hill people is the word I got."

When she looked at her brother's face, Colleen's stomach did a flip flop. "Be careful, Sam," she put in quietly. "There's Pinkerton detectives everywhere, spying on the union. They are just trying to stir up our men and make them do something stupid. Don't talk to anybody you don't know!"

"Awww Sis. They can't do nothing to us! That's what's going to break the damn company. I heard they're paying out thousands of bucks for the agents and guards to protect the scabs. Besides, the union's got help coming in from all over. Lawyers too, and I heard from one of the bosses that we have more than $10,000 in the bank!"

Unions from across the country were ready to back the miners in the fight that was sure to come. The Union Pacific brought in two cars of provisions, gaily decorated, from the miners' union at Butte, Montana. According to the paper at the time it was more than $2,400 worth of supplies including ten tons of flour, thirty-five sacks of beans, five caddies of tobacco, six cases of tomatoes, six boxes of dry apples, four chests of tea, three cases of baking powder, ten kegs of syrup, twenty-five boxes of codfish, fifteen boxes of soap, twenty cases of coffee, three tons of bacon, two tons of sugar and ten boxes of smoking tobacco.

* * * *

Colleen continued to worry and hope for a paying job. She took temporary jobs caring for children and helping with housework, but she knew it was not enough. Polly was old enough now to do a lot of the work at home, especially now that summer was coming, and she'd be out of school. One day Sam told Colleen he'd heard that they needed someone to work part time in the dry goods store, so she walked downtown to get the mail and see about it.

The day was balmy and clear with a brilliant blue sky overhead and birdsong in the air. She spotted two mountain bluebirds sitting on a fence near Main Street. It was almost enough to make her forget her troubles. She remembered Granny's saying that bluebirds were a sign of good luck. She fervently hoped so as she watched them take off. They flashed and sparkled in the sunlight, dark blue jewels against a light blue sky.

She walked to the store first. She didn't know the new owner and it took all her courage to go in, but she knew she must do it. Her legs felt like rubber but she took a deep breath, entered and looked around. She saw a man behind the counter and walked resolutely over to him.

He looked up without smiling. "May I help you?"

She tried to keep her voice from quivering. "I heard you might need someone for part time work."

"No," the owner said curtly, "I'm afraid that job has been filled. Business is real slow right now, as you probably know."

Colleen nodded and tried to smile, but it was more of a grimace. "Thank you anyway," she said. "If you hear of anything I'd appreciate it. My name's Colleen, Colleen McCarthy."

The store owner nodded with a frown. "Yes. I know who you are." She nodded, cheeks burning, looked down at the floor and turned to leave. Was it her imagination or did he mean he knew who her brother was? She walked quickly out of the store and down the street to the post office. The post master handed her two letters. One was a bill from the catalog company. She glanced at the other one and her heart did a somersault when she saw the name in the corner. Ryan Kelly! She thanked the post master, blushed and turned quickly away from the counter so he wouldn't see her reaction. Her mood shifted in a moment from dejection to euphoria. She wanted to fly; she wanted to yell; a hundred bells went off in her head. Her feet never hit the ground as she walked out the door. She thrust the treasure into her dress pocket until she found an empty bench along the street. Then she sat down, tore open the envelope and read the message.

> *Dear Colleen:*
>   *I am writing to let you know I haven't forgotten about you. I wonder how things are going for you and your family. You probably heard we had to leave Wardner pretty fast. We walked over the mountain and now we both have jobs here in Missoula and are doing ok. I've been saving my money and not doing much except working and going fishing when I get a day off. The boarding house here is nice. Sean and I have a room to ourselves, a window and a nice desk where I'm sitting now as I write this.*
>   *I think of you often and am sorry I couldn't come to see you in those weeks before I left but you understand.*
>   *Things are bound to get better. Write me back if you can.*
>
> *Your friend,*
> *Ryan*

Colleen put the letter back in her pocket and ran all the way home. She knew she couldn't tell her parents or anyone, but she planned to answer him back as soon as she had a minute's free time. She thanked her lucky stars that she was the one who always picked up the mail.

*   *   *   *

Ryan worked at a lumber mill in Missoula, but the lure and excitement of the beautiful Coeur d' Alene country kept calling him back. Like the creeks weave through the rocks to the rivers and the rivers run inexorably to the wild and restless sea, he was pulled to the silver-lined mountains. He got a letter from Colleen not long after he'd written her, and he knew he had to see her some way, some time. His mind wandered across Lookout Pass with the memory of her intense blue eyes and sweet laughter. He daydreamed of the time the conflicts would subside and he would be able to return to Wardner and resume their courtship. Sean knew, also, that it wasn't just the pull of the mountains and the sparkling rivers that drew his nephew, but he was ready to go as well. Always restless and ready to move on, he was ready just about anytime he had a few dollars in his pocket.

Days were warm now, and sunlight coaxed dogtooth violets and trillium from the rocky soil along the wild Clark Fork River. Ryan spent his Sundays hiking and fishing along its banks. Around the middle of May, he came back to the boarding house and delivered five large trout to the cook. Sean was having coffee with some others around the long table in the dining room and he joined them.

"Well, I ain't hankering to get my damn head blown off," one of them said.

"Me neither. No job is worth it. I'm staying right here." Sean grinned. He knew without asking what Ryan would say.

"Where?" Ryan asked as he sat down. "What are you talking about?"

Sean ignored him and addressed the others. "Now Ryan here, he's a corker, he is." He turned and looked at his nephew, "Faith, and you won't be fussing about a few bullets, will you?"

"What's going on?"

"There's a train coming through out of Bozeman," Sean told him. "Loaded with workers all the way from Minnesota heading into the Coeur d' Alenes. It has armed guards too. The mine owners are going to keep their mines operating no matter how many guards it takes to do it."

Ryan's eyes lit up. Here was their chance! Soon dinner was served, though, and talk changed to other subjects.

Sean wasn't at all sure going back across the mountains was wise. That night in their room he tried to talk Ryan out of going back. "It's a dangerous place for the likes of us," he told his nephew. "We'd be much better off keeping our jobs here and saving our money."

"Well, I like it over there. I aim to get back sooner or later, and with all the protection, I can't see that the union's going to dare even show their face!"

Sean just shook his head. He knew he wasn't going to talk him out of hopping the train for the Coeur d' Alenes, but he felt he had to try.

He went downstairs to the toilet and met one of the men who had been discussing the coming train at the table earlier. He had a newspaper in his hand. "You see this article?" he said as he stopped Sean in the hall. "It's just what I was sayin,' a body's liable to get his self shot over there."

Sean took the paper, dated May 14, and read it. It said just what he'd been trying to tell his nephew. He realized it might make an impression on him, so after he returned from the outhouse, he took it up to their room. Ryan was lying on the bed, reading a tattered copy of "Harper's Monthly." Sean held up the Coeur d' Alene Press and pointed to the article. "See what I've been saying? This paper says just what we already know. Now just listen to this:"

Approaching a Crisis

"*That the long continued strike in the Coeur d' Alene mines is rapidly drawing to a crisis there can be no doubt and if that point is passed without bloodshed the people will breathe easier and their apprehensions be relieved; but from present indications the difficulty will not be settled without trouble of a serious nature. ... the mine owners are determined to operate their mines and for this purpose are importing non-union miners from the east. ... on the other hand the miners, while protesting that they will not resort to violence, are receiving guns and ammunition in large quantities. Several cases of guns and ammunition were loaded on the boat last Wednesday for the miner's union....*"

Ryan shook his head. "Well, I don't care. I think it will be alright. I still want to go, and if you want to stay here, that's alright." He was adamant and Sean had promised their parents they would stick together no matter what, so within a few days they paid $7.55 for a ticket and hopped on board the Northern Pacific passenger train. They joined over seventy workers, mostly Swedes, Finns and Italians, and armed guards from Duluth, heading west over the pass.

Talking to the miners from the East, who had been on the train for two days, Sean and Ryan could tell they had no idea where they were going or what they were getting into. The two newcomers weren't about to fill them in, either.

Sean was worried about what they might find. They were told they would work at the Union Mine and that all was serene there, the troubles had settled down, and besides that they would have protection. He took it all with a grain of salt, but he didn't say much to his obstreperous nephew. He could tell that Ryan was tickled pink to be heading back.

The train they took consisted of an engine, baggage car, three coaches and a caboose. Ryan settled back in the seat, which smelled of tobacco and grease, and watched the world flash by out the window. This was the life! The Northern Pacific, the life line of the west, had only had this Coeur d' Alene branch open less than a year, and it connected Wallace and Wardner to Missoula and the lines that led all the way across the country to the east coast.

Sean and Ryan had come west on a train like this, and it was a thrill to be riding across the country once again. Ryan planned to write his mother as soon as he got there to describe the whole marvelous trip.

They traveled through pine forests and along pristine creeks. Meadows quilted with wild flowers, brilliant yellow balsamroot, wild iris and lilies, moved past as he daydreamed. In one of the meadows, he saw a mother bear and twin cubs digging in the soft warm earth looking for roots and grubs. He nudged Sean who was dozing in the seat next to him. "Look at that, Sean!" But by the time his uncle focused on the scene it was gone.

They rolled to a creaking stop at the terminal at Saltese to get water from huge tanks along the tracks, and to load up on fuel. Ryan got out to stretch his legs and look around. He watched another engine which was being moved onto the tracks and realized it was hooking on to their train. One of the trainmen walked by and he asked him, "What is going on? We need two engines?"

"Yes, we do. We need a helper engine. From here up to the top is fourteen miles of four percent grade. It's a tough pull."

When Ryan returned to his seat, Sean pulled out some bacon sandwiches and a bottle of water which they shared for lunch.

The locomotive shuddered and strained as it started up again. As the miles sped by, the rhythm, the clickety clack of the wheels on the track, was a soporific lullaby and Ryan's head began to nod. He stretched his long legs out into the aisle, and soon he was sound asleep.

A few minutes later, however, he awoke with a start and looked out. The engines had slowed, and steam burst out from the pipes with a loud whoosh! WHOOSH! The cars behind them shuddered, creaked, rattled and groaned as they started up into the steep and rugged Bitterroot Mountains. Ryan stared out the window for hours as the miles slid by and the spectacular scenes changed like a kaleidoscope.

He watched the deep evergreen trees and snow-patched meadows roll past as they slowly gained altitude. Then they were in snow, but the tracks were cleared. They chugged past gigantic outcroppings of rocks, orange tinged, white streaked, gray, reddish brown and ocher, as if they'd been painted by a mighty hand. Solid rock walls, which had been blasted away to make a bed for the track, were sometimes within feet of his window, and other times the light went out and it was pitch black as they chugged through tunnels One was more than 650 feet long as they threaded their way slowly up the richly forested mountains.

They reached the summit of the pass and Ryan read a sign along the tracks that said, Coeur d' Alene Divide…Idaho: Montana, elevation 4,680 feet." They stopped briefly, then started up and the train gained speed as they headed down the mountains. This part of the ride, from here to Mullan, was touted as some of the most spectacular scenery in the west.

They went over several gigantic wooden trestles which spanned the river or deep canyons. One, at a place called Dorsey, was several stories high and looking out from the train window, the sheer magnitude of the country took Ryan's breath away. Since he couldn't see the trestle under them, he felt as if the train was flying. The cars banged, screeched and shuddered as the engine chugged across the spindly trestle.

Later on, they came to a huge S shaped bridge over three hundred feet long where the track looped back on itself. Ryan looked straight down hundreds of feet into the canyon and the mountains spread out for hundreds of miles in every direction. The late afternoon sun reflected off of the rust-red lichen-patched cliffs. At the bottom, the river sparkled like a ribbon of silver. A deer stood on a ledge on the opposite side and looked up, alert with the noise of the train.

They soon reached the deep valley of the Coeur d' Alene River. They stopped at Mullan to unload freight and passengers, then headed on toward Wallace.

Northern Pacific Train on one of the many magnificent wooden trestles on the Idaho side of Lookout Pass.
Special Collections and Archives, University of Idaho Library, 16-24-1

~ CHAPTER SEVEN ~

June, July, 1892

I stood by a city prison,
In the twilight's deepening gloom,
Where men and women languished
In a loathsome, living tomb.
They were singing! And their voices
Seemed to weave a wreath of light,
As the words came clear with meaning:
Workers of the World, unite!
                    Laura Payne Emerson
                    Little Red Songbook

The union leaders in the Coeur d' Alenes got word of the train coming in loaded with workers and armed guards, and they set out to see that they were stopped. Sheriff Cunningham had a warrant for the arrest of the leaders of the fifty armed guards hired by the mine owners to protect the scabs on the train. The Idaho State Legislature had approved a law in 1891 to enforce the section in the State constitution which provides *"that any association, corporation or company which shall bring or aid in bringing into this state any armed or unarmed force for the purpose of suppression of domestic violence, shall be guilty of a felony."*

The leaders of the guards were to be charged with "impersonation of a U. S. Deputy Marshall." The sheriff took a Union Pacific Train to intercept the car loads of workers at the switch point outside Wallace and make the arrest.

Ryan and the others on board knew nothing of these events. They expected to stop at Wallace at the usual station before going on to Gem and the Union Mine and mill. Somehow the engineer of the train, Levi Hutton, guessed what was happening and as they approached the town, instead of slowing down they speeded up! As it dawned on the passengers that something was amiss, they all crowded to the windows to watch excitedly as they gained speeds to over fifty miles an hour. They saw the houses and buildings of the town flash by as they hurtled on and careened up Canyon Creek, sparks flying from the rails like fireflies.

The deputies' train raced to intercept them, but the "train load of scabs and Hessians" as Adam Aulbach later called them in the Wallace Free Press, had passed the switches just moments before the other train arrived. The loaded train roared right up the canyon without slacking its speed and stopped at the depot at the base of the hill near the mill. The sheriff and his deputies arrived shortly after.

Sam, Herbert and dozens of union members were there to meet the train of scabs. They stood stone-faced, with fists raised and rifles at the ready as the workers piled out of the cars. Ryan and Sean hopped down with their packs, looked at the mob, then looked at each other. It didn't look like this was the peaceful camp that the owners had described.

The miners from Minnesota were confused and scared. Even though the "troubles in the Coeur d' Alenes" had been reported across the country, nobody had told them what a hornet's nest they were getting into.

Sean frowned, shook his head and shrugged his shoulders. They were here now; there was nothing to do but go ahead.

Their greeting committee, the union men, many of them armed with Winchesters, yelled and threatened them. "Get back on that train, Scabs! You ain't wanted here!"

"If you want to live, get out of here!"

"Go back to the holes you crawled out of, scum!" Sam yelled.

The union mob, fuming with resentment and ready to explode, harassed the workers as they marched in a body up the hill toward the Union Mill. Ryan kept his eyes straight ahead purposefully. "Surely they won't shoot us," he thought, but he expected to hear the roar of a rifle at any minute and his eyes darted beside the trail to see where he could dive for cover. The union mob, however, allowed them to pass without incident. The chief of the guards and others had been arrested on the spot and escorted back to the train to return to Wallace. Some of the scabs decided not to work as well, and many of the union men, including Sam and Herbert, boarded the cars to return to Wallace.

Ryan, Sean and the others got to the safety of the mill, which was heavily guarded, and reported for work.

Sam and the union men on the train were furious. They intended to go en mass to Wallace to demand their rights as union workers and protest the importation of hundreds of scabs. They wanted action. It was common knowledge that the owners had sworn never to hire another union man. Men who wanted to work would have to sign a Yellow Dog Contract where they swore they would not join a union now or in the future. Records with lists of miners' names were kept by the mine owners. If a miner had one X beside his name it meant he was a union member; two X's meant he was a dangerous agitator, and three X's meant he was a dangerous unemployed worker. Sam had two marks beside his name.

Millions of dollars in wages and profits had been lost, and the mine owners were ready to go to any extreme to get control of the situation. They put up the following notice at their closed mines:

> *"Union miners will be hired at this mine on condition they withdraw from the union. This is the last chance, and if the old hands do not take it, outside miners will be imported and exclusively employed."*

Governor Willey proclaimed that he would declare martial law if any more threats or actual violence occurred.

When Sam and the others arrived at the Wallace Depot, the tension was palpable. They spilled from the train and joined the crowd of other union members and sympathizers waiting for them. The town boiled with fear, anger and uncertainty. Rumors of violence and threats of violence traveled from house to house and mouth to mouth as the union men assembled outside the depot. Soon the rumble of their heavy boots echoed in the streets as they marched on the boardwalks of the town. Grim-faced, Sam and Herbert kept pace with the others, double file, up Cedar Street to the miners' supply store.

Knots of business men and townspeople lined the streets and watched as they went by, some with fear and disgust, others with curiosity, apprehension or worry, and a few with downright hatred. "It's the damn Irish that are the real troublemakers," one older man in a suit and vest told his friend under his breath.

"You ain't just a woofin!" his buddy said out of the corner of his mouth. "We're getting rid of the damn heathen chinks all through these parts; it would be good to get rid of the god eating Micks right along with them!"

"Amen to that! Wrap their stinking prayer beads around their necks and send'em all back to where they come from."

"I think all we'd have to do is give them papists a shillelagh and all the bad whiskey they could drink and the bastards would kill each other off afore too long!" They laughed as the rag tag band of miners went past.

When the contingent arrived at the Miners' Supply Store, Thomas O'Brian stood on a chair to address the crowd. The faces looking up at him were exhausted, frustrated and bitter. The winter had been long, cold and dark and their rage had gradually grown, like an icicle hanging precariously above a door, with each passing week. The weight of their anger and sense of injustice had to crash down sooner or later. Out of work and out of hope, they had struggled to feed their families while talk of enormous profits and mansions being built in Spokane continued to reach their ears.

O'Brian spoke for reason and restraint. "Now men, we want no violence. We have the law on our side. The hired army leaders are in custody. You only hurt our cause when you lose your temper. Keep cool, and we'll win this battle yet! Please return to your homes," he admonished, "stay out of the saloons and have patience." The men quieted down and soon dispersed.

Things settled down for a few weeks, but the miners' anger and frustration festered as they saw hundreds of non-union workers arriving daily to take over their jobs. Fear grew in the canyons like a cancer, overriding the reason and sense that O'Brian, and the others tried to maintain. The companies had the government on their side and Sam and the Unionists felt they were being strangled day by day and week by week.

* * * *

On a warm morning on July 11, Sam wolfed down his biscuits and gravy and headed for the door.

"Where are you going so fast?" his mother asked. She didn't know that the fabric, the warp and weft of the whole community, and all the thriving villages up and down the canyon, was to be ripped apart on this day like it had never been torn before.

"Herbert says we're all supposed to get over to Canyon Creek as fast as we can. There's a train coming in with a lot of miners on board. It started at Burke and there's to be a big demonstration there. John Maloney, that new guy from Butte, is the leader."

Colleen came into the room. "Why are they all going to Canyon Creek?"

"You've heard me talk about old Esler, the owner of the Frisco Mill there at Gem?"

"Yes. He's dead set against the Miner's Union."

"Yeh, he hates our guts. He's tried to cut the wages before and threatened to bring in scabs if we don't accept it. That S. O. B. says he'll even shut down the mine before he'll pay shovelers and carmen $3.50."

Colleen shook her head and frowned. "You know they're talking about bringing in military troops to guard the mine."

"I know it. But we're not going to be stopped. They can bring in the U. S. Army for all we care. We're not backing down. Everybody knows Esler's out to bust the union. I have right here a piece that was in the Wallace Press. Just listen to this!" He took a wrinkled page from his pocket and read:

> "Esler, the scab hunter and hounder of the Irish race, did not serve his country when his flag needed defenders, yet this blatant advocate of wage reduction wants the army of the United States to slap the glorious flag about his carcass and protect it with bristling bayonets."

Clara bit her lip and looked at her son. "Sam, why don't you just stay out of it? It's not going to do you any good to get involved. There's going to be trouble."

"I've got to go, Ma. I've got to help out our men." He walked across town and caught up with his friend. They arrived just as the train pulled in, swung on board as it stopped, and joined hundreds of other miners. Workers from mines up and down the canyon were on board. Many of the men wore masks and most carried guns. Sam and Herbert stood jammed against the wall of the car along with others from Wardner and Kellogg.

"What's going on?" Sam asked one of his friends.

"You know Jack Bailey?"

"Sure. What about him?"

"He's crookeder than a dog's hind leg."

"What do you mean?"

"He's one of them Pinkerton agents!"

Sam looked at his friend in disbelief. "No, that's not possible. Why, he's one of our best men. He's one of our officers! He's recording secretary for the Gem!"

"It's true, Sam. I didn't believe it at first but now I do. Did you ever wonder how the Owners seemed to know things before we do? And remember how he got special permission to take the books back to his room?"

"Yes, that's right. But still I just don't believe …."

"Well, he took those minutes home so he could copy them."

"Who said this? Where's the proof?"

Several of the others came to join them, signs of shock and horror on their faces. One of them spoke up. "It's true. We've checked it out. Seems like one of those fallen women over on Cedar Street, name's Ruby …" he peered around the group and grinned, "… some of you might know her … anyhow one of her customers had a little too much whiskey and he bragged about it. Seems he knew Bailey down in Nevada."

"Then you know that young German boy named Henry who's one of our members?" he continued. "They say he's so lonesome for his mother and sisters that he pays good money just to sit and talk with this here Ruby." They all laughed. "Anyway, seems like she told him."

Sam shook his head. He felt as if he'd been punched in the stomach as the news sunk in. "I knew the Pinkertons were everywhere, but I just can't believe that Jack Bailey is one!"

"I smelled a rat months ago. Yep. That guy was slicker than a gravy sandwich. Just too smart, too nice to be real!"

"We know for sure," John Maloney joined in. "Seems that Henry told O'Brian and the others and they put a tail on him and sure enough, he was leaving Gem and walking to Wallace after dark to mail his reports. The way I heard it, the report would go back to the Pinkerton offices in Minnesota, then be sent back to the powers that be here."

Sam just shook his head and the train started off as the men continued talking.

"Where is that son of a bitch now?"

"We don't know for sure but as soon as we get to the canyon we'll find out."

"Killing is way too good for him!"

"He's about as low as snake shit in a wheel track!"

"I say we tie him to the train and let it drag him to death when it takes off!" They laughed bitterly.

Chapter Seven

"I think we should poke out his eyes and cut his lying tongue from his damn mouth!" Herbert put in.

Sam was outraged. "After all these months we trusted him! How could any man be that low down? How could he sit there in the Silver Pick with Pa and the others, buy them drinks and joke around when all the time he's choking the life blood out of our lives?"

"One word. Easy to explain, M-O-N-E-Y. Those Pinkertons make lots of it," Maloney said. "They don't care if they sell their souls to the devil or anybody else!"

Sam sat down and put his head in his hands. The train bumped and rattled on the tracks as it gathered steam and headed up the canyon toward Gem. He felt as if somebody had died. He was heartsick, scared and ashamed too, for having admired the man so much.

Skillet, his dad's old drinking buddy, came over and squatted beside him. He touched the younger man's arm. "Don't take it so hard, son. It ain't a easy lesson, I know, but it's a damn important one. Life ain't fair. It never has been and never will be. We all got hood winked by that low down bastard."

Sam looked up and nodded. "I guess so. But we were fools!"

The train traveled along the main track to Wallace, then turned up Canyon Creek past the union mill where the trouble had been before. Farther up the canyon was the town of Gem and right above Gem was the Frisco mill and mine. The concentrating mill that processed the raw ore was lower in the canyon. Above the mill, farther up the draw, was the mine itself, where the raw ore was mined from the underground shafts.

The train pulled into the station at Gem and the men piled out. More than half of them carried guns, Colt revolvers, Winchester rifles, and even a few old muzzleloader shotguns. Many of the guns had been stolen from the armory at Wallace. Other union members were on the platform waiting for them.

"Anybody seen Bailey?" they asked them.

"We saw him go into the boarding house up the street about an hour ago." The mob took off running. They got to the house, thundered up the steps to the porch and pounded on the door.

The landlady stood behind the door wringing her hands. She'd been warned they were coming. "What do you want?" she called through the door.

Maloney answered, "Bailey here?"

"No. He left."

They pounded again. "Open the door!"

"No, I tell you he's not here." Her little boy, a child of about five, cried in the background.

"One more time!" Maloney yelled. "Open this here door or we'll break it down!" The woman ran upstairs with the child and they crashed the door in and ran into the house, guns drawn. They found her holding the boy and shaking in the corner of the hallway.

"Where'd he run off to? He's a gone sucker and you better not be helpin' him neither! We don't aim to hurt you or your young 'un, but you'd better tell us where he is!"

She shook her head. "I-I swan! I don't know anything. You can look around here all you want." About a dozen men searched every room but he was nowhere to be found. Sam, Herbert and the others waited outside seething with rage and frustration.

Only minutes before, Bailey had sawed a hole through the floor of his room, escaped underneath, and the landlady had moved a trunk over the hole. He wiggled his way under the floor to the front of the building and crawled under the boardwalk, where he crouched, waiting for them to leave.

The union men were in a fury when the others came out and said they didn't find the agent. Bailey listened from where he was hiding under their feet.

"We'll get the traitor if it takes a week!" Sweat dripped down Sam's collar from the heat, tension and fear as he went with the others up and down the street, guns drawn, looking behind buildings and inside wagons. They trooped into Dutch Henry's Saloon where a few more stragglers joined them, then back to the street. The hollow sound of dozens of boots echoed as they stamped along the boardwalks. Storekeepers stayed inside and women and children hurried into the houses and locked the doors.

At last the heat of the moment was too much for some of them to bear. Gunfire exploded from the mob, then more shots were fired into the air and into the buildings. Dust, confusion and chaos grabbed the town and held it in terror. Several people ran outside and took off on horseback to tell the owners in Wallace what was happening. The nearest telegraph was there, and the union men later heard that A. M. Esler, manager of the mine, escaped by special train to safety in Spokane.

Suddenly the mob heard shots coming from the direction of the mill. Sam's heart beat like a fist on a wooden door as they headed toward the sound. As they ran up the hill they saw one of their men running toward them.

The man was a mess. He shook with anger and fear as they approached him in the dusty road. One arm hung limp to his side and blood dripped from his fingers. "I was just trying to walk past the mill to get over to see my folks when one of those damn guards stopped me. Said I couldn't go across there! I told him to kiss my Royal American, then he come at me. I got in the first lick and he went down like a ton of bricks, but then them other guards come out shooting!" He looked down at his arm. "Bastards just winged me though!"

The men exploded. Their eyes were wild with fury as someone yelled, "We ain't taking it no more! NO MORE!" Two or three more shots were fired in the direction of the mill. The guards and others from the mill came down the hill, guns blazing.

Sam and the others scattered from the road and hid behind trees, rocks, whatever they could find. When the shooting stopped and the guards had gone back to their stronghold, they cautiously came out. That was when they saw one of their men lying in the dust on the road.

As they got closer, Sam recognized him, and he knew he was dead. "It's old Skillet!" He said as he came up to the little cluster of men surrounding the body. Sam picked up the old man's body and fought back the tears as they carried him back down the hill to the town.

They deposited the body near the train and rushed back up to join the fray. They found Maloney and the others in a huddle behind the buildings, discussing their tactics.

They were furious and eager to fight to the finish. "Let's go get the scumbags out! We've got enough guns!" Then one of the men took up the chant and others joined in:

>Onward Christian Soldiers
>Rip and tear and smite
>Let the gentle Jesus
>Bless your dynamite!

"Got a lot of dynamite too. It's on the train we came on. Didn't you know?"

"We could blow the whole dam building sky high!"

"Where did that come from?" Sam asked. He was ready to do whatever they could. If his heart was sick before, it was broken now after seeing the dead eyes of his old friend.

"Didn't you hear they ordered the engineer to get more boxcars back there in Wallace? That's why we stopped at the McDonald powder house. Loaded up with Giant powder, we are!"

Sam looked at him skeptically. He shook his head and frowned, not really believing there was any plan of that sort.

One of the older men looked worried. "I'm not sure about this, men. I was back in Chicago during the Haymarket trials. The feds just picked up any miners they could find, guilty or not, and executed them to teach the union a lesson. It wasn't pretty. We can't fight the whole damn country!"

Maloney wasn't in a mood to think of consequences. He ignored the warning. "Let's go on up and tell them to send the scabs out," he yelled. "Give the cowards a chance to give up before we blow them to smithereens!"

They went back to the train, climbed aboard and ordered the engineer to move closer to the mill. The mill was a huge four-story wooden building. When they stopped, Sam and the others piled out. Company men and guards came out of the mill with their guns drawn. Several of the union men approached them, guns at the ready. They stopped a hundred yards away.

"Get out of here or we'll shoot!" One of the Pinkerton guards yelled. The men advanced.

"Send all the scabs out! Give us the dirty scabs and we'll go!" Suddenly a shot rang out and one of the unionists was hit in the shoulder. They saw they were at a disadvantage and left a few men to hold the point while the rest ran around to the hillside at the back of the mill where they found cover behind stumps and rocks. The guards came around and fired. They hid behind barricades of lumber and cordwood as they shot at the intruders. The canyon echoed with the blasts of weapons as the miners opened fire with a barrage of lead. Two guards fell, and their companions dragged them back to the building.

The Pinkertons and scabs held their ground, and so did the miners. Smoke, dust and the smell of gunpowder boiled up from the clearing around the mill. Sam and Herbert stayed in the boxcar, wide-eyed and scared. Later they heard the shooting stop and looked out.

Two union men lay on the ground dead. Then the gunfight resumed. Sam couldn't make out who the dead men were. He shook his head and shuddered as the full impact of the situation hit him, and he and Herbert hunkered back down inside. Then more shots echoed up the draw.

"Dang I wish we had some guns!"

Herbert's face was as white as a sheet. "I just wish I was out of here!"

During another lull in the fight Maloney conferred with the other shooters. "We can't hold out here much longer. Our guns are too light."

"Not only that but those bastards have piles of ammunition in there. We've got to think of something."

They decided to send the dynamite down the tramway. They went above the mill, loaded it on, lit the fuse and sent it barreling down the mountain toward the mill. Before it got to its destination, however, it detonated and blew the tramway into a worthless pile of steel. Then Maloney had a better idea. He poked his head into the boxcar. "We need some men to run up to the penstock and see if it's guarded!"

Sam, cramped and restless, jumped up and looked at Herbert. He nodded. "We'll go!" The older man thrust a gun in Sam's hands as they jumped down and ran through the trees. Glad for some action, they ran up the mountain to the large wooden flume that carried water down the mountain to the mill. The flume was connected to a big iron pipe, called the penstock that carried the water to the waterwheel to power the mill. Since the mill wasn't running, there was no water in it now.

When they reached the sluice at the top, the boys couldn't believe their eyes. "Hot dog!" Herbert yelled. Nobody was there. Sam looked around; all was quiet except for the distant crack of the rifles down below. He wasn't sure what the others planned to do, but he knew something was about to happen. They raced back down the mountain.

"There's not a soul around the penstock," Sam said as soon as he got Maloney's attention. The older man dodged behind the boxcar to reload as he breathlessly gave them instructions.

"Go back there and help those fellows. We're going to give them Pinkertons the surprise of their lives!" Sam and Herbert joined a group of men who were taking two fifty-pound loads of dynamite off of the boxcar.

Maloney joined them and they carried the boxes of dynamite up the mountain. Giant Powder was the miners' best tool. They lived with the enormous power of the explosive every day, respected it and feared its ability to change the course of rivers and bring down mountains. But, unlike old-fashioned black powder, it was stable and could easily be transported or even cut with a knife. When they got to the penstock they put their cargo down and surveyed the scene.

Maloney chuckled. "Well boys, you know what they say, 'one man armed with dynamite is equal to a regiment of militia!' He nodded to Sam and Herbert. "You were right, boys. Looks like we've got clear sailing."

Sam bit his lip. Would this really work? It seemed too simple. Yet the shock of seeing their men killed in the gunfight below drove them on.

They diverted the small amount of water in the chute and carefully opened the boxes of explosives. Herbert and Sam stood a short distance away and watched.

They made several bundles of dynamite and sent them careening down inside the penstock. On the last one they placed a long fuse and lit it. From years of experience, they knew how long the fuse would take to reach the powder and they were right on target. After lighting the fuse and sending it down, they all ran back into the trees, then turned and high-tailed it down the hill. They soon came within sight of the mill far below, and just as they did, they stopped in their tracks. A deafening boom reverberated down the canyon and the ground shook under their feet. The sound was heard for miles. They stood frozen as they watched the mill as it flew up into the air, then burst into a million pieces. The timbers of the roof of the building flew through the air, and pieces came close to hitting them where they stood. Smoke and dust billowed from the area like a volcano where the mill had been. Sam's eyes were wide, and he stood entranced, in shock at the force of the explosion. Somehow they hadn't really believed such a scheme would work.

"Yahoooo!" Herbert yelled as he threw his hat into the air. "That'll teach them cussed capitalists!" They ran down to their companions who cowered in the woods nearby. As the smoke and dust settled, pieces of wood and metal continued to fall for several minutes.

"You should have seen them Pinkertons!" one of them yelled as they joined the group. "They run out the back door like a bunch of scared old hens. Ever one had a white handkerchief wavin' from his gun!"

"That was a sight for sore eyes! Yes sir!" another of the men joined in. "I never seen so many white flags in my life, except on the clothesline at washday!"

After the splintered timbers and metal stopped raining from the sky and the smoke cleared, Sam and the others ran to where the battle had been fought. They found two other dead union men, and eight more seriously wounded. One had been blinded by debris from the explosion and another was bleeding profusely from a head wound. Another had taken a bullet in his shoulder. Near him was a young man about Sam's age who cried out with pain. "Help me, somebody! I can't feel my legs!"

The casualties sat on the ground, dazed, bleeding and disoriented.

Maloney and another man had worked as orderlies in the war. They soon had the wounded miners bandaged up and ready to be moved.

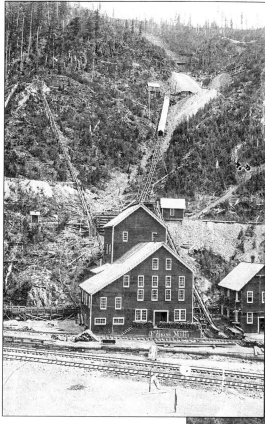

The Frisco Mill at Gem could process 200 tons of ore a day. Ore was brought down by a gravity tramway. It was one of the largest mills in the district and was lit by electricity.
Special Collections and Archives, University of Idaho Library, 8-X1023A

When the boxes of dynamite reached the mill, the building exploded. People said the boom could be heard ten miles away.
Special Collections and Archives, University of Idaho Library, 8-X1023B

They carried their comrades down the hill to town, where they found quilts and tarps to wrap the bodies, and carried them to the train.

They lay the bodies out in the back of the train car, found seats and settled down on board, then the euphoria and excitement of the battle drained away. The enormity of the destruction they'd caused to the mill gradually sank in, and like a fog rolling in to the mountains, silence settled over the group. Herbert was quiet as a mouse and Sam bit his lip to hold back the tears. He clenched his hands to keep them from shaking. They all sat quietly, subdued, each one dealing with the shock of the events in their own way.

What would happen to them now? They all wondered but no one voiced that concern. Maloney ordered Levi Hutton, the engineer, to head to Wallace.

* * * *

At Wardner that day, Colleen and the family was no more worried than usual. They figured Sam was taking part in another demonstration. Colleen was more and more worried about her mother, she hadn't given much thought to Sam. She hated to leave Clara alone for very long. Like a tangled skein of thread, reality was mixed with imagination and nightmares in her mother's mind.

"You see that man out there behind the fence?"

Polly looked out the window. "I don't see anything, Mama."

"See? Can't you see him, there? He just looked over. He's watchin' this house, he's watchin' us!"

Polly looked again, scared and not trusting her own eyes. She shook her head and called her sister. "Colleen, come here! Ma says there's somebody out there!"

Colleen came into the room and looked. "No, there's nobody there. Mama, just try to rest," she said as she led her mother away from the window. She sat down next to her and tried to reassure her, but Clara was distraught.

"I-I know there's a man out there!" She shuddered. "Even when I close my eyes I can see him. He's waiting. Now I don't want you girls goin' outside, you hear? It's not safe!"

"Mama, please. Don't scare the girls."

Later on that morning Colleen saw her mother standing at the back door looking out at the road, terrified, getting up courage to run to the toilet. Finally she looked both ways, ran as fast as she could to the outhouse and slammed the door behind her. Colleen met her when she came breathlessly back in the house. "Mama, I'll go with you next time."

Later, though, Colleen was gone downtown to the store, and Clara used the chamber pot instead of venturing out. She surreptitiously poured the contents out the window, ashamed and disgusted with herself.

Her moods and fears changed in the blink of an eye. By that afternoon she seemed almost like her old self; the demons had vanished into thin air. She even baked a batch of cookies. The kitchen was hot, and when the chores were done Colleen asked the girls if they'd like to go on a picnic. "We'll leave some dinner on the stove for Pa, in case he comes home, but we'll probably be back before he shows up."

Annalee's eyes sparkled. "That will be fun! Can we take our fishing poles?"

"Sure! We'll see what you can catch."

"Can mama come too?"

They looked at Clara hopefully and she nodded and smiled. "If you're not goin' very far."

"I know a nice place along the creek that's not more than half a mile from here," Colleen told them. They gathered up a blanket and filled a basket with cheese, bacon sandwiches, apples, a jar of canned tomato juice and cookies. Then the four of them struck out up the road.

They soon arrived at the spot along the creek. It was shady and pleasant under the pine trees and they spread the blanket on the mossy bank. The smell of pine needles and damp earth permeated the air. Clara sat down on the blanket while Colleen took out the food.

"This is nice!" Polly said with a wide grin. "We ought to do this every day; it's so cool and sure better than eating at home!" The girls put small chunks of cheese on their hooks and dropped the lines in the water.

Within minutes Annalee had a tug on the end of her line. "I got one!" she cried excitedly.

"Well, pull him out!" Colleen called to her. She yanked a bright silver trout about five inches long up on the bank, then stood proudly watching it flop.

"Can we keep him?" Annalee asked as Polly and the others came over to see the catch. Polly reached down, grabbed the fish and took the hook from its mouth. She looked at Colleen.

"He's not big enough to keep, sugar," Colleen said. "We need to put him back in so he can grow. If you catch a bigger one, though, we'll cook it up for dinner tomorrow.

The girls caught three small fish about eight or nine inches long that they carefully placed in the basket. "Nice pan-size trout," Clara declared. They ate their dinner as the sun began to settle on the mountains to the west, and the light came slanting through the trees. As they walked home together, Colleen was happier than she'd been for a long time. Each time Clara had a good day, Colleen thought the bad times were over, and things would be all right. It was wonderful to have her mother back with them. If only Sam had been there, it would have been perfect. She would soon find out where Sam had been while they were sitting in the peaceful glade by the creek.

*   *   *   *

After the explosion at the Frisco mill, Sam and the other union members arrived at the Wallace depot to a huge crowd of union sympathizers. Cheers and yells of approval echoed up and down the street from every side as they piled out of the train. Other citizens, women and children and men who didn't support the violence, stayed indoors or observed the fracas with grim faces.

"Down with Capitalists! Workers unite!"

"That'll show the bastards!"

The union men cradled their dead and wounded in their arms as they took them out of the train and placed them in wagons. They then fell in behind the wagons to march up the street to the Miner's Hospital, where they were met by Sister Joseph and Sister Madeline who ran the hospital. The wounded were moved onto stretchers and taken inside a temporary building near where the new three story hospital would soon be completed, then they continued on to Worstells Undertaking Parlor with their sad cargo.

Sam's Uncle Alfred stood silently on the boardwalk in front of his store and watched worriedly as they went past. He saw his nephew in the crowd and started to wave, but thought better of it and Sam didn't look his way. Most of Alfred's fellow businessmen were on the side of the owners and denounced the miners as anarchists, thugs and "wild eyed lunatics." It was best not to show his support. He sure didn't support the violence and destruction that people said went on at Gem, yet he felt for his sister's family and agreed with their demands for the most part.

He and Mattie followed the events with heavy hearts. The next week someone brought a copy of the July 12, New York Times newspaper into the store. "Did you see this, Mr. Buchanan? The Coeur d' Alenes is famous all the way back to New York City!"

Alfred frowned and shook his head. "I hate for this beautiful country to be famous for death and destruction," he said as he took the paper, read the headline, "*Western Miners at War*," and the following article:

> "*Nine Men Killed and the Frisco Mill Blown Up*
> *... a miner from Gem started for Burke. When opposite the Frisco Mine he was fired upon. He ran back several hundred yards to Gem, where the shot had been heard, and soon the miners in the town gathered with arms. They marched in a body toward the Frisco Mill, directly in front of the mine. When scarcely within rifle range a volley from the Frisco Mill greeted the miners. They scattered and a regular battle ensued.*
>
> *A number of miners were killed and six wounded during the engagement. The miners, in the meantime, went up the canyon above the mine and loaded a car with 750 pounds of giant powder. This they sent down the track toward the Frisco Mine. Directly in front of the mill an explosion occurred, shattering the mill to splinters, making it a complete wreck. The non-union men then showed the white flag and surrenderd....*"

Alfred didn't get to see his sister Clara very often since he didn't see eye to eye with her husband, Joe. He knew Joe didn't support his wife and children like he should, that he was a heavy drinker, and there was little that Alfred could do about it. He, although the younger of the two, had always felt protective of his sister partially because they'd been orphaned as children.

"I sure don't know what's going to happen with Clara and the children," Alfred had said to his wife that morning. "You know Sam is into the struggle up to his eyebrows, and the whole family is suspect because of it."

"I know. I don't know why the company can't pay decent wages. Bunker Hill makes more for its investors and pays less than any of the other companies."

"It says right here in the paper what Joe and the others are up against. They can't make a living on three dollars a day. A single man with no family to support pays out $30 for board, $20 for clothes, $8 for a bunk, and other expenses that come to at least $15. That leaves only about $30 a month for everything else! Men with a family are in the hole every month."

"Not only that, but they risk their lives and health every time they go down into the mine. I don't think I could do it for any amount of pay. It's inhuman!"

"They feel they have no choice. Joe isn't trained for anything else, and of course Sam, even as bright as he is, followed right along in his footsteps."

"I wish we could help them some way."

"We've been through this before. It's stubborn pride, that's what it is, but Joe is not likely to change."

Now Alfred continued to watch the swarm of union men roar down the street. He, like most of the other citizens of the town, was horrified at the audacity of the mob and couldn't quite believe that the huge mill at the Gem had been totally destroyed.

All along Cedar Street people rushed to get out of the way of the wagon with the dead and wounded and the grim marching miners. Women and children watched from the windows. Ruby and the other girls at Miss Bessie's house craned their necks and took turns looking out from their lace-curtained windows on the second floor.

Sheriff Cunningham wired Governor Willey for troops. The Governor replied that they should exhaust their civil power first, so the Sheriff called men from Wallace, Murray and Wardner to help quell the riot. At the appointed hour few showed up. They refused to fight a war against their neighbors and friends.

The union men left off the bodies of their comrades and proceeded to union headquarters where they planned their next move. It didn't take them long to go to the next step.

As darkness came down they moved en mass like an angry cloud of hornets out of the headquarters and to a warehouse where boxes of guns had been stashed earlier. Then they proceeded out of town and down the river. They followed the railroad tracks toward Wardner. A wagon with five or six men accompanied them with the boxes of guns. Just below town they commandeered two flat cars of the Northern Pacific Railroad, and with the downgrade they soon rolled down to Wardner Junction. Along the way they acquired a load of dynamite from George Crane's Powder House.

When they got to the Junction they proceeded to the Bunker Hill Concentrator along the tracks. The new five story building was the largest of its kind in the world at 447 feet long and 72 feet wide. More than three hundred men worked here during the day, but tonight it was quiet. The union miners piled out of the train and surrounded the building with Winchesters at the ready while Maloney and others went under it and surreptitiously packed a ton and a half of Giant Powder under the crushers of the mill.

It was near midnight when the deed was done, and Sam and the others who lived in Wardner went home. The rest camped out nearby and waited for morning.

Sam crept into the house as quietly as he could. He was totally exhausted but so excited from the days events that sleep would not come. He lay wide awake for over an hour and went over every aspect of the situation. He dreaded the morning when he would have to tell his father that Skillet was dead.

The next morning he told them about the gun battle and how Skillet was one of the first to fall to the enemy's fire. Joe just looked at his plate and grunted. He shook his head. "Well, I'll be dammed!" was all he said.

Sam related the rest of the events of the day before. "When the building exploded people said the boom could be heard ten miles away! It was blown to smithereens! Big timbers flew through the air, and it's a wonder somebody wasn't hit by them."

Joe looked up at his son. "I hope you know your goose is cooked. There'll be hell to pay!"

"I know, Pa," he said quietly, a shadow fell across his face. "They didn't really intend to blow it up, but after we found out about that spy Bailey, the men were ready to explode themselves!" He grinned wryly and continued. "That mill looked like a pile of old matchsticks!" he said as he helped himself to more cornmeal mush and canned peaches. Joe nodded with approval, and the little girls gazed at their brother with their usual adoration, but Clara and Colleen just shook their heads and sighed. Where would it all end?

At the break of dawn the next day the union leaders and others went back and attached the fuses to the dynamite they had planted, then proceeded to wait for the mine officials to show up.

It wasn't long before mine manager, V. M. Clement, and others arrived. "What do you want?" Clement demanded.

"Take all the scabs out of the country or we'll blow this place to kingdom come!"

"You wouldn't dare! Get off this private property!"

"You heard what happened up at the old Frisco? We've got the dynamite placed. All we have to do is light it!"

Clement knew that state and federal troops were coming, so he put them off for a day.

The next day, however, he decided he couldn't jeopardize the mill. He backed down, the union miners withdrew the explosives and dispersed.

Clement immediately discharged more than three hundred non-union workers from the mill and the mill was shut down. Sam and Herbert, jubilant with victory, walked down to the junction with hundreds of other union members to watch the scabs leave. They cheered and jeered as the workers straggled out of the camp with their blankets and possessions on their backs.

✒ CHAPTER EIGHT ✒

July, August, September, 1892

Come all you exploited workingmen
And fight for Freedom's cause,
For you are bound, both hand and foot,
By capitalistic laws;
Your voices you can raise no more,
Your lips you now must seal,
For if you rise to speak a word
A gun-man's at your heel.

James J. Ferriter
Little Red Songbook

The miner's were ecstatic with the sight of hundreds of scabs leaving the valley. Free drinks were the order of the day at the Silver Pick, and Sam and Herbert both felt it was only a matter of time that the Owner's Association would adjust their thinking, but their victory was short lived.

The union leaders knew better from the beginning. They feared the worst. Many were very aware of the brutal repercussions to union activities in other areas, and the violence here was some of the most destructive of property in union history. They waited for the next shoe to drop.

Receiving other urgent messages in Boise, Governor Willey realized the enormity of the situation and sprang into action. On July 12th martial law came down on the beautiful mountains and deep canyons of the

Coeur d' Alene country like a thunderbolt from hell. The Governor proclaimed Shoshone County in "a state of insurrection and rebellion." Colonel James Curtis, commander of the Idaho National Guard, issued orders to his troops. They were to shoot anyone found in the act of blowing up railroads, bridges, mills or other property.

Colleen, Annalee and Polly walked downtown a few days later. It was early in the morning but the air was already hazy with pollen from pine trees in the surrounding mountains. The day promised to be a scorcher and Polly was anxious to get back home to finish up the hem of a skirt she was making.

As they left the post office, they noticed a soldier tacking up a notice on a post outside. They waited until the soldier left, then went over to read it. Four or five others came out of the stores nearby to see what was happening.

Annalee craned her neck to see what it was. She tugged at Colleen's skirt. "What does it say?"

Colleen read the following so all could hear:

Wallace Idaho
Idaho National Guard
July 15, 1892

To the officers and members of the Coeur d'Alene Miner's Union whether permanent or temporary: You are hereby commanded to surrender yourself and your arms to the commanding officers or troops at your respective localities. Protection under the law will be guaranteed. All good citizens of this county are requested and commanded to aid in identifying and arresting those who do not surrender.

Acting for the Governor,
James F. Curtis, Col.
Headquarters, Idaho National Guard,
Commanding.

The girls continued down the street, but one of the men who had been standing in the back waited until all were gone. He watched the soldier turn the corner a block away, then surreptitiously went up to the notice, ripped it down and tore it into shreds.

As they walked home, Annalee frowned and asked her sister. "Do they mean Sam?"

"Yes, honey, I'm afraid they do."

"Will he do that? Turn himself in to the soldiers?"

Colleen frowned and shook her head. "I don't think so."

Few union men heeded the order and Sam wasn't about to cooperate. They waited for the next move. The mine owners had Sheriff Cunningham removed from office, since he had sympathy for the miners, and named their own man as sheriff, the same man who was the company doctor before the union got its own hospital.

The state sent six companies of Idaho's National Guard into the county. Governor Willey also sent an urgent message to President Benjamin Harrison asking for federal troops.

Many leaders in the Silver Valley felt there was no need for martial law or federal intervention. Editor Aulbach was furious with the governor and was never shy about stating his opinions in his paper. He described the governor as *"His 'accidental' Excellency, Governor Willey (by the forbearance of God and the stupidity of the Republican Party, Chief Executive of Idaho)."*

Trains began to roll into the canyon, one after the other, with cars and cars filled with soldiers. Companies of Infantry from Vancouver Barracks, Fort Sherman, Fort Spokane and Fort Missoula swelled the ranks of the army to over 1500. Five hundred men were stationed at Wardner.

News spread quickly across the country of the events in the Silver Valley, and reporters, many of whom didn't know where the new state of Idaho was until the story broke, arrived by train and stage coach to write and photograph the results of the explosion and resulting martial law. They kept the telegraph line warm and the operators busy sending out their urgent reports.

*   *   *   *

Ryan and Sean left the country right after the battle at Gem. After the reception they'd received when they arrived, the tensions and dangers they'd faced every day in town, and finally the battle and explosion at the Frisco, even Ryan was ready to throw in the towel. They knew the Union Mill, where they worked, could be next.

They took the train to Spokane the next day and soon found a boarding house in the booming city. In the days after they arrived, they followed the events in the Coeur d' Alenes with heavy hearts. The papers were full of pictures and stories of the devastation of the mill and the union's activities. Ryan, especially, was shocked at the violence and the amount of damage done. He read everything he could find about the situation and worried about Colleen and her family.

He came into his and Sean's room on July 17th with a newspaper. "I'm glad we got out of there when we did, Sean," he said as he sat down on his cot across the room from his uncle. "I think the trouble is far from over. Just listen to what the Coeur d' Alene Miner had to say:"

> The struggle between the mine owners and the union developed a new phase this week that will make it (the Coeur d'Alenes) more famous in the annals of labor troubles than anything that occurred during the past months of peaceful warfare. The Winchester has taken the place of argument and Giant Powder has been substituted for arbitration.

Sean also had a newspaper. He took a Spokane Daily Chronicle from the table nearby. "Yes, it was good that we left, but sorry I am for the people there at Wardner. It's a blooming tragedy, it is, for a fact. Take a look at this." He handed Ryan the paper and he read the following:

> The strictest military regulations are enforced. Permits from commanding officers are required to leave town.
> A company of soldiers under Captain Luhn guard the Bunker Hill mill. A line of guards two miles long stretches from the mill to the mine. A company under Captain Bisbee protects the mine.
> Twenty-five of the Missoula infantry, sturdy Ethiopian warriors who fought the savage Sioux under captain Sanborn, are camped along the Northern Pacific tracks north of Wardner.

*   *   *   *

Wardner was an anthill crawling with soldiers. Armed men in military regalia marched through the streets. The sound of their loud voices and heavy boots permeated the air. The echo of military boots on the boardwalks was music to shopkeepers and others. It meant law and order and protection against thugs and outlaws.

For the McCarthys and other union members and their families, though, it was terrifying. The blue-coated soldiers overran the town, and their presence heightened the already volatile situation. Tension, suspicion and anxiety settled in the valley like a toxic fog and there was more hard drinking and less good natured banter at the Silver Pick. Fistfights and bitter arguments broke out among the union members and their families over nothing; a wrong word or dirty look could set them off.

Just outside of town, on one of the few level areas, where the ball field used to be, the military set up camp. More than a hundred canvas tents sprouted up like mushrooms.

The troops fanned out through the towns and countryside. Anybody not in uniform was suspect, and there seemed to be no rhyme or reason for taking certain men prisoner and not others.

Thomas O'Brian and some of the other known leaders and officers of the union were arrested immediately and put in the guard house. Then the military went to the Miner's Union Supply Store and seized all the arms and ammunition. The hunt for the rest of the union agitators was on, but they didn't have a clue who many of them were.

They rounded up and arrested hundreds of men, many of whom had nothing to do with the violence. Then there was the problem of what to do with them. At first they crammed them into boxcars and when they were full they put them in an old barn down near the Union Pacific tracks. Soon three hundred fifty men were crammed into a space 150x50. Hay was scattered on the floor and they curled up on the floor or the ground outside with no blankets and no toilets. Within two days the stench was horrible, and each day it became more unbearable.

The prisoners were set to work constructing a large log structure like a corral near the railroad tracks at Wardner Junction to hold more of the hundreds being arrested. Called the Bull Pen, the walls of the stockade were fourteen feet high, and when finished it consisted of four sheds and a large open area in the middle. Most of the prisoners were outside, since the sheds were used by the guards.

It wasn't just union men who were arrested. Editor W. A. Stewart of the Mullan Mirror was arrested for publishing "seditious materials." He was thrown in the Bull Pen for printing pro-union articles and demanding that the prisoners be treated fairly. His wife took over the paper and continued his work. They couldn't arrest a woman, but the authorities summarily confiscated her printing plant and promised her they'd let her husband go if she quit publishing the paper. She did, and Stewart was released. Soon after that the owners used the printing press to publish a paper for "The Coeur d' Alene Industrial Union" which was not a union at all but an arm of the Mine Owners Association.

A curfew was put in place and the town and the whole mining district was under siege. All saloons were ordered to close at midnight. The community was in tatters with sides taken and emotions high. Rumors flew from kitchen to saloon to church to bedroom, but nobody really knew what to expect next. The company people, most of the store owners and non-union miners, welcomed the troops with open arms.

In Wallace, Colleen's Aunt Mattie and Uncle Alfred were horrified at the violence at the Frisco Mill, but they were also appalled and sickened by developments afterward. Day after day they read and heard of the

State and Federal troops entered Wallace and Wardner to place the
Coeur d' Alene country under martial law.
Special Collections and Archives, University of Idaho Library, 8-X489

Hundreds of men, guilty and innocent, were arrested and held in the bull pen.
Special Collections and Archives, University of Idaho Library, 8-X27

arrests and of the Bull Pens in Wallace and Wardner. They knew Sam would probably be arrested if he hadn't been already. They'd sent a letter to Clara but had heard nothing.

Alfred came home for lunch on July 23rd, poured himself a cup of coffee, and spread a newspaper beside his plate. As Mattie dished up bean soup, he sipped his coffee as he scanned the front page of the Coeur d' Alene Barbarian. Then he put his cup down and shook his head. "Now just listen to this, dear:"

> "Reign of Anarchy Ended"
> "Now that the troops have possession of the country and martial law is declared it is to be expected that revolution and anarchy will come to an end. It is sincerely to be hoped that the frenzied men will come to their senses; that law and order will be restored and that those who have been defying the laws of the only country on earth that gives them their full rights as men and citizens will be brought to a realizing sense of the gravity of their offense."

Mattie shook her head. "I surely wish we'd hear something from Clara. They all must be beside themselves with worry. I heard today that Wardner's like a graveyard."

"Wallace isn't much different."

"Seems a little dramatic to call those miners 'revolutionaries and anarchists.' They don't want to revolutionize anything. A decent wage and safe working conditions don't seem to be much to ask."

In Wardner, the women and girls stayed off the streets as much as possible, but Colleen had to go to the store and post office. One Saturday she kept her head down as she hurried up Main Street a few days after martial law was established. It was only nine in the morning, but already getting hot, and she planned to get right home to help Clara cook the meal for the day so they wouldn't have to have a fire in the stove that afternoon. She held her skirt up with one hand to keep it out of the dusty road.

Suddenly a wagon full of soldiers pulled by two horses roared past her, and she was engulfed in a cloud of dust. She stared after them with disgust and dusted off her hair and dress as best she could.

When she got to the post office, there was a line waiting at the counter. Several of the people in line were soldiers. The one directly in front of her was an officer. He was chatting with a young soldier not much older than herself, who was ahead of him. The younger man was in fine spirits. "This operation shouldn't last long, I'm thinking. These hooligans and agitators will melt away like butter on a hot stove soon as we grab hold of the ringleaders."

The officer chuckled. "You're right. We've taken the monster by the throat and we're going to choke the life out of it!" Then he turned and glanced back at Colleen. She stood still as a statue and looked at the floor, but a shiver of fear went down her back. Sam is part of that monster, she thought.

On her way home, a clot of soldiers jeered as she went by. They hooted, whistled and yelled after her. "Now ain't that a picture fit to paint! I'd give my eye teeth for that little cherry!"

"Where are you going, Bonnie Irish lass? Said your prayers today to the Dago pope in Rome?"

"Come here, girl. I want to give you something!" She never gave them the satisfaction of a glance, never slowed her pace or speeded up, but kept her eyes on the road as her cheeks burned.

As soon as she was out of their sight, she ran the rest of the way home. Her legs shook and her breath came in gasps when she got to the house and slammed the door behind her.

"What's the matter, Colleen? You look like you're being chased by the devil!" Polly said as she finished drying a plate and put it in the cupboard.

"No," her sister said as she caught her breath. "Just couldn't wait to get back here and help you with the dishes! You poor girl!" she said as she gave her a hug. "Where's Annalee? It's her job to dry."

"Mama's pinning up the hem for her new dress." Colleen heard them in the other room and smiled.

Annalee hated to stand still long enough to have her dress measured on her little frame. "Are you done yet?" she whined.

"No, and if you don't be still I'm going to get this all crooked, and we'll have to start over!"

"Well can't you hurry up some? I swear you're as slow as the seven year itch!"

Clara laughed at that and gave her a good-natured swat on her behind. "And you are like a little flea on a hot stove!"

Later that day Colleen got her two sisters together. "Now, I want you both to listen to me. You are NOT to go downtown by yourselves for any reason! You hear me?" Annalee squinted at her with a frown, but said nothing.

Polly looked at her curiously. "Why not?"

"Because the town is crawling with soldiers, that's why. Now promise me you'll stay home unless some of us go with you."

As martial law took hold, like a noose that choked the life from the town, the authorities continued to arrest every man, young or old, who looked suspicious. On July fifteenth, they rounded up more than five hundred in Milo Gulch alone. They snatched several from the Silver Pick, including Joe McCarthy. He was standing at the bar when a soldier came up to him and grabbed him by the arm.

"You're under arrest!"

"What for? I haven't been anywhere near them explosions!"

"Do as we say and you won't get hurt. Get over by the door and line up." Joe joined several others along the wall.

"Empty your pockets!" They searched each one and confiscated pocket knives, guns and anything else they could find.

One of the younger men glared at them. "We got rights! This is part of the United States of America!"

"You can't arrest us without charges!" another one yelled.

"Charges hell! We don't need no charges. You're lucky we don't shoot you down right here for what you've done. You're all in it, one way or the other, nothing but anarchists and thugs."

"You got proof we were at Gem?" Joe said.

"Yeh, we got proof, you scum bags. Proof you Irish are a pack of wild dogs that need some taming!"

One young man shook with terror as they pushed him toward the door. "I got a wife and a sick baby at home. I live right over yonder on that street; can I just run over to that house and tell them? Then I'll go with you."

"We got orders. You're in custody. Shut up and get over there!"

Clara heard that Joe had been taken down to the old barn with the others and she and Colleen walked there to see him.

When they got close, one of the guards blocked their way. "Nobody allowed without permission from the commanding officer!" The imposing dark man was part of the contingent of black soldiers from Ft. Douglas. They surrounded the tall fence and guarded the entrance.

The young guards carried rifles with bayonets and they followed orders. No family members were allowed in to see the prisoners, and Clara and Colleen turned to go back home.

Walking along the street, they overheard a couple of soldiers talking. One nodded toward a black soldier across the street. "Why'd they bring those darkies in here anyway?"

"That's the Buffalo Soldiers. They've got no use for the Irish or for their unions. Them coloreds won't have no more mercy on the sons of bitches than they would with rattlesnakes!"

When Clara and Colleen told Sam about Joe's arrest that night, he was outraged.

"He hasn't been involved with any of this!"

"It don't matter. There's no rhyme or reason to any of it. Maybe they got the wrong McCarthy!" Clara said.

"You think I should go down and turn myself in and they'll let Pa go?"

"Don't you do nothing of the kind, Sam," Colleen said. "Let the old buzzard stay there. Maybe he'll straighten out some in there."

Her mother looked at her and frowned. She didn't like that kind of talk, but then she nodded. "Well, you are probably right. Besides they probably wouldn't let him go anyway, then we'd have both of you in there!"

"Did you hear about those trainloads of scabs coming back in?" Sam said.

"Yes, we heard about it. Anybody who wants to work will have to sign a paper swearing they are not or never have been a member of the union."

"They can't do this!"

"Looks like they can, son," Clara answered. "The law is with the power and the money."

That evening Clara begged Sam to get out of town. "Pack some food and go up into the mountains. You know they are going to grab you. You're too well-known, especially by that traitor Bailey that you were so friendly with!"

Sam grimaced. "Nope. I'll take whatever they dish out. I'm not about to turn myself in, though. Those hyenas will have to come and get me. I'm staying close to home for awhile, Ma."

"I can't believe it's come to this," Colleen said. "Our own government, the United States of America, is taking up arms against us! And we were so proud to become the forty-third star!"

Clara shook her head sadly. "Those rich fat cats could have done the right thing to start with and none of this would have happened!"

"They could bully us, starve us, and treat us like dirt under their feet, but they haven't broke us yet. If I go to jail, I'm ready," Sam declared.

On July 22nd, Joe and several others were released without explanation. He came home exhausted and shaking with fever. Racked by a hoarse cough, he told them about the conditions inside the Bull Pen. Clara gave him some of Dr. Gunn's Onion Syrup, while Colleen fixed dinner. When they all sat down to eat, her mother just rearranged the food on the plate and went back to bed soon afterward.

A few days later Herbert was picked up and hauled off to the Bull Pen.

The shopkeepers and company men were furious at the behavior of the miners, but they were further outraged when some of the soldiers in the Wallace militia called in to enforce martial law refused to take arms against the unions. The talk in the saloons was of little else.

"They ought to line the whole damn union up and shoot them! And all the traitors who refuse to fight! They're nothing but terrorists!" the local tailor said as he sipped his beer at the Golden Nugget.

"It's a damn crime when men in the army refuse to do their job!" another one sitting down the bar put in. He picked up a copy of the August 20, "Coeur d' Alene American" from the counter and said "Listen to this!"

> *"Down With Mutiny:*
> *"It will be remembered that when the Coeur d'Alene riots commenced the Wallace militia broke ranks. Some of them joined the insurrectionists, and one or two went so far as to steal the state's guns and turn them over to the rioters.... When a soldier publicly, ostentatiously, mutinously, in the presence of the colonel of his regiment, proposes three cheers for an assassin, an anarchist and a dynamiter and thus seeks to signify approval of the murder and riot which he is sworn to suppress, no penalty can be too severe, no disgrace too deep."*

Sam was cagey as a cat and managed to elude the authorities for a month, but on August 15, he was more restless than usual and took a chance. The day was humid and overcast. Thunderstorm clouds were piled up in the sky above the mountains to the west like whipped cream tinted purple, blue and gray.

He went down to the drugstore for a bottle of soda water. As he came out of the store he saw a knot of men along the street. He kept a close eye out for soldiers, but since he didn't see any, his curiosity got the best of him and he approached the crowd to see what was happening. He recognized several of the group. At the center of the crowd was a friend from his class in school, a boy who was only about five feet tall and 125 pounds, whose name was Arthur. Sam didn't remember him being involved with any of the union activities.

The sheriff had him by the arm as he struggled to get away. Shopkeepers and people on the street crowded around to watch. "I've done nothing wrong! Let me go!"

"We heard what you said, boy, back there at the barber shop. You and your kind are a threat to the peace of this town."

"I stand on the free soil of America! I can say anything I want!" He spat on the ground and with that the sheriff, who was about twice the size of the boy, smashed him hard alongside the head.

"Shut up or you'll get more of the same!"

Arthur staggered back, dazed. "What's the matter, Doc? I ain't done nothing!"

The sheriff hit him again and a small trickle of blood came out of his mouth. "I said shut up!"

"I am in free America! I have a right to talk!"

The sheriff, by way of an answer, smashed him in the head again and dragged him away.

Mattie and Alfred read an account of the event in the Wallace Democrat the next day:

> "... *Our worthy sheriff struck the boy four times in all, much to the edification of the silk Stocking bank street crowd of Mine Owners and trucklers to that organization. After the sheriff had beaten the boy unmercifully he grabbed him by the collar and yanked him to the goal ....*"

They had still not heard from Clara, and hoped that Sam, if he had been arrested, at least went peacefully.

Sam, watching the beating from the edge of the crowd, could stand it no longer. He ran after them and yelled. "That man has done nothing wrong! What are you taking him for?"

At that instant he felt a vice grip on his shoulder and his arms were roughly pinned behind his back. He was suddenly surrounded by armed soldiers. "Come along peaceable now and there'll be no trouble. You're Sam McCarthy!"

Sam struggled but he knew there was no use fighting. "We have rights!" he said as they marched him off with several others.

"Bullshit! Anarchists don't have nothing! You pigs are terrorists and you were right in the thick of it." He put the gun to Sam's head. "I've a good mind to blow your head off! You want me to settle your hash like what that kid got? Just keep talking!"

Sam was marched to the Bull Pen and shoved inside with the others. The first thing that hit him was the smell. He blanched at the stench of urine, vomit and body odors of more than four hundred men. As soon as he caught his breath and adjusted to the smell he looked around. He'd heard that Herbert had been taken two weeks before. He soon saw him slouched against the wall on the far side. It looked like he was sleeping. Dozens of men were plastered there in the dust since it was the only area that had any shade.

He went over and touched his shoulder. "Herbert, wake up. It's me."

His buddy opened his eyes and looked around with a dazed expression. "Who, who's there?"

"It's me, Sam. They got me today."

Finally Herbert focused his eyes. "Well, I'll be damned! Ain't you a sight for sore eyes! I figured you to be up in the mountains!"

"No, I've been around. Are they feeding you?"

"Not at first. Just bread and water. It makes a body feel real tired. Now we get a little water two times a day and some food. Last time, I think it was yesterday, they brought in some kind of slop. I tried to eat."

Night came down, like a nine-pound hammer driving steel, and even though the days were warm, even hot, the usual evening chill settled over the canyon. Sam and the others shivered in the cold. His stomach growled from hunger but no food or water was offered.

The next day he found other friends, and he and Herbert listened as some of the prisoners joked and sang songs to pass the time. In any group of Irish or Scots there were always a few who knew the words and tunes to dozens of songs. They sang songs from the civil war, like "Tramp, Tramp, Tramp, the Boys are Marching," and work songs like "Patrick on the Railroad," but their sentimental favorites were always the old Irish tunes like "Shenandoah" and "Green Grow the Lilacs." Sam and Herbert didn't join in.

That evening Herbert came over and squatted next to Sam. "What did we get ourselves into, old buddy?"

"I wouldn't change one damn thing!" Sam said defiantly. They need us as bad as we need their damn jobs! If I had the chance I'd blow them all to hell!"

Herbert looked nervously around and frowned at his friend. "Don't talk that way. They'll hear you. Nothing to do now but hunker down and wait." But 'wait' was a word foreign to Sam's ears.

That night a thunderstorm moved into the valley with a vengeance. Thunder cracked and boomed and lightning lit up the sky. Then the heavens opened up, and it poured buckets of rain within an hour. It drenched the men who chose to be huddled outside rather than packed like sardines in the sheds. Muddy ground and wet clothes added to their misery.

The next morning the storm was over, but the tops of the mountains were hidden behind wispy gray clouds and the temperature dropped. Sam sat with the others, silent and subdued. His stomach ached and he ate a little of the mush that was sent around. By the second night he was pale, resigned and unusually quiet. It was almost impossible to sleep with the coughing and vomiting of the prisoners. On the third day, a large trough of some kind of mixture of half rotten meat and vegetables was brought in and the men scooped it out with their filthy hands or they had none at all.

The day after Sam was arrested, Clara heard a loud bang on the door around dinner time. Joe was still downtown. Clara opened it to a pair of soldiers. They informed her that Sam was in custody. She just stood like a rock and stared at them; her face drained of color.

Colleen came out of the kitchen. "What is it, Mama?" she said, but she knew the answer.

One of the soldiers started to step inside the door, but Clara stood her ground. He backed off. "We know your boy, Sam, was in on the dynamiting of the mill. Now if you can tell us who was with him we've got orders to go easy on him."

"We don't know anything. How do you know he was part of it?"

"It's secret information, ma'am. Now what can you tell us?"

"We can't tell you anything!" Colleen pushed her way in front of her mother. "Now you've done your job, you can leave our porch!" The two turned around abruptly and headed back to town. Clara, now shaking and crying, closed the door and slumped to a chair nearby. Colleen helped her to the bed, where she took some medicine that the new druggist had given her, called coca cola. He said it would help with her sleep since it had cocaine in it.

Joe came home a little later and the four of them sat down to eat. Colleen told him Sam was in custody. He just said "Dammit to hell! I told him to stay out of town!" and the rest of the meal was eaten in silence.

As the girls did the dishes, Polly and Annalee were quiet and anxious. "What will they do to Sam?" Polly finally whispered.

"He'll be all right. He's young and strong and they can't keep hundreds of men locked up down there forever," Colleen assured her with brave words that she didn't feel. "In a few minutes I'm going to take some food down to him."

"Can we go too?"

"No, sweetheart. You need to stay here in case Mama needs you."

When the kitchen was cleaned up and the girls were settled, Colleen put potatoes and meat into a pot with a lid and set out for the prison. As she made her way down the hill, the sun, setting on mountain silhouettes, was a brilliant orange, and the sky was streaked with salmon and rose colored clouds. Ordinarily she would have stopped and stared at the glory of the scene, but she hardly noticed. She hurried faster since it would soon be dark, and she didn't like being out after dark with the town full of strangers.

When she got to the camp and approached the structure, the guards stopped her outside the walls. She handed over the food and told them who it was for. Later she learned that the prisoners never got any of the food the families brought. It was eaten by the guards.

It was an exciting time for some of the townspeople. The ladies, wives and daughters of the shop owners and company men, the so-called "better element," were all aflutter, excited by the arrival of soldiers. They gave dinners for the officers and invited them to their homes for tea.

Colleen went over one morning to visit with Sally. It was a warm sunny morning and she hadn't seen her friend since Sam was arrested. She found her outside. They chatted as Sally washed clothes. She had a bench outside the door with two small wash tubs on it. Inside the first tub was a scrub board and she took a blouse, dipped it in the soapy water, scrubbed it on the rough surface of the board, then dipped it again in the soapy water, squeezed it out and put it in the clean rinse water in the second tub.

"Are you going to the dance tonight?" Sally asked her as she wrung out the blouse and hung it on a line nearby.

Colleen sat down on the porch step. "What dance?"

"They're having a dance for the officers. The Law and Order League and the APA are putting it on. All us girls are going."

Colleen just looked at her, dumbfounded, for a minute. "Don't you know what that APA is?"

"Not really. I know a lot of the shopkeepers belong to it. You know Ma, she don't join much of anything."

"Well, Sam said it's called the American Protective Association. And guess who they are protecting America from? Us!"

"That can't be right! Are you sure?"

"Yes, I'm sure. They hate all us Catholics, especially the Irish ones! Did you hear they've taken Sam now?"

"No! I'm sorry to hear that."

"It was bound to happen. You know he was in on a lot of it."

Sally shook her head. "I know he was. It's too bad but what they did was awful. Blowing up the mill and all."

Colleen's jaw stiffened. "They were fired on first," she said, her voice rising. "The mine owners have been trying for months to get our men to do something bad so they could arrest them. I'm sure they're happy now." She got up from the porch and faced Sally. Her voice shook. "You're going to a dance for the soldiers? If that don't beat all. You think I could go down there to that hall and smile all pretty and dance with the men who are starving my brother, beating him and keeping him prisoner!"

Sally blushed, looked down at the ground, then looked worriedly at her friend. "I guess you're right. I'm sorry about everything." Colleen shook her head and turned to go, her eyes brimmed with tears. Sally called after her as she walked away. "Now come back and see me Colleen! Don't get all huffy about this!"

Colleen walked quickly down the road toward her house. Tears blinded her eyes and she wiped them away angrily. How could people give parties and dances for these men who had taken over their town? How could they even be civil to officers who were starving Sam and the others? She went home, dejected and discouraged.

* * * *

The days dragged by and August turned into September. Every day was shorter than the one before. Frost etched the grass along the road and many nights a thin coat of ice formed along the edge of Milo Creek. By noon it was warm, though, the ice evaporated like a miner's pay on Saturday night, and the days were golden.

Colleen tried to keep her mother's mind off of Sam. She told her it couldn't be much longer, the men were getting more food, and they now had blankets and quilts to ward off the freezing nights. With the publicity, the authorities were finally shamed and frightened into improving conditions. Each day Colleen went down to the Bull Pen, but often she wasn't able to see Sam.

She and Clara walked downtown one afternoon to get some embroidery thread. Clara was embroidering some new pillow cases. She was calm and focused when she had handiwork to do, but otherwise she was morose, distraught and disconnected to what happened around her. She seldom left the house except at her daughter's urging.

On this day she was in a good mood for once, and Colleen felt hopeful. The heat of summer had melted away up the cool draws, leaving crisp clear air and sunny skies in its place. The sky, an uncanny bright blue, stretched above their heads like a giant blanket. The closer mountains that surrounded the deep canyon stood in silent splendor fringed with firs and cedars. Behind them the misty blue shoulders of higher peaks reared up, and behind them still stood the jagged ridges of the Bitterroots, dark navy blue and miles away along the Montana border. They were stitched to the sky with brilliant white lace, the first skiff of snow of the season.

As they walked back home they suddenly heard gunshots from down the canyon, toward Wardner Junction. Colleen's heart skipped a beat. She quickly recovered, though, and assured Clara it was probably the soldiers doing target practice.

Today Clara was talkative. "You remember that man with the wagon who came through here last fall with the apples and peaches?" she said.

"Yes, they were sure good, weren't they? I could die for a peach cobbler right now."

"He was the spittin' image of my uncle. The one who raised me."

Colleen's ears perked up. If she could just get her mother talking, maybe she could understand her better. "You never have told me much about your uncle and aunt. What were they like?"

"Oh, they were fine people. Salt of the earth .... You haven't heard anything about the fruit man this year?"

"No, but I'll ask around. I think he came from down in the Walla Walla country. We could sure use some more fruit for the winter."

"Yes, but he charged an arm and a leg for it, I'm not sure we could afford to pay his prices even if he did show up."

"I'm glad we've got all those tomatoes put up. We could live on canned tomatoes and venison if we have to."

"How many jars did you say we have?"

"Close to two hundred. That's a lot of tomatoes! I thought I was going to turn into a fat juicy tomato before we got them all in the jars!" They walked past two horses and said good morning to an old man who busily forked timothy hay into a feed trough nearby. Colleen smiled, glanced at her mother, then looked more closely. Clara had stopped dead still in the road as soon as she smelled the hay, a stricken look on her face.

"What is it, Mama?"

"Nothing. Nothing. I'm doing fine." Her face was white, as if she'd seen a ghost.

"It's just a couple of old horses, nothing to be afraid of!"

"I'm not afraid!" Clara snapped at her, her mellow mood gone in a second. "You think I'm afraid of a dad gum horse?" Colleen shook her head and didn't answer as they continued up the road to the house. It seemed there was no rhyme or reason to her mother's tempers and anxieties, and more often than not, she bore the brunt of her anger.

The next morning Colleen left early to go get the mail. Her mind was on her brother and what might happen next. She knew he wouldn't talk, and she didn't know how he could stand being cooped up with hundreds of other men with nothing to do. It was a recipe for disaster. She also worried about her mother. She knew Clara was getting worse. There were times now when she didn't make sense, and there was no one to talk to about it. She had tried to talk to the visiting priest a few months ago, but he just patted her on the shoulder and told her he'd keep her in his prayers. God's will he said.

Every day she looked for a letter from Ryan. She hadn't heard from him since before the explosion at the Frisco. He had written once while he was back in Idaho, but that was all. She went to the counter and greeted the mailman as he went to look in their box. He came back with a letter and she held her breath. Yes! It was from him, but the return address said Spokane.

September 5, 1892
Dear Colleen:

Thank you for your letter. I'm sorry I've taken so long to answer. I've been reading about the arrests and the Bull Pens. I'm sorry your brother was involved in the trouble. He's a good man and I know you must be very worried about all that has happened.

I was sorry I couldn't see you while I was at the Union Mill, but with the way things were going, I think you understand. We worked for a couple of months there, but after the mill at Gem was dynamited we realized the Coeur d' Alenes are not a good place for us right now. That was too close for comfort. I was given a gun but never had to use it. I thought it would be awful if I had to shoot at your brother.

As you know I'd rather be horse whipped than go down in the mines anyway. I've got a job here in Spokane mucking out stalls at the livery. I'd sure rather muck horse puckey than those blessed rocks but it don't pay much. At least I can stay up in the daylight where a man is supposed to live. Sean got on with the railroad, a good paying job. I plan on starting to school at the new college as soon as I save some money.

This city is booming! The big fire they had never slowed things down much. There's big fancy brick buildings going up in every direction. You should see it! They have a brand new trolley system and a body can ride one of them trolleys clear out to Twickenham Park where they have some mighty good baseball games. Someday I'll take you there.

That's all for now. Write back to me when you can. You can send it to this address. Sean and me are staying at a real nice boarding house and we'll be here for awhile. Hoping to hear from you I am and that you are doing all right.

Sincerely,
Ryan

⁀ CHAPTER NINE ⁀

September, October, November 1892

You will eat, bye and bye,
In that glorious land above the sky;
Work and pray, live on hay,
You'll get pie in the sky when you die.

You will eat, bye and bye,
When you've learned how to cook and to fry;
Chop some wood, 'twill do you good,
And you'll eat in the sweet bye and bye.
                    Joe Hill
                    Little Red Songbook

Sam, Herbert and a few others were not idle in the Bull Pen stockade. Sam kept track of the days by making a mark with his fingernail on the fence. On the fifth day he and Herbert hatched a plan of escape. They stationed some men as lookouts and started digging a tunnel under the fence. With their bare hands or anything else they could get, they dug and deposited the dirt unobtrusively behind the shed. Day after day they worked. It gave them a purpose and a focus and helped to pass the long days. Sam could stand the conditions as long as he was occupied. By September 10, they had a tunnel 75 feet long and 30" wide. Then the inevitable happened. A guard got curious and discovered it.

As punishment, early the next morning, Sam, Herbert and about six others who were known to have been involved, were ordered to dig a trench inside the enclosure to thwart any other attempts at escape.

"That's all you Irish know how to do, anyway," the guard barked with a sneer. "You can dig holes and your old ladies can be washerwomen!" The prisoners just looked at him. "Here's the shovel. You know an Irish spoon when you see one, don't you! Now get started!" he pushed Herbert with the butt of his gun.

Herbert glared at him with contempt and stayed rooted where he was. "No, sir. I'm not working!" Each of the others took their cue from him, responded in like manner and sat down on the ground.

"Go ahead, kill us. Then see what happens!" Sam said defiantly. "You won't get away with it!"

The guard left to report the rebellion to his superiors. He came right back. "If you don't work, line up over there! You'll wish you did, you sons of bitches!" Sam lined up with the others in the hot morning sun. "Now, stand up straight! Attention! Now stay there! Any man who moves will be shot!"

One hour went by. Then three. It was hot, especially for September, and the sun hung like a red hot branding iron over the valley. By early afternoon, the temperature hit 72. Four more hours passed, then five. Sam's eyes blurred from the heat and the sun. The high of the day was 77 degrees.

They were given no food or water and were not allowed to relieve themselves. Wet stains appeared on some of their pants. Still they stood. Sam gritted his teeth and looked at Herbert. They locked eyes and each made a fist in defiance. Bile rose in Sam's throat. His stomach rumbled and he thought he would be sick, but he managed to overcome it. Another hour passed and the dizziness came and went in waves. His knees felt like rubber, but he looked at the sky and willed himself to hold on. Four ravens circled high overhead, attracted by the putrid smells of the Bull Pen, or did they smell death? He wondered.

He tried to concentrate on something far away from this nightmare. In his mind he went on a journey up into the cool woods above the town where the huckleberries were found. He knew the days were getting shorter, and the long cold winter lurked just around the corner. That meant if a person was real quiet standing in the draws above the town, he could hear the bull elk bugle a challenge to the other bulls on the far distant slopes. He thought about huckleberries, and elk and cool mountain streams.

He pictured the river, clear and cold, and the trail he often followed along the mossy bank under golden cottonwood trees to his favorite fishing holes. He imagined each rocky outcropping, each stand of trees, and each gentle bend in the river. He visited a place where the creek gurgles over huge boulders and splashes into a deep hole. That's where the fish would be and he could see them swimming languidly in his mind's eye.

Then he was jarred back to reality. The acrid smell of human waste, sweat and filth brought him back with a jolt. Arthur, the boy who was arrested with him, suddenly fell out of line on his face in the dust. He'd fainted, and the guards casually came over and dragged him away. Sam and the others listened fearfully for a shot, but all was still.

At five that evening, as the heat of the day began to dissipate and the sun edged toward the mountains, the guards ordered them back to the main prison yard. They were given water but no food until the next morning, and then it was bread and water. Sam curled up in a ball and slept for fourteen hours straight.

Soon after this, Herbert was released and Sam felt more despondent than ever.

In Wallace, Alfred and Mattie went to the post office each day, anxious to hear of Clara's family, but all they heard was rumors and wild tales about what was happening in Wardner. Wallace was also under siege.

On September 22nd, Alfred leaned against the counter of his drugstore with the *Wallace Democrat* open in front of him. He nodded as he read the editorial which accused the other paper in town, the *Coeur d' Alene Miner*, of being:

> *"persistent in upholding the extraordinary methods of martial law at the expense of civil rights, and continually reiterating that 'it meets the approval of our best citizens.' Now we would like to know who are our best citizens? Are they the ones who have the money of the country and the toadys of aristocratic tastes?.... ... the Republicans of Idaho have gone to tyranny, conspiracy, falsehood and criminal injustice to gain them very questionable ends in Shoshone county. 'Gold or money,' it has been said, 'is the root of all evil.' But we in Idaho can exclaim with profound sorrow: 'Oh! Lead, what crimes and injustice have been committed in thy name!'"*

A friend of his came up just as he finished. Alfred motioned to the paper. "Now this piece has got it just about right. It's dead wrong to bring U. S. troops against our own citizens! It's against the laws of the state and the country!"

The man was non-committal. "It's sure an ugly situation any way you look at it."

"Have you heard any news from Wardner? Mattie's been worried sick. I would have taken the train down there but for the travel restrictions."

"Yes, I heard your brother-in-law and nephew were taken in but Joe was released."

"I figured Sam would be taken. He was in on it I know."

* * * *

At Wardner, the crowded conditions, lack of sanitation and little food in the bull pen contributed to the unrest of the prisoners, and constant surveillance by the soldiers added to the tension. Tempers were short, anger was just below the surface among the men, and old grudges and feuds surfaced. One day a prisoner had a box of chewing gum that his mother had brought him. A man who sat next to him along the fence grabbed some of the gum and the first man erupted with rage. He smashed the man's nose in and a fight ensued. The two men were both covered with blood before they were forcibly pulled apart by the other prisoners. The guards did nothing.

Sam kept quiet and away from the troublemakers as much as he could. For the first time in his life he felt real depression, and the days never seemed to end. Finally September dragged to a bitter end, and he had forty-six marks on the fence. Then October, that spectacular golden month in the northern mountains, crept into the canyons, painting the trees along the river yellow and orange and rust. Days were blessed with brilliant blue skies, and nights shivered with crisp frost.

Little changed in the Bull Pen, each day ground grimly to a merciful close, only to start over again the next morning. If Sam hadn't kept track, he would have lost count of the monotonous days and cold, miserable nights. Nothing much happened. Of and on, some prisoners were released, but Sam was never one of them. His fiftieth day of captivity came and went.

Without his friend Herbert and with nothing to do, he became more and more agitated as time went by. He was an action-oriented person, and boredom by itself was torture for him. Patience wasn't his strong point, and like a caged lion, he paced the perimeter of the stockade and ate barely enough to keep alive. Periodically the guards isolated him and tried to get him to confess and give information, but he steadfastly refused. At one point they took him into the shed and gave him coffee and a small piece of cake.

"Now son," one of them told him. "Your mother is very sick. If you will just tell us who all was involved in the explosion, we'll let you go."

Sam glared at them with hatred. "You go to hell! And before you go, you can kiss my foot! I ain't telling you beans!" He was put on bread and water for several days.

The other prisoners gambled and whiled the time away any way they could. They even played cards with some of the guards, but Sam would have none of it. He kept to himself.

On his fifty-seventh day of captivity, near sundown, as the sky was ablaze with salmon-colored clouds that billowed up from the purple ridge of mountains to the west, Sam paced around the wall of the enclosure near the gate. Suddenly a young woman with two toddlers hanging onto her skirts came up.

She asked to see her husband. "I heard my husband, Michael O'Reilly, is terrible sick. I would like to see him."

The guard shook his head. "No. Nobody allowed in here."

"Please, sir. Just for a minute. He needs medicine for his ailment. It won't take any time at all. I have it here, with me, see?" She took out a small medicine bottle. The guard moved menacingly toward her. Sam looked around. None of the other guards were near. He stood plastered along the fence just inside the gate and watched and listened.

"You heard me. You can't see him. Come back next week when the commanding officer is here. Move on, now." Instead of leaving, the woman stepped boldly toward him and tried to push him aside. Surprised at her audacity, the soldier held the gun across his chest and used it to shove her back. The toddlers screamed and she staggered back. At that instant Sam saw his chance. He ran out the gate. The guard wheeled around, but Sam shoved him to the ground and took off running.

The guard got up on his knees, yelled "Halt or I'll shoot!" and got a bead on Sam's back. The other guards, who had been inside the compound gambling with the prisoners, ran toward the gate, guns at the ready. Again the guard yelled, "Halt! Or I'll shoot!"

Sam didn't slow down. All that was in his mind was getting out of the stinking Bull Pen and into the open air away from the guards and the misery and hopelessness they all felt. His legs churned as he ran through the dry grass. He was thin and emaciated after weeks of little activity, but still strong with youth and desperate determination.

He felt he could run forever into the crisp October evening and he headed for a stand of pine trees a short distance away. It was the kind of day he loved. He could see the trace of snow on the high mountains in the distance as he gasped the clear mountain air for breath.

He glanced back over his shoulder just as the rifle in the guard's hands cracked. A bullet whizzed near his head and he kept running. He could hear the shouts of the soldiers as they started after him. Other shots split the silence of the evening, and the sounds echoed up the canyon. He was almost to the trees when a bullet tore through the air and slammed into his back. He fell, face down, into the dry brown grass of the field. Writhing with pain, he turned over, eyes to the sky, then the light in his eyes dimmed and sputtered out like old candles at the bottom of the mine shaft.

When the light went out of Sam's eyes, the light for Clara, Colleen and the family went out at that moment as well. The fabric of their life, worn thin and bare for months, was now in shreds. A messenger came to the door within an hour. When he knocked on the door, Colleen was the one to answer. He told her what happened and offered his condolences. The color drained from her face and she reeled back as if she'd been hit with the bullet herself. She couldn't breathe. She couldn't speak, and the man standing in front of her was a blur. She grabbed hold of the door jam and leaned her cheek on the rough wood.

She stared at him and shook her head with disbelief. "No, you've got the wrong house," she finally said; her voice sounded far away, like someone else's voice, and she felt as if she were out of her body looking down at herself.

"Sam McCarthy was the boy's name. This is his house?"

"Yes, but it can't be."

"I'm sorry, ma'am. He assaulted the guard and ran from the stockade. The men have orders to fire. He was told to halt, he was given warning more than once, but he just kept on."

"Where is he? Take me to him." She turned and called out to her mother. "Mama, I'm going downtown for a minute. I'll be right back." She needed to see for herself before telling her mother. She followed the soldier down the hill to the union hall.

She entered the door of the hall and it was so dark she couldn't see anything. Then her eyes adjusted and she saw him. She saw Sam, her dear brother, lying on a table near the back of the dim room. Her father had arrived before her. He sat stony-faced in a chair near the stove with a glass in his hand.

She glanced at her father, nodded, then ran to Sam and dropped to her knees. His face was white like granite, and she smoothed the hair on his forehead and held his hand. It was cold and lifeless. Several of his friends were there, standing in mute silence. She stayed for an hour; she honestly thought she would never move again. Finally one of the older men came and knelt beside her. "Come on now, Colleen, dear. Let me take you home."

She dragged herself up and let him lead her out of the building but as they left Main Street she told him to go back. "I'll be fine now. Thank you." She needed to be alone and to walk slowly on this, one of the longest walks of her life, back to the house to tell her mother and sisters.

Clara collapsed when Colleen told her and Polly sobbed as if her heart would break. Annalee cried, but she really didn't believe her big brother wouldn't come back. He was too important in her life and she believed in magic. Joe never came home at all that night. He came home the next day, disheveled and morose. He had nothing to say about planning the funeral, and Colleen was relieved when Sally and her mother came over to help.

The next few days were a blur. The first night a wake was held. Candles were lit around the room and around the coffin. Colleen, Clara, Joe and the girls sat on chairs nearby throughout the day and night watching over the dead. The tradition harked back to the old country where the watchers guarded the dead to ward off evil spirits and prevent them from entering the body. People streamed through the house bringing food and drink, songs and music. The coffin was walled off from the all-night party with a blanket. Games were played, and Colleen and the girls were cajoled into taking part a few times.

The next day Alfred and Mattie pulled up in front of the house in a fine carriage with two spirited black horses. Colleen never knew how they got word, but they brought food and presents for everyone. The younger girls, especially, were comforted to have them there.

The next day was Sunday, and it happened to be the Sunday that Father Keyzer was scheduled to have mass in Wardner. He alternated Sundays between Wallace, Wardner, Mullan, Burke and Murray. The mass was held in the union hall, and the place was packed with Sam's friends and fellow union members. They buried Sam up on the hill at the cemetery just outside of town near Granny's grave.

Clara's brother and sister-in-law were devastated at the way Sam died, but their grief at the loss of Sam was almost overshadowed by their shock and dismay at Clara's condition.

They tried to talk to Joe. "She is not good, Joe. You need to get her some help."

Joe just shook his head and looked at them as if they were strangers. "She's fine. We don't need any help from you. This is none of your affair. You know Clara's always been puny. This is just hard on her. She'll be doing fine with Colleen here to help."

Before Alfred and Mattie left to go back to Wallace, they got Colleen aside and told her she must send them word if they could help in any way.

"I promise. I will let you know, but we'll be fine. Mama will get better in a few days, I'm sure, and we girls can do most of the chores." Pride formed those lies and platitudes that rolled out of her mouth like thread from an almost-empty spool.

Things didn't get better, though. Joe was often gone for days at a time, and he had always withdrawn from his wife when she had her "problems." Clara cried every day and left most of the work to the girls. She didn't seem to care whether Joe or anyone was there or not. She even ignored the two younger girls, something she'd never done before. Colleen was glad that Polly and Annalee had school to go to.

In the days that followed, there were times when Clara was uncontrollable. "No!" she screamed. "Get away from me! You can't do this! Please!"

"Mama, I'm just going to comb your hair. You haven't combed it for two days." Colleen took her mother's arm and tried to get her to be still. Her dress was dirty and she'd slept in it the night before. Clara pulled away, slapped her arm, and ran back to the bedroom.

Colleen followed her to the door of the room and watched as Clara curled into a ball on the bed, mumbling and crying. "No, don't make me. I didn't mean to Mama ...."

"It's ok, mama," Colleen said. "I won't do anything, but you need to eat something. You'll feel better if you do." She went back to the kitchen and put a stick of wood in the stove. The girls were due home from school soon and she'd hoped she could get her mother to clean up before then. She made some tea and took it to the bedroom. "Here, I made you some nice tea. Remember what Granny always said, a cup of tea works wonders."

Clara looked at her with anguished eyes. "Tea won't fix this," she said savagely, but she reached for the cup with trembling hands. After she sipped briefly, Colleen put the cup on the table near the bed, sat with her for a few minutes, then returned to the other room and slumped into a chair. She had lived with this terrible black hole, this empty abyss in her heart since the loss of her brother a week ago. Why couldn't her mother realize the pain they were all in? She, Colleen, was still alive. She wanted to scream out, "I'm here!" Annalee and Polly were still here. It was as if they didn't count; as if Sam had been the only one that mattered.

She yearned for Granny and closed her eyes to conjure her up. She remembered their conversation which seemed so long ago now, even though it had actually been a little over a year, when they met their neighbor who was all crippled up.

She could hear Granny's dear old voice saying how you keep on. "Yes. You just put one foot in front of the other and keep on. Nothing to it," the old woman said. "Just keep on keeping on. Day by day. The Lord gives you this one day to do with ...." Finally Colleen got up and went into the kitchen to make some bread.

*   *   *   *

Gradually most of the prisoners that were still held in the Bull Pen were released on bond but some were transported to Boise to stand trial. Herbert went down to the train station with a lot of the other miners to watch as about twenty-five of them were marched under guard to board the train for Boise.

November 19, 1892, martial law was officially rescinded, and soon after winter moved into the canyons with a vengeance. The wind howled and blizzards shut off the roads for days at a time. Three people were caught in an avalanche outside Wardner and suffocated before they were found. If it weren't for wild game some neighbors gave them, provisions delivered from unions in other states and those dozens of jars of tomatoes, Colleen thought they would have starved. But somehow they managed. Polly took over some of the work that Sam used to do. She shoveled the path to the outhouse and hauled in wood.

Joe did little to help. He chopped wood when he was in the mood, but mostly he lived in his own world. He seldom spoke when he was home. One day he came home and sat down at the kitchen table. Colleen was peeling some potatoes that were sprouted and wrinkled up but still edible. She looked up and noticed him watching her with more of a hang dog look than usual.

He had something on his mind; she could tell. He looked at his oldest daughter wretchedly. "I'm going away," he said shortly. "Hoping to find work down in the Palouse country." He took a twenty dollar bill from his pocket. "Here's a few bucks. I'll send some more when I can." Colleen just looked at him and nodded. What could she say? "One less mouth to feed," is what she thought. She nodded.

He got up, went to the bedroom, told Clara that he was going, packed a few things and left.

Colleen sat in stunned silence for several minutes, then went in to see how Clara took the news. She was half asleep. "Did pa tell you he was going away?"

"Uh-huh," her mother mumbled, turned over and went back to sleep.

One afternoon about two weeks later, after she was finished with the morning chores, Colleen decided to go for a walk up on the mountain. Clara seldom left her room now, and she was often hostile, but Colleen confided in no one, not even Sally, since she seldom saw her friend anymore. With the work and her mother and sisters to look after, there was little time left in the day. But she thought she would burst if she couldn't get some exercise and fresh air. She went in to tell her mother she was going.

Clara sat in her chair by the window with her embroidery in her lap. The large ragged stitches went every which way, and the colors bore no resemblance to the pattern of wildflowers printed on the flour sack. Colleen had watched her mother's beautiful work deteriorate week by week; the threads were a tangled skein. She was just glad when Clara picked up a needle now, no matter what the outcome looked like.

Colleen went and knelt beside her. "Mama, I'm going on a little walk. I won't be gone long. You'll be OK, won't you?"

Clara looked at her with wide eyes. Then her eyes narrowed and glazed over. She nodded and her mouth formed a tight line. "Yes, you go. You just go and leave me here!" her voice rose angrily. "All alone. By myself. I'll be just fine!"

Colleen hesitated, but she felt she was going to scream and throw something if she couldn't get out at least for a few minutes. There were times her feelings scared her. She wanted to shake her mother, even slap her to get her to come back to reality, make her come back as she used to be, and even though she never followed through, just the feeling frightened her and made her ashamed. She put on her boots, grabbed her coat and her wool stocking cap and went out the door.

When she came back an hour later, Clara was gone. She searched the house and yard. She called, but no one answered. Finally she headed toward town. When she got near Main Street she saw a crowd of people. She got closer and saw Clara sitting on the ground, a blanket wrapped around her, surrounded by onlookers.

"She's crazy as a loon!" one of the men said.

Another one laughed and shook his head. He spit tobacco into the dust at his feet. "Yes, sir. Plumb out of her skull!"

"I heard her running down the road, screaming like a banshee!"

Colleen pushed her way through and knelt beside Clara. "Mama, what happened?" Her mother just stared at her with empty eyes and pushed her away. Colleen stood up and noticed that Sally's mother was there.

Maggie came over and put an arm around her. "She was out here in the road, without a coat, talking crazy and sitting here in the snow," she said quietly. "I just happened to be walking by. I tried to help her up, but she acted like I wasn't there. Just kept mumbling."

Colleen sagged against the older woman. She felt as limp as a dish rag. "I'm sorry. I shouldn't have left her alone. I knew she was bad today."

"It's not your fault, child. Way too much has been put on your shoulders. We need to get her some help." Then she looked around at the crowd and yelled at them. "Will some of you gawkers make yourself useful? Go and get that new doctor that just come to town!" Before the doctor arrived, Clara stood up, looked around and seemed to be aware of things. Colleen and Maggie led her back home and the doctor came to see them that afternoon.

Maggie and Sally came with Colleen to put Clara on the train for Spokane the next day. The doctor sent his wife to go with her. The insane asylum was there, and they would know what to do, he said. Colleen felt as if the pieces of her world, like the leaves on the trees, were being swept away, one by one, and she was left to face the wind. It was all she could do to keep from shaking. She held herself together as best she could, hugging herself, hands cupping each elbow. Sally and Maggie stood with her, and they all watched in silence as the train pulled away.

Feelings washed over her, one after another. Worried, numb, sad, exhausted and relieved, her thoughts were a tangle of confusion and guilt at the relief she felt. She was also frightened to think of where her mother was headed. The new doctor had assured her it was different now, but she'd heard of that place where they put crazy people. A friend of hers from school had gone there to watch the loonies a few months ago, and she'd told Colleen about it. They had an outside pen where people could come and laugh at their antics. They even threw sticks and pebbles in to get a reaction from the inmates, and if a patient roared and growled and lunged at them through the fence his rage was greeted with howls of laughter. How could it be her mother was going there? Why had it come to this? Her shoulders sagged. If she'd only been a better daughter ....

After the train left, she walked back with her friends to their house.

"Come in, girl. Visit for awhile," Maggie said gently. "I had no idea your Mama was so bad. I'm so terrible sorry. Come in. I'll make us some tea."

Colleen held back her tears and bit her lip. "I'd better not. The girls will be coming home from school. But thank you."

She walked on to the house. When she opened the door, everything was as usual. The kitchen table was there, chairs, water bucket, stove, and she thought to herself, "How could this be? When so much has changed." The house was eerily still, though, and it had a new emptiness.

She made a fire and put the kettle on. 'When trouble brews the tea brews,' she thought, and somehow she felt Granny was nearby.

Her hands shook as she took cups from the cupboard, looked in the safe for some bread and thought of how she would tell her sisters. She heard a knock on the door and put the things on the table before answering it. It was Maggie. Though Colleen had spent a lot of time at her house, Mrs. O'Sullivan had been at the McCarthy's only a handful of times. She carried a plate of oatmeal cookies in front of her like a shield.

"Come in."

"No, that's fine, child. I thought you might could use some sweets."

"Oh, yes, the girls will be here any minute and all I had was some bread and jam. Are you sure you can't come in for a minute?"

"I think you probably need to talk to the girls alone. But do come over tomorrow, and if you need anything, dear, you know we are close by," the older woman said as she prepared to leave.

"I know and thank you. I'll do that. We'll be all right." Colleen held back a sudden rush of tears. "Thank you."

Polly and Annalee burst through the door a few minutes later. Colleen had the cookies waiting for them. She gave them each a hug and told them. "Mama has gone away for awhile. You know she's been sick for a long time, and the doctor says the people at the hospital can help her."

"What's wrong with her?"

"It's called a nervous breakdown."

"What's a nerve break up mean?" Annalee asked. "Did Mama break her arm?" She remembered when Sam had broken his arm and there was talk of "nerve damage."

"She said break down, not up, you ninny!" Polly said, poking Annalee in the ribs.

"She will get some help there, and then be back home before you can say scat!" Colleen continued. She knew how to smooth things over, put things in the best light, she'd learned that much from her mother years ago.

As night shadows lengthened on the snow outside the door, Colleen got the girls to bed, then sat in her mother's rocker by the window and debated what to do. Finally she crept up the ladder to the loft and lay wide eyed for hours. She went over and over in her mind all that had happened and pictured what the future held. Worries marred the smooth soft cloth of sleep like stains on a favorite skirt. She managed to clear up one, when two more would appear. Would Clara be able to come back home soon? Would her father send money as he'd promised? If she just had a job, she could take care of her sisters, but most businessmen in town were still angry with the miners and felt Sam "had it coming." It wasn't likely they would hire his sister, at least not for weeks or maybe months.

The next morning she got up, made the fire and started on breakfast. When the girls came down she managed a smile for them, just as if it were another normal day. While Annalee was gone to the outhouse, Polly quizzed her sister on what was happening.

Colleen tried to reassure her. "Mama will be back before long," she told her. "And I have most of that money that Pa left for us. That will last for awhile, and he said he'll send more." After the girls left for school and the dishes were done, she collapsed in a kitchen chair with a cup of tea. The haunted look that had lurked in her mother's eyes now crept into hers.

After awhile she got her coat, boots, gloves and hat and went for a walk up the hill into the woods. The sun bathed the cold winter forest with a glorious light, and the sky was robin's egg blue. The mountains ringing the valley were gilded with gold. Better than Lydia Pinkham's tonic, better than the priest's prayers, almost better even than a letter from Ryan, the pine-scented mountain air renewed her spirit. As she left the gulch behind, the air became clearer. Crisp, clean and sharp as a whistle, it filled her lungs and caressed her face. The country enveloped her, held her tight and soothed her soul. Alive and constantly changing, yet always the same, it performed its magic as she intuitively knew it would. New snow etched each tiny stem and branch with inches of white, and it clung to one side of the rough-barked pine trees. Then a slight breeze stirred in the tops of the trees and sparkling snowflakes filled the air.

As she approached a large old cedar, a great horned owl flew silently from its branches. She stood mesmerized as he swooped silently through the snowy trees, then sailed up, up into the sky. She smiled and continued walking, higher and higher until finally she stopped at the top, took a deep breath and looked down on the town. People, horses, wagons and animals, miniatures of themselves, went about their business. The Bull Pen would soon be only a memory, she thought, but it would always be a scar on her soul, and the trials and bitterness it brought to the people here would last for a long time.

She sat down on her favorite rock for several minutes. She thought of Sam, recalled his cocky grin, his heart and eyes wide open to life, his strength and stamina and determination to right the wrongs of the world. It was hard to realize he was really gone. He is gone, she told herself for the hundredth time, just like Granny is gone. Are they in another place? Another dimension? I hope with all my heart there is a heaven and the two of them are smiling down. I don't know; I doubt it, but I do know my brother won't live his life here on this earth with me. I will never feel his hand in mine again. He won't walk these trails or sit down at the table or swoosh down the mountain behind me on the sled. Yet I am here, she told herself stubbornly. Like it or not. I am here left to live, left to live for Sam as well as for me. Then another thought dawned on her. Sam and Granny are still here too, with me, inside me, in my bones, my heart and in my blood. I can close my eyes and conjure them up and as long as I can do that, maybe they're not really dead. She took some comfort in these thoughts and realized she must be getting back.

Before she could get up she heard something, a movement directly behind her. She turned to see a young buck standing in rigid attention, his antlers shining in the sunlight at the edge of the trees. He stared at her with dark, liquid eyes. She looked back, suddenly filled with a deep unexplainable peace. After several seconds of communion he finally turned and walked regally back into the forest. She sighed, got up and headed down the hill.

When she approached the house she heard the crack of an axe and then she saw Herbert at their woodpile, splitting wood. "Ahhh, Herbert, you don't need to do that! Polly needs the exercise."

Sam's friend stopped and wiped his brow. "Oh yes. I need to do this, and anything else around here you need done. I just heard this morning about your ma. I-I don't know what to say."

"You don't need to say anything. It was coming on for a long time, and the doctor says she'll get some help now." She nodded at the pile of split wood. "Thanks. Will you come in for a minute?"

"Not now. Soon's I'm done here, I need to head home. I'll be back in a day or so though."

Colleen walked down to see Maggie and Sally. Maggie had been awake most of the night as well, thinking about the little family and what was going to happen to them.

"I'm not fixing to pry," she had told Sally that morning, worry etched on her full, kind face, "but that girl can't shoulder the load all by herself."

"I think she's been shouldering more of a load than we knew for quite some while."

Her mother nodded sadly.

When their friend came in, Maggie and Sally each gave her a hug. She sat down at the familiar table as Sally gave her a cup of coffee and placed a plate of warm cinnamon rolls in front of her. "How are the girls?"

"They are doing all right. I'm hoping Ma will get better and be able to come home before too long." Maggie frowned and nodded. She suspected it would be quite a long time before Clara was able to care for a household. They talked of the trial coming up in Boise for the miners still held and other matters.

Then Maggie gently broached the subject of the situation at home. "Your Pa left a few days ago?"

Colleen immediately stiffened up and looked down at her cup. "Yes, ma'am. He left us money though, and he'll be back probably before long."

"Do you know where he went to? Have an address?"

"He's just down in the Palouse country. Near Moscow I think, but I don't know." Then she added quickly, "We'll be just fine, though. Like I said, he left us grocery money and said he'll send more. We have a good store of canned venison and tomatoes, some green beans."

"You'll need to let him know about your ma."

Colleen bit her lip and said nothing for several seconds. She took another bite of the sugar-coated roll, wiped her fingers on her napkin, then looked at her friend and smiled a wan smile. "I expect I'll write and let him know as soon as he sends his address." To herself she added, "as if it would do any good. We're better off without him."

Maggie persisted. She felt bad about making the girl uncomfortable, but knew it was the right thing to do. "And what about your aunt and uncle in Wallace? Have you sent word to them? I met them at the funeral. They seem like nice folks."

Colleen set her jaw and looked toward the door. In fact she had been thinking of this, but now that Maggie brought it up, she resisted the idea. She couldn't imagine tearing the fabric of lies her parents had so persistently woven to keep their troubles to themselves. If she let them know, if she let them in, it would be like betraying them all, and she knew her Pa would be furious when he found out. Clara, herself, had kept her brother at a distance, knowing his disapproval of her husband. "I'm thinking on it," Colleen finally said.

After a few seconds of silence, the talk turned to other matters, then Colleen got up from the table to leave. "Thank you so much for the coffee and roll."

"You don't need to hurry off now. Here, have a little more coffee and another one of these rolls."

"No, thank you. I need to get back home," she squared her shoulders and smiled. "We'll be fine. Honest. My Mama was married and had two babies by the time she was my age."

Maggie nodded, smiled and bit her tongue. "Not a very good recommendation," she wanted to say, but of course, she didn't. Instead she thrust a plate into Colleen's hands. "Here's some rolls for the girls. You come back soon, you hear?"

Her visitor smiled and nodded, then added impishly, with a trace of her former spirit, "I'll be back for sure, when are you making cinnamon rolls again?"

A week went by. Colleen wrote to Ryan and told him some of what had happened. She just said her mother was in the hospital, and she didn't know when she'd get to come home. The things Maggie had asked her kept gnawing at her mind. She knew she needed to write her aunt and uncle. If she didn't tell them, they'd probably hear the story from someone. People traveled from Wardner to Wallace all the time now that they had the train, and bad news flies, while good news crawls.

After the girls left for school a couple of days later, she reluctantly got her ink pen and paper, sat down at the kitchen table and composed a letter. She had decided to tell them everything. She remembered Sam's stern lecture that day in Wallace, about their relatives and how it was important to see them. Clara was, after all, Alfred's sister. He and Mattie deserved to know the truth.

CHAPTER TEN

December 1892 – April 1893

I want to feel no Iron Heel shall disgrace our peaceful shore;
That all the world may do away with war...
I love to dream the old, old dream, that tomorrow I will find
Men of a kindred mind... who love their fellow kind.
I long to make this plea, say not that it cannot be,
I want to see the whole world free from the chains of slavery.

T-Bone Slim
Little Red Songbook

few days after they received Colleen's letter, Aunt Mattie and Uncle Alfred arrived in Wardner and drove their carriage directly to the house. It was about eleven in the morning, so the girls were in school. Colleen had dreaded their arrival and yet when their buggy pulled up to the door she was glad to see them, which surprised her. After they were settled at the kitchen table and tea was poured, she began to tell them the circumstances of the last few weeks since Sam's death. She had rehearsed the chronology of events and calmly explained, as best she could, what had happened up to the day that Clara was taken to Spokane. Gradually, as she talked, a feeling of relief came over her like a warm quilt on a very cold day.

"I shouldn't have left her," she said, her voice finally shaking. She crossed her arms in front of her, cupped each elbow with the opposite hand, to hold herself together. "I knew she was bad that day …."

Mattie got up from her chair and knelt beside her niece. She wrapped her big arms around her and said sternly. "Now you listen to me, child. None of this was your fault. None of it! You're a strong girl and we know enough to see you've worked very hard to take care of things." Colleen felt a tear roll silently down her cheek. It was the first time she'd cried. She brushed it away, but more came, and suddenly it was a torrent. Her shoulders shook and she buried her face in her hands and sobbed. It was as if she couldn't stop, and the grief of losing Granny, then Sam and the struggle with her mother's illness finally overcame pride and determination.

Alfred got up and awkwardly hugged her as well. "Mattie is right. We knew Clara needed help long ago, but we didn't know what to do, with your Pa feeling like he does." He glanced at his wife. "I need to go down to the mercantile, dear; I'll be back in an hour or so."

Mattie put the kettle back on the stove and went outside for a few sticks of wood. She stoked the fire and straightened the kitchen as her niece's sobs gradually abated. Finally, when the tears were all out, Colleen wiped her eyes and blew her nose on the handkerchief that appeared on the table. She looked at this big woman, her aunt, with new feeling. "I'm real glad you and Uncle Alfred came," she said quietly. "I know the girls will be thrilled to see you."

"We'll be glad to see them, too." Mattie poured them both tea and sat down across the table. "I think it's time I told you some things about this family. All these years, I've kept the silence. That's the way Alfred wanted it. He said, 'what's done is done, it's water under the bridge,' but he's grieved about it for years, and when we got your letter saying Joe was gone and what had happened to Clara, we decided it was time."

"When I said it's not your fault, I really meant it," she continued. "It's not your mama's fault either, bless her heart, or even your pa's, as ornery and no account as I think he is. You see, your mama had to marry your pa."

"You mean, she was …, you know, in the family way?"

"Well, yes and no, it's not that simple. It's worse than that, and your mama's mind just couldn't take it."

Colleen looked at her aghast. What could possibly be worse?

"You've heard that pious old platitude, that the Good Lord never gives a body more than they can handle?"

"Yes."

"Well I'm here to tell you, that's a pile of crap!" Colleen stared at her aunt with shock that she'd use such language. The older woman continued. "People crumble, honey. People fall under their burdens, and some don't get up. And it's not their fault and it's not God's will." Colleen just stared at her. Mattie continued with a sigh, "I believe in God as much as the next person, but I sure don't think he's directing everything that happens. If he is, he's doing a mighty poor job of it," she said with a wry laugh.

Colleen remembered Granny saying, "God gives you this day to do with …."

Mattie went on. She too, had rehearsed this conversation. "You know Clara was just nine and Alfred was five when their parents died."

Colleen nodded. "I know they were raised by their aunt and uncle there in Pennsylvania."

"Yes. The children didn't know them before. It must have been hard on the old folks, too, never having been around children. They lived on an old run-down farm miles from town. It was especially hard for Clara; she missed her comfortable home, her friends and her mama a lot."

"But it was good that they had a place to go besides the children's home."

"That's right, dear. And they were good people, but not educated like the rest of the family. They were real strict and old. Religious, strict and ignorant," she said grimly. "And stupid!" she added triumphantly. "Really stupid!"

Colleen's eyes widened. She'd never heard anyone talk like that. "Mama never seemed to talk about them much, except to say they were kind to take them in."

"Kind, yes, but they did something, made a decision, that caused a lot of heartache. The tears you shed today partly come from long ago, more than twenty years ago, from a time and a place that you don't even know. They spring from a deep and putrid well that's been covered up and left to sour for too many years."

"Granny said she needed to tell me something one day, but then she up and died!"

"I know dear, but even your granny, that dear woman, didn't know the whole story. They never told her the part her own husband, George McCarthy, that evil devil, played. I hope he's rotting in hell! He was at the bottom of it."

"Mama never liked him. She put up an awful fuss when Pa moved him into the house."

"And rightly so!" Your pa was always browbeat by his old man. Never had a lick of sense. I swear he never thought one single idea for himself his whole life. What happened was this …."

The sun still beat down on the hayfield even though the shadows were long as Clara finished raking the last of the hay. Almost 16, she and Alfred usually helped their uncle with the hay, but today her brother was sick and she'd been in this field about two miles from the house since early morning. Sweat ran down her face, and she took her hat off to wipe it as she walked to the edge of the field to get a drink from the water jug. Chaff from the hay prickled her skin, and the hot dust made her eyes water.

She poured some water in her hand and washed her face, then lifted her shirt and splashed water on her breasts. Then she noticed their neighbor, George McCarthy, walking across the field toward her. He lived about a half mile up the road. She quickly put her shirt down and took a drink as he approached.

"Howdy there, Miss Clara," he said as he got closer. "Mind if I get a drink?" Clara looked at him, puzzled. She could tell he was drunk, which was usual. Her uncle said the man was fine until about noon, but after that it was best to let him be. But why would he be out here in the field this time of day?

"Is your uncle around?" he said grinning at her, pretending he hadn't seen him leaving on his horse, going toward town.

"No, Sir. He's gone into town to get a part for the wagon. I'm just finishing up the raking." She turned and reached for the water jug when he grabbed her from behind. Clara had no experience with men. She couldn't imagine what was happening, but when he grabbed her arm, she fought back.

"Let me go! What are you doing? No! No!" She struggled and kicked but he was strong, and she was tired from a day of hard work. He pushed her backward onto the hard ground, held her down with his left arm while he tore her pants off with his right.

It was over in a few minutes, and he left without a word. He left her there, bleeding and broken, like a beautiful doll, cast aside. She lay in the hay stubble for about thirty minutes, absolutely still, trying to understand what had happened. She finally got up slowly, tried to fix her clothing and wandered around in a daze, looking for the hay rake.

She went to the water jug and washed her face, then got the rake, finished the hay and walked slowly back to the house after the scorching sun disappeared behind the trees. When she arrived, her aunt was just taking a cake out of the oven and didn't turn around as she started up the stairs. "I'm not feeling very good," Clara told her. "I won't be wanting any dinner."

It was three or four days before she told what happened.

Mattie continued. "What he did to her was horrible, but what came next was just about as bad. If I live to be a hundred, I'll never understand it. Alfred listened at doors and put it all together. He was just a kid at the time, eleven years old, and didn't know much being a farm kid like he was, but he figured it out. You see, when Clara told the old people what happened and said she had lifted her shirt to cool off, they acted like it was her fault. They were horrified, terrified and ashamed, ASHAMED of the girl who was like a daughter to them.

For days they discussed what to do. What to do with HER, not what to do with George McCarthy! Clara never left the house, and Alfred heard her crying in her room for hours. He felt so bad, but didn't know what to do. He heard them talking and planning. His sister, so sweet, so innocent, was damaged goods in their eyes, and his uncle never once looked her way or spoke directly to her after that. She would never get a husband now, those old fools thought. That thinking wasn't all that unusual among a lot of God fearing people back there."

"So what happened?" Colleen asked. She thought her heart would break for her mother.

"Two months later she came up expecting."

Colleen's eyes widened and she gasped. "You mean I ...."

"No, child. She lost the baby later on."

"What did they do?"

"Well, the old fools went and talked to George, unbeknownst to his dear wife. They told him they knew what happened. He blustered and denied it, and they went back home, thinking that now their girl was a liar as well as a fallen woman."

"But a few days later George paid them a visit. He brought his boy Joe, who was nineteen at the time and had mostly mush between his ears. They struck a deal. Joe would marry Clara, make an honest woman out of her, and solve their problem. It was all very hush, hush."

"Why didn't mama put up a fight? Why didn't she say, 'no'?"

"You don't understand, child. Things were different then, even worse than it is today. She had nobody to talk to except the priest, and I'm sure he told her to obey her parents and accept her lot. She was going to have a baby. She believed her aunt and uncle, that she was no good, and no other man would ever want her now, that she was dirty and doomed to hell. She just went along with it, thinking she had no choice. And Joe, well, he never had a say in the matter either, although he probably was more than happy about it. Clara was a pretty girl, and smart, but she never went back to school after that. They were married, and

George McCarthy gave them some land and a little house. Then she lost the baby, but the die was cast. You know the rest."

"Granny tried to help Ma, always stuck up for her."

"I know. She was a good woman and done the best she could. Now she's gone, and thank the Lord she never knew what really happened. May she rest in peace … and may the old man fry in hell for eternity!"

Colleen sat back in her chair, dizzy from this information and overcome with deep sadness for her mother.

Alfred and Mattie stayed for two days, and they discussed the situation. They had decided even before they left Wallace what would be best for the little family, but they needed to bring Colleen around to the idea. She had, in many ways, been the head of the family for sometime, and she was proud of the fact that she could take care of her sisters.

"There is no earthly reason for you three girls to stay here," Alfred told her. "We have a large house; why sometimes the two of us get lost in it!"

Mattie laughed her big laugh. "That's the honest truth!" she said, her shoulders shaking with mirth at the idea. "The other day your uncle here was missing for seven hours before I located him in the attic!" Colleen laughed. She marveled at the easy give- and-take between them.

"Besides," her uncle said. "This idea is purely selfish. It would be wonderful for us to have you and the girls."

"The school is nearby, too, and I know Polly and Annalee would love it there," Mattie said.

"Well, I hate to leave here. We have friends and neighbors here who can help us, and I know I'll get work soon. Then we can manage."

"I know you could, dear," Mattie said gently.

"A job!" Alfred put in, his eyes lighting up. "I plumb forgot that part of it. I always need good help at the store. You can work for me as long as you need to, but I was thinking you would be going to school before long."

Colleen's heart did a flip flop. School! The very word was magic. She had put the idea of higher education completely out of her mind, an impossible dream. She could think of only one more reason for refusing, and that was a weak one. "But what if Pa comes back? He'll be furious if we're not here."

"We'll worry about that when it happens. As soon as we hear from him, we'll write and let him know. He said he'd send more money?"

"Yes, but he hasn't yet."

"I'm thinking Joe might be relieved to know you girls are taken care of. He's not an evil man, just proud and stubborn," Mattie said.

Colleen nodded. The more they talked, the more she knew it was the right decision, and finally she agreed. Mattie was ecstatic, and Alfred just beamed.

The house, since it was rented, was no problem; and the next week they packed up their clothes, cleaned out the kitchen and prepared to move.

Colleen paid a visit to Maggie and Sally the day before the wagon was coming for their things. Since Sam's incarceration she hadn't visited with them as much; she'd felt separated from them somehow, but her friends were pleased to hear the news.

"We'll sure miss you around here," Sally said, "but how exciting to work at the store!"

"Yes, and you should have seen Polly and Annalee when we told them! They were simply giddy!"

"I'm so glad, dear," Maggie said as she gave her a hug. "Your uncle and aunt are real fine people. It won't be the same around here, with you and your family gone, but you'll write us, won't you?"

"Oh, of course! I'll write and let you know how things are going. And Wallace isn't so far. You can come and visit us."

"We'll do that!"

* * * *

When they first arrived in Wallace, the two younger girls couldn't believe their eyes at the luxury. They had visited their aunt and uncle's house only briefly once or twice, sitting stiffly in the parlor. Now they were amazed at the size and elegance of the two story frame house that stood on the hill overlooking the town. They explored the house from the basement, which had a huge coal furnace, to the dark and mysterious attic which was reached by a ladder that came down from the ceiling on the second floor.

The house had a huge porch across the front with a porch swing, and there was a balcony on the second floor. From there it seemed you could see for a hundred miles.

The sitting room had chairs and a settee, upholstered with gold brocade with fancy wood-carved legs and arms. In one corner it had a large player piano, and on a table nearby, a graphophone with real records that played music. Annalee was enthralled with the piano, and within weeks she was enrolled for lessons.

The dining room featured a large cherry wood table with eight chairs, and above the table was a chandelier that was possibly the most beautiful thing they had ever seen. When it was lit, it was like a hundred stars twinkling right above their heads.

The gas lights throughout the house were fascinating, and they had some electricity as well. At first the lights seemed so bright it hurt their eyes after the soft light of kerosene lamps, but they soon became used to it. Polly discovered quickly the better light for reading, and after two weeks she couldn't imagine reading by lamplight. All three girls liked to read, and they loved the rows and rows of books in the library.

The spacious kitchen in the house was marvelous as well. It had a modern gas refrigerator, a shiny linoleum floor and water coming out of a faucet! It was all so new and wonderful that the girls even liked washing dishes, except they were nervous about breaking the fine china that the family used every day.

Polly and Annalee shared a room upstairs, not because they needed to but because they wanted to. Neither of them had ever slept in a room, or even a bed, alone. Colleen had a room next door, but it seemed so big and strange that many nights she crept into their room and snuggled up with one or the other of her sisters.

Colleen wrote to Ryan and told him her new address in Wallace, and of the house where they lived. She told him how exciting it was to have a real job working in her uncle's drugstore and how she was saving her money to go to college. She also shared her worry about her mother with him. She said she had written to her but had not yet received a reply.

The days gradually settled into a comfortable pattern. She loved working in the store, and the girls made friends at school. The events of the previous months seemed almost like a dream, or rather a nightmare, but the repercussions and antagonism between the mine owners and workers continued for years.

They followed the news of the union prisoners and what was happening in Boise. As the months passed, most of the prisoners were released on their own recognizance. State and federal charges, however, were brought against Thomas O'Brian and dozens of the other leaders. Jack Bailey was the star witness against all of them. The trials continued all winter. Alfred read in the paper that thirteen unionists were convicted of contempt of court. He read out loud to Colleen and Mattie. "It says here that thirteen were convicted, and they found four others guilty of criminal conspiracy."

"It's too bad about Mr. O'Brian," Mattie said. "From all I heard he did everything he could to keep the unions from violence."

"That's what Sam always said," Colleen replied. "He's a good and fair man." A few weeks later they read in the Spokane paper that the United States Supreme Court had overturned the conspiracy charges and a federal judge released the two men still held on contempt.

* * * *

Winter dissolved into spring. Colleen had found new trails to explore in the mountains above Wallace, and the day she discovered the first waxy yellow butter cups twinkling among the moss and needles of the forest floor, she ran all the way home to show Mattie.

Since December, she'd been counting the days, and finally the time that she'd been dreaming of arrived. The last Saturday in March, she stood on the platform outside the depot in town with her aunt, uncle and sisters.

She would take the Northern Pacific train west from Wallace to the Mission, where she'd board the steamer, Georgia Oakes, ride down the river to Coeur d' Alene Lake, then cross the lake to Coeur d' Alene City, where she'd board another train for Spokane.

She was dressed for travel, and her eyes sparkled with excitement as she bent down to adjust the laces on her patent leather boots. She wore a new cloak of soft brown wool with a smart, new, English wool felt dress hat to match, and she carried a small cloth embroidered handbag with fifty dollars tucked away inside. She clutched the bag tightly. It held not only her money, which she'd saved diligently from her work in her uncle's store, but the address of Alfred's friends in Spokane where she would be staying. Her trunk, a small flat-topped metal one with leather handles on the ends, stood nearby ready for the conductor to load.

Annalee fidgeted and investigated every corner of the station while Polly stood, sad-faced, as if she would cry at any minute. Finally Alfred said to his wife, "Well, my dear. I must be getting back to the store. We're getting a shipment, and I just saw the wagon going up the road. Would you want to stay and see her off and walk on home with the girls? The train is due anytime now."

"We'll do that," his wife answered. She looked at Polly, then inquired of her husband, "Would you be needing Polly to help out this morning?" Polly's eyes lit up, and she looked hopefully at her uncle.

He smiled at her. "I sure could use some help, Polly. Now that your sister is leaving me, would you like to?"

Travelers going to Spokane would take the Northern Pacific train west from Wallace to the Mission Landing, where they'd board the steamer, Georgie Oakes, ride down the river to Coeur d' Alene Lake, cross the lake to Coeur d' Alene City, then board another train for Spokane.

Special Collections and Archives, University of Idaho Library, 6-096-4a

She nodded vigorously, and smiled. "Yes Sir."

"Well, you'd better come with me then." He gave Colleen's arm a squeeze. "You be sure and write us every week, you hear?"

She smiled and took his hand. "I will, Uncle Alfred, for sure. And thank you. I will be seeing Mama and will let you know how she is."

"You tell your mother that as soon as she gets better we have a room all ready for her here. And try to get her to write us."

Colleen hugged her sister, "You write to me every week, ok?"

Polly nodded, her eyes glistened with tears. "I will."

Soon after Alfred and Polly left them, they heard the locomotive give a mighty whistle as it approached the town. Then there it was, filling the air with smoke, steam and noise as it hove into sight, a wondrous black beast that breathed fire and carried people away in its belly. Excitement filled the air as the passengers gathered valises, bags, hats and canes, clutched their tickets and prepared to climb aboard.

Colleen turned to her little sister and held back tears as she hugged her tightly. She whispered in her ear, "Mind Aunt Mattie and work hard in school. See to it that Polly behaves herself!" Annalee drew away, looked up at her quizzically, then giggled at the thought.

Colleen turned to her aunt. "I'll write every week," she said as she gave her a hug. "Thank you for everything." Then she turned quickly and walked to the conductor, who stood at the bottom of the steps taking tickets.

She climbed the steps and entered the compartment. The smell of tobacco smoke, oil and stale bread wafted her way, and she quickly found an empty seat by the window and looked out to wave at Mattie and Annalee. She couldn't believe she was really here, going to Spokane, and Ryan was going to meet her.

As the train pulled away and she finally looked around the car, she saw a familiar blond head three seats in front of her on the opposite side. Could it be? Yes, she could tell as the girl turned her head that it was Ruby. Colleen got up to go and say hello, noting the older girl's smart hat and fine broadcloth coat. What really caught her eye, though, as she got closer, was something in her friend's lap. Yes, her fingers were flying and she had a ball of yarn in a bag on the seat beside her. She was knitting.

 BIBLIOGRAPHY

Aiken,Katherine G. *Idaho's Bunker Hill*. Norman, Oklahoma: University of Oklahoma Press, 2005

Aiken,Katherine G. *Fire in the Hole*. Interview on the Internet

Bankson, Russell A. and Harrison, Lester S. *Beneath These Mountains*. New York: Vantage Press, 1966

Brainard, Wendell and Chapman, Ray. *Golden History Tales*. Kellogg, Idaho: Progressive Printing, 1998

Brown, Ronald C. *Hard-Rock Miners*. College Station and London: Texas A & M University Press, 1945

Cloman, Flora. *I'd Live it Over*. New York, Toronto: Farrar & Rinehart, Inc., 1941

Dary, David. *Seeking Pleasure in the Old West*. New York: Alfred A Knopf, 1995

Emmons, David M. *The Butte Irish: class and ethnicity in an American mining town*. 1875-1925. Urbana Illinois: University of Illinois Press, c1989

Fahey, John. *Days of the Hercules*. Moscow, Idaho: University Press of Idaho, 1978

Foote, Mary Hallock. *A Victorian Gentlewoman in the Far West*. Henry E. Huntington Library & Art Gallery, 1972

Forster-Priesmeyer, Emma Louise. *Gunfighter Ethic on the Industrial Frontier, a social and cultural history of the Coeur d' Alene mining district*. Moscow, Idaho: University of Idaho Thesis, 1991

Greenway, John. *American Folksongs of Protest*. New York: Barnes, 1960

Grover, David H. *Debaters & Dynamiters, The story of the Haywood Trial*. Corvallis, Oregon: Oregon State University Press, 1964

Hanson, Donna M. *Frontier Duty: The Army in Northern Idaho, 1853-1876*. Moscow, Idaho: University of Idaho Library, 2005

Harriman, Job. *The Class War in Idaho*. New York: The Volkszeitung Library, 1900

Hart, Patricia and Nelson, Ivar. *Mining Town*. Seattle and London: University of Washington Press, 1984

Holbrook, Stewart. *Wildmen, Wobblies & Whistle Punks*. Corvallis, Oregon: Oregon State University Press, 1992

Hutton, May Arkwright. *The Coeur d' Alenes; or, A tale of the Modern Inquisition in Idaho*. Wallace, Idaho: M. A. Hutton, 1900

I. W. W. *Little Red Songbook*: First published around 1909, the songs grew out of the Union movement that began in the 1890's in the Coeur d' Alenes and across the country. The authors of the lyrics at the start of each chapter are as follows:
> Chapter One: To the tune of "Power in the Blood" by Joe Hill
> Chapter Two: by Joe Hill
> Chapter Three: by James J. Ferriter
> Chapter Four: by Ralph Chaplin
> Chapter Five: Written in Leavenworth Penitentiary by Ralph I. Chaplin
> Chapter Six: by Laura Payne Emerson
> Chapter Seven: by Laura Payne Emerson
> Chapter Eight: by James J. Ferriter
> Chapter Nine: by Joe Hill
> Chapter Ten: by T Bone Slim

Lukas, J. Anthony. *Big Trouble*. New York, New York: Simon & Schuster, 1997

Magnuson, Richard G. *Coeur D'Alene Diary*. Portland OR: Binfod & Mort, 1968.

Magnuson, Robin. *The Socialist Tradition and the American Novel*. Moscow, Idaho: University of Idaho thesis, 1979

Olsen, Gregg. *The Deep Dark*. New York: Crown Publishers, 2005

Phipps, Stanley S. *From Bull Pen to Bargaining Table*. Moscow, Idaho: University of Idaho thesis, 1983

O'Sullivan, Sean. *Legends from Ireland*. Totowa, New Jersey: Rowman and Littlefield, 1977

Schrier, Arnold. *Ireland and the American Emigration 1850-1900*. Minneapolis, Minnesota: University of Minnesota Press, 1958

Siringo, Charles A. *A Cowboy Detective, A true story of twenty-two years with a world-famous detective agency*. Lincoln and London: University of Nebraska Press, 1988. Reprinted from the 1912 edition published by W. B. Conkey Co., Chicago

Siringo, Charles A. *Riata & Spurs*. Boston, New York: Houghton Mifflin, 1927

Smith, Robert. *Coeur d' Alene Mining Wars of 1892, A case study of an industrial dispute*. Corvallis, Oregon: Oregon State University Press,

Stegner, Wallace. *Joe Hill*. Lincoln and London: University of Nebraska Press, 1950

Stoll, William T. *Silver Strike*. Little Brown & Co. 1932. Reprinted Moscow, Idaho, U of I Press, 1991

Warren, Sidney. *Farthest Frontier*. New York: Macmillan Company, 1949

Wood, John V. *Railroads Through the Coeur d' Alene's*. Caldwell, Idaho: Caxton Printers Ltd., 1983

Wyman, Mark. *Hard Rock Epic*. Berkley, LosAngeles, London: University of California Press, 1979

Strahorn, Robert E. *The Resources and Attractions of Idaho Territory*. Moscow, Idaho: University of Idaho Press, 1990. Originally printed in 1881 by the Idaho Territorial Legislature

Newspapers:

Coeur d' Alene American, Wallace Idaho, 1892-1893
Coeur d' Alene Barbarian, Wardner/Wallace Idaho, 1892-1893
Coeur d' Alene Miner, Wallace Idaho, 1890-1893
Cocur d' Alene Press, Coeur d' Alene Idaho, 1892-1896
Mullan Tribune, Mullan Idaho, 1891
Spokane Daily Chronicle, Spokane Washington, 1891-1892
Wallace Democrat, 1892-
Wallace Press, 1891-1903
Chapter 2:   Mullan Tribune, August 22, 1891
Chapter 6:   Coeur d' Alene Barbarian, April 30, 1892
              Coeur d' Alene Press, May 14, 1892
Chapter 7:   Wallace Press, Adam Aulbach, editor
              New York Times, July 12, 1892
Chapter 8:   Coeur d' Alene Miner, July 16, 1892
              Spokane Daily Chronicle, July 16, 1892
              Coeur d' Alene Barbarian, July 23, 1892
              Coeur d' Alene American, August 20, 1892
              Wallace Democrat, October 6, 1892*
Chapter 9:   Wallace Democrat, September 22, 1892

* Note: This article was quoted at a different time in the story to fit with the story line.

ORDER FORM

Ninebark Publications
Box 8915-3
Moscow, Idaho 83843
Fax: 208-882-5763

Pat Cary Peek
www.patcarypeek.com
pcaryp@moscow.com

To order *Silver Threads, War in the Coeur d' Alenes* or *Cougar Dave, Mountain Man of Idaho* by Pat Cary Peek, send to the above address:

Name of book	No. of copies	Price Each	Total
		$14.95	
		$14.95	

Idaho residents add   6% Sales Tax $ .90   _____

Add Shipping:
$2 for 1 book, $3 for 2-3 books, $4 for 4-5 books,

Total   _____

Ship to:
Name: _____

Address: _____

City: _____ State: _____ Zip: _____

Phone: _____

Payment:

_____ Check or money order enclosed
(Checks payable to Ninebark Publications)